BIG
TROUBLE

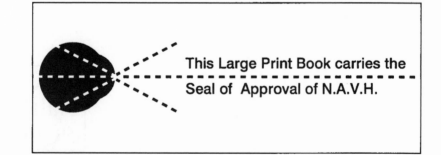

This Large Print Book carries the
Seal of Approval of N.A.V.H.

BIG TROUBLE

Dave Barry

G.K. Hall & Co. • Thorndike, Maine

Published in 2000 by arrangement with G. P. Putnam's Sons, a member of Penguin Putnam Inc.

G.K. Hall Large Print Core Series.

The text of this Large Print edition is unabridged.
Other aspects of the book may vary from the original edition.

Set in 16 pt. Plantin by Rick Gundberg.

Printed in the United States on permanent paper.

Library of Congress Cataloging-in-Publication Data

Barry, Dave.
  Big trouble / Dave Barry.
    p. cm.
  ISBN 0-7838-8924-0 (lg. print : hc : alk. paper)
  ISBN 0-7838-8930-5 (lg. print : sc : alk. paper)
  1. Advertising executives — Florida — Coconut Grove —
Fiction. 2. Family — Florida — Coconut Grove — Fiction.
3. Coconut Grove (Fla.) — Fiction. 4. Large type books. I. Title.
PS3552.A74146 B54   2000
  813'.54—dc21   99-055839

For Michelle

Acknowledgments and Warning

I'll start with the warning: *This is not a book for youngsters*. I point this out because I know, from reading my mail, that a lot of youngsters read my humor books and newspaper columns, and I'm thrilled that they do. But this book is not for them, because some of the characters use Adult Language. I did not necessarily *want* the characters to use this type of language; some of them just went ahead and did. That's how some characters are.

And now for the acknowledgments:

I want to first thank my editor at Putnam, Neil Nyren, who proposed the idea of my writing a novel, and made it sound like a lot of fun. Neil was always supportive and has given me excellent advice, so I forgive him for the fact that he never told me, back at the beginning, that I would need to come up with characters *and* a plot.

I thank my agent, Al Hart, who also encouraged me to take a stab at fiction. I always listen to Al, who has calmly steered my writing career through many a stormy sea, with one steady hand on the tiller and the other wrapped around a refreshing beverage.

I am very lucky to have, as friends, some wonderful novelists who were generous enough to share their wisdom with me when I actually started writing this book and discovered that I had no idea what the plot was. I especially want to thank Carl Hiaasen, who is the master of the genre I tried to write in — the Bunch of South Florida Wackos genre — as well as Stephen King, Elmore Leonard, Paul Levine, Ridley Pearson, and Les Standiford, all of whom basically said not to worry too much about the plot at the beginning, except Ridley, who is *extremely* organized and already knows what he will have for breakfast on May 12, 2011 (tea and an English muffin, unbuttered). I also thank Jeff Arch for his words of encouragement, even the Yiddish ones that I did not understand.

I thank my amazing research assistant, Judi Smith. I'm always calling Judi up and asking questions like, "How much milk does an average Tahitian coconut contain?" And within ten minutes she has somehow gotten hold of the world's foremost authority on Tahitian coconut milk, and she'll call me with *reams* of information, and I'll say, "Whoops, it turns out that I don't need that after all," and *still she never gets mad.*

I thank Luis Albuerne and Bobby D'Angelo, who told me helpful stuff about police procedures and fighter jets, respectively. I probably got it all wrong, but that's not their fault.

Finally, I thank all of you who've supported me over the years by reading my columns and books, and who are now (except for the youngsters) following me into the Realm of Fiction. I hope you enjoy reading this book as much as I enjoyed writing it. Once I figured out what the plot was, I mean.

ONE

Puggy had held down his job at the Jolly Jackal Bar and Grill, which did not have a grill, for almost three weeks. For Puggy, this was a personal employment record. In fact, after a career as a semiprofessional vagrant, he was seriously thinking about settling in Miami, putting down roots, maybe even finding an indoor place to sleep. Although he really liked his tree.

Puggy liked everything about Miami. He liked that it was warm. He liked that most of the police seemed tolerant of people like him — people who, merely by existing, tended to violate laws that solid citizens never even thought about, like how long you were allowed to sit in a certain place without buying something. The attitude of most of the police down here seemed to be, hey, you can *sit* all you want; we're just glad you're not *shooting*.

Puggy also liked the way, in Miami, you were always hearing people talking Spanish. This made Puggy feel like he was living in a foreign country, which was his one ambition, although the only time he had ever actually been abroad was four years before, when, after a long and confusing weekend that began in Buffalo, he was briefly detained on the Canadian side of Niagara Falls for urinating in the Ripley's Believe It or Not Museum.

The funny thing was, Puggy had not been trying to get to Miami in particular. He had left a homeless shelter in Cleveland and started hitch-hiking in the general direction of south, looking for a warm place to stay the winter; the trucker who picked him up happened to be heading for the Port of Miami, right downtown.

As good fortune had it, Puggy arrived on election day. He'd been on the street for less than an hour when a white van pulled up next to him. The driver, an older man, said something in Spanish and showed him a ten-dollar bill. Puggy, assuming the man wanted a blow job, said "Not interested." The man immediately switched to English and explained that all Puggy had to do, for the ten, was vote.

"I'm not from here," said Puggy.

"No problem," said the man.

So Puggy got into the van. En route to the polling place, the older man picked up seven other voters, all men, some quite aromatic. At the polling place, they all walked right inside and the man told them what to do. The poll workers did not seem to have any problem with this.

When it was Puggy's turn to vote, he gave his name, per instructions, as Albert Green, which he spelled "Allbert Gren." The real Albert Green was a person who had died in 1991 but still voted often in Miami. Puggy cast Mr. Green's ballot for a mayoral candidate named Carlos somebody, then went outside and collected his ten, which looked like a million dollars in his hand.

Puggy had never voted for anything before, but on that magical day, riding around in the white van, he voted in the Miami mayoral election four times at four different polling places. He got ten dollars each for the first three times, but the fourth time, the van man said the price was now five, and Puggy said OK. He felt he had already gotten a lot from the city of Miami, and he didn't mind giving something back.

Puggy cast his last ballot in a part of Miami called Coconut Grove; this is where the van man left him. There were palm trees and water and sailboats gently waggling their masts back and forth against a bright blue sky. Puggy thought it was the most beautiful place he had ever seen. He was feeling good. He was warm, and he had thirty-five dollars cash, the most money he'd ever had at one time in his life. He decided to spend it on beer.

He scouted around for a good spot, quickly rejecting the tourist bars in the central Grove, where a beer could cost five dollars, which Puggy thought was way high, even for a guy who was pulling down ten dollars a vote. And so, after wandering to the seedier outskirts of Coconut Grove, Puggy found himself walking into the Jolly Jackal Bar and Grill.

The Jolly Jackal was not upscale. It would have needed thousands of dollars' worth of renovation just to ascend to the level of "dive." It had a neon sign in the window, but part of it wasn't working, so it just said "ACKAL." When you walked in the front door, you could see straight back through the gloom to the toilet, which had lost its door some years back when a patron, frustrated in his efforts to operate the doorknob, smashed his way in with a fire extinguisher. The bar was dark and rancid with stale beer. The TV was tuned to motorcycle racing. There were names scrawled on the walls, and crude drawings of genitalia. Puggy felt right at home.

He sat at the bar, which was empty except for a bearded man at the far end, talking to the bartender in a language that wasn't English, but it didn't sound to Puggy like Spanish, either. The bartender, a thick man with a thick face, looked at Puggy, but didn't come over.

"I'll take a Budweiser," Puggy said.

"You have money?" the bartender said.

Puggy was not offended. He knew he looked like he didn't have money. Usually, he *didn't* have money.

"I got money," he said, and he put all of it, three tens and a five, on the bar. The bartender, saying nothing, uncapped a longneck and set it in front of Puggy. He took Puggy's five and replaced it with three dollars and two quarters. Then he went back to the bearded man and said something foreign, and they both laughed.

12

Puggy didn't care. He was figuring out, at a buck fifty a beer, how many beers he could buy. He couldn't pin down a definite number, but he knew it was going to be a lot. More than ten. He might even get some Slim Jims, if they had them here.

Puggy was on his fourth beer when a couple of guys came in, one called Snake, whose T-shirt said "Gators," and one called Eddie, whose T-shirt said "You Don't Know Dick." They both wore cutoff jeans and flip-flops, but their feet were black with dirt, so it almost looked like they were wearing socks.

Snake and Eddie referred to themselves as fishermen, although they did not fish. They did live on a boat; it had been abandoned by its legal owner because it had no engine and would sink if it were moved. Snake's and Eddie's actual source of income was standing in front of vacant parking spaces in Coconut Grove, and then, when a tourist car came along, directing the driver into the space, making arm motions as though this were a tricky maneuver that had to be done just right, like landing the space shuttle. Then Snake and Eddie would stand close by, waiting for a tip, which usually the tourists gave them, especially if it was dark.

Puggy figured that Snake and Eddie must have been to the Jolly Jackal before, because as soon as they walked in, the bartender was coming toward them, pointing back at the door, saying "Out! I tell you once before! Out!"

13

"No, no, man, no," said Eddie, holding his hands up in front of his chest, making peace. "Look, we just wanna couple drinks. We got money." He was digging into his cutoff shorts, pulling out some quarters, some dimes and pennies, putting them on the bar.

The bartender looked at the money, saying nothing.

"OK?" said Eddie, settling at the bar to Puggy's right, one stool away. "OK," he said again, because he could see the bartender was going to let them slide. Snake sat on the stool to Eddie's right. Eddie pointed at the cluster of coins, said, "We'll take whatever much this'll get us."

The bartender, still saying nothing, counted the money, sliding the coins off the bar one by one into his hand. He put out two glasses and filled them with clear liquid from a bottle that had no label, then walked back to the bearded man.

"Asshole," remarked Eddie, to Snake.

Puggy, as soon as he determined that the situation was not going to require him to duck, went back to watching the TV, which was now showing pickup trucks racing. Puggy had never thought of that as a sport, but his policy with TV was, if it was on, he'd watch it.

It was maybe twenty minutes later that he decided to take a leak. He started to pick up his money, and he realized that some of it was gone. He wasn't sure how much exactly, but he was definitely short at least a ten.

Puggy looked to his right. Eddie and Snake were both looking at the TV, looking interested, like it was showing naked women, instead of pickup trucks.

"Hey," said Puggy.

Eddie and Snake kept staring at the screen.

"Hey," repeated Puggy.

Snake kept staring at the screen. Eddie turned his head to look at Puggy, a hard look.

"You got a problem, chief?" he said.

"Gimme it back," said Puggy.

"*What?*" said Eddie, screwing up his face, trying to make an expression like he had no idea what Puggy meant, but overdoing it.

"I said gimme it back," said Puggy.

"What the *fuck're* you talking about?" said Eddie. Now Snake was looking, too, both of them starting to turn toward Puggy on their stools.

Puggy knew, from experience, that this was one of those situations where he could get hit. He knew he should give it up. He knew that, but, shit, *ten dollars*.

"I said," he said, "gimme . . ."

Eddie's punch didn't hurt so much, because he was still a whole stool away, and the punch caught Puggy on the shoulder. But when Puggy fell over backward to the floor, that did hurt. Then Snake was coming around from behind Eddie, stomping with the heel of his flip-flopped foot, trying to get Puggy in the face. Puggy curled up and pressed his face in where the bar met the floor, not planning to fight, just trying to ride it out. The floor smelled like puke.

Snake was making his fourth attempt to stomp Puggy's face when there was a ringing "bong" sound and Snake went down. This was because the bartender had hit him in the head from behind with an aluminum softball bat. The bartender had never played baseball, but he had a nice, efficient swing. He preferred the aluminum bat because the wood ones tended to break.

With Snake down, the bartender turned to Eddie, who was backing toward the door, hands up in front of him, the peacemaker again.

"Listen," Eddie said. "This ain't your problem."

"YOU are problem," said the bartender, taking a step forward. You could tell he expected Eddie to run, but Eddie didn't. This is because Eddie could see that Snake — who could take a bat to the head better than most — was getting to his feet behind the bartender, picking up one of Puggy's longneck beer bottles. The bartender didn't see this, but Puggy saw it, and for no good reason he could think of, even later, he rolled over and kicked out hard, his left foot catching Snake's right leg just above the ankle. The ankle made a cracking noise, and Snake, saying "unh," went down again, dropping the bottle. The bartender spun back around, saw Snake on the floor, spun back to see Eddie going out the door, then spun back to Snake again. Leaning over,

16

holding the bat like a shovel, he gave Snake a hard poke in the ribs.

"Out!" he said.

"He broke my ankle!" said Snake.

"I break your head," said the bartender. He gripped the end of the bat, cocked it for a swing, waited.

"OK OK OK," said Snake. Using a stool for support and keeping an eye on the bartender, he pulled himself up, then hobbled to the door. When he got there, he turned and pointed at Puggy, still lying under the bar.

"When I see you," Snake said, "you're dead." Then he pushed open the door and hobbled outside. Puggy noticed that it was dark.

The bartender watched Snake leave, then turned to Puggy.

"Out," he said.

"Look, mister," said Puggy, "I . . ."

"Out," said the bartender, gripping the bat.

Puggy got to his feet, noticing, as he did, that he had peed his pants. He looked on the bar. His voting money was gone, all of it. Eddie must have grabbed it while Snake was trying to stomp him.

"Oh, *man*," said Puggy.

"Out," said the bartender.

Puggy was starting toward the door when, from the other end of the bar, the bearded man, who had watched the fight, not moving from his stool, said, in English, "You can stay."

The bartender looked at the bearded man,

17

then shrugged and relaxed his grip on the bat.

Puggy said, "I got no money. They took all my money."

The bearded man said, "Is OK. No charge."

Puggy said, "OK."

He was drinking his second free beer, feeling better again about how the day was going, except for peeing his pants, when the door opened. He flinched, thinking it might be Snake come back to kill him, but it was a guy in a suit, carrying a briefcase. The suit went to the far end of the bar and started talking foreign with the other two men. Then the bearded man called down to Puggy.

"You want to make five dollars?"

"Sure," said Puggy. This was some town, Miami.

It turned out that the job was moving a wooden crate out of the trunk of a Mercedes parked outside. The crate was very heavy, but the bearded man and the man in the suit did not help. Puggy and the bartender, breathing hard, lugged the crate inside, past the bar, past the toilet, down a hallway to a room that the bearded man unlocked, which took a while because there were three locks. The room was bigger than Puggy thought it would be, and there were other crates inside, different sizes. They set the crate down and went back out. The bearded man locked the door and gave Puggy a five-dollar bill.

"You are strong," he said.

"I guess," said Puggy. It was true, although a lot of people didn't see it because he was also short.

"Come back tomorrow," said the bearded man. "Maybe I have another job for you."

That was how Puggy began his employment at the Jolly Jackal. Usually he came to work in the late afternoon and stayed until Leo (that was the bartender's name) or John (that was the bearded man's name) told him to go home. Some days they didn't need him to do anything, but they let him stay anyway. When they did need him to work, it was always moving heavy crates — sometimes from the Mercedes to the room; sometimes from the room to the Mercedes. Each time, when it was done, John gave him a five. One time, Puggy asked what was in the crates. John just said, "Equipment."

Mainly, Puggy watched TV and drank beer, which Leo almost never charged him for. It was like a dream. If Puggy had known jobs were like this, he would have tried to get one a long time ago.

At night, when they told him to leave, he went back to his tree. He had found the tree on his third night in Coconut Grove. He'd spent the first two nights in a park near the water, but some kind of nasty ants were biting him, plus, on the second night, from a distance, he'd seen Eddie and Snake go past, heading toward the dinghy dock. Snake was limping.

So Puggy went looking for another place. He

discovered that, if you walked just a short way in Coconut Grove, you could be in a whole different kind of neighborhood, a rich people's neighborhood, with big houses that had walls around them and driveway gates that opened by a motor. There were strange trees everywhere, big, complicated trees with roots going every which way and vines all over them and branches that hung way out over the street. Puggy thought it looked like a jungle.

He found a perfect tree to live in. It was just inside a rich person's wall, but across a big, densely vegetated yard from the house, so it was private. Puggy got into the tree by climbing the wall; he was a natural climber, even after many beers. About twenty feet up in the tree, where three massive limbs branched off from the trunk, there was a rickety, mossy wooden platform, a kids' treehouse from years before. Puggy fixed it up with some cardboard on the platform and a piece of plastic, from a construction site, that he could drape over the top when it rained. Sometimes he heard people talking in the house, but whoever they were, they never came back to this end of the yard.

Late at night, there was always music coming from one end of the house. It was some kind of music with a flute, soft, coming through the jungle to Puggy. He liked to lie there and listen to it. He was very happy the way things were going, both with his career and with his tree. It was the most secure, most structured, least turbulent existence he had ever known. It lasted for almost three weeks.

"I look at this ad," the Big Fat Stupid Client From Hell was saying, "and it doesn't say to me, 'Hammerhead Beer.' "

Eliot Arnold, of Eliot Arnold Advertising and Public Relations (which consisted entirely of Eliot Arnold), nodded thoughtfully, as though he thought the Client From Hell was making a valid point. In fact, Eliot was thinking it was a good thing that he was one of the maybe fifteen people in Miami who did not carry a loaded firearm, because he would definitely shoot the Client From Hell in his fat, glistening forehead.

At times like these — and there were many times like these — Eliot wondered if maybe he'd been a bit hasty, quitting the newspaper. Especially the way he'd done it, putting his foot through the managing editor's computer. He'd definitely burned a bridge there.

Eliot had spent twenty-one years in the newspaper business. His plan, coming out of college, had been to fight for Justice by using his English-major skills to root out and expose corruption. He got a job at a small daily newspaper, where he wrote obituaries and covered municipal meetings in which local elected officials and engineering consultants droned on for hours over what diameter pipe they needed for the new sewer line. Eliot, listening to this, slumped over a spiral reporter's notebook covered with doodles, figured there was probably some corruption going on there somewhere, but he had no idea how even to begin looking for it.

By the time he'd moved up to the big-time city newspaper, he'd given up on trying to root things out and settled into the comfortable niche of writing features, which it turned out he was good at. For years he wrote about pretty much whatever he wanted. Mostly he wrote what the higher honchos in the newsroom referred to, often condescendingly, as "offbeat" stories. They preferred *issues* stories, which were dense wads of facts, written by committees, running in five or six parts under some title that usually had the word "crisis" in it, like "Families in Crisis," "Crisis in Our Schools," "The Coming Water Crisis," et cetera. These series, which were heavily promoted and often won journalism contests, were commonly referred to in the newsroom as "megaturds." But the honchos loved them. Advocacy journalism, it was called. It was the hot trend in the newspaper business. Making a difference! Connecting with the readers!

Eliot thought that the readership of most of these series consisted almost entirely of contest judges. But more and more, he found himself getting ordered to work on megaturds, leaving less and less time for him to work on stories he thought somebody might actually want to read.

The end came on the day when he was summoned to the office of the managing editor, Ken Deeber, who was seven years younger than Eliot.

Eliot remembered when Deeber was a general-assignment reporter, just out of Princeton. He was articulate and personable, and he could be absolutely relied on to get at least one important fact wrong in every story, no matter how short. But Deeber did not write many stories; he was too busy networking. He rose through the ranks like a Polaris missile, becoming the youngest managing editor in the paper's history. He was big on issues stories. That's why he summoned Eliot to his office.

"How's it going, Eliot?" Deeber had said, starting things off. "Everything OK with you?"

"Well," said Eliot, "I'm kind of . . ."

"The reason I ask," said Deeber, who was not the least bit interested in whether or not everything was OK with Eliot, "is that John Croton tells me you haven't turned in a thing on the day-care project."

The day-care project was the current mega-turd. It was going to explain to the readers, in five parts with fourteen color charts, that there was a crisis in day care.

"Listen, Ken," said Eliot, "There are already five people working on the . . ."

"Eliot," said Deeber, the way a parent talks to a naughty child, "you were *given an assignment*."

Eliot's assignment was to write a sidebar about the Haitian community's perspective on the day-care crisis. Deeber believed that every story had to have the perspective of every ethnic group. When he went through the newspaper, he didn't

23

actually read the stories; he counted ethnic groups. He was always sending out memos like: *While the story on the increase in alligator attacks on golfers was timely and informative, I think more of an effort could have been made to include the Hispanic viewpoint.* The main reason why Deeber's car ignition had never been wired to a bomb is that reporters have poor do-it-yourself skills.

"I know I had an assignment," said Eliot. "But I've been working on this story about . . ."

"The pelican story?" sneered Deeber. Eliot thought Princeton must have a course in sneering, because Deeber was good at it.

"Ken," said Eliot, "it's an incredible story, and nobody else has it. There's this guy, this old Cuban guy in Key West, and he trains pelicans to . . ."

"Drop bombs," sneered Deeber. "It's the most dumb-ass thing I ever heard."

"Ken," said Eliot. "This guy is *amazing*. He actually tried to use a trained pelican to *kill Castro*. Something went wrong, maybe the bomb malfunctioned, maybe the pelican got confused, but the thing apparently blew up outside a hotel in downtown Havana, sprayed pelican parts all over a bunch of French tourists, and the Cuban government claimed that it was some kind of atmospheric . . ."

"Eliot," said Ken, "I don't think we're serving our readers with that kind of story."

"But it's *true*," said Eliot. He wanted to grab Deeber by his neck. "It's a *great* story. The guy

24

talked to me, and he . . ."

"Eliot," said Deeber, "Do you realize how *important* day care is to our readers? Do you realize how *many* of our readers have children in day care?"

There was a pause.

"Ken," said Eliot, "do you realize how many of our readers have assholes?"

Deeber said, "I see no need to . . ."

"All of them!" shouted Eliot. "They all have assholes!"

Quite a few people in the newsroom heard that through the glass wall to Deeber's office. Heads were turning.

"Ken," said Deeber, "I'm *ordering* you right now to . . ."

"Let's do a series on it!" shouted Eliot. "RECTUMS IN CRISIS!" The entire newsroom heard that.

Deeber, aware that people were watching, put on his sternest expression.

"Eliot," he said. "You work for me. You do what I tell you. I gave you an assignment. If you want to keep working at this newspaper, that assignment will be done, and it will be *in here*" — he pointed to his computer — "before you go home tonight."

"Fine!" said Eliot. He stood up and crossed around to Deeber's side of the desk, which caused Deeber to scoot his chair backward into his credenza, knocking over several journalism contest awards.

25

Eliot said: "How about I put it in there RIGHT NOW?"

Then he put his left foot through Deeber's computer screen. His foot got sort of stuck in there, so when he yanked it back out, Deeber's whole computer crashed to the floor. In the newsroom, there was a brief but hearty outbreak of applause.

Except for the time a drunk loading-dock employee drove a new $43,000 forklift into Biscayne Bay, nobody had ever been fired from the newspaper faster than Eliot. His coworkers expressed their sympathy and support; in fact, Eliot became a minor cult hero among reporters all over the country. But it was pretty clear he wasn't going to get another job in journalism, especially not in Miami, where he wanted to stay so he could be near his son, Matt, who lived with Eliot's ex-wife.

And so Eliot became Eliot Arnold Advertising and Public Relations, working out of a small office in Coconut Grove. At the beginning, he spent most of his time going around begging people to become his clients. But after a couple of years of hard work, he'd reached the point where he spent most of his time going around begging for his clients to pay the money they owed him. Either that, or he was listening to clients tell him why his work was not acceptable. This is what the Client From Hell was doing.

The Client From Hell's latest brainstorm was Hammerhead Beer, which tasted so awful that the first and only time Eliot put some in his mouth, he spat it out on his desk. Eliot thought Hammerhead Beer was an even worse idea than the Client From Hell's previous project, a theme park for senior citizens called Denture Adventure.

But the Client From Hell actually paid his bills some of the time, so Eliot had developed an advertising concept for the beer. The Client From Hell was looking at it, and offering his usual thoughtful brand of criticism.

"This sucks," he said.

"Well, Bruce," said Eliot, "I tried to . . ."

"Listen," said the Client From Hell, who did not believe in letting other people finish their sentences as long as he had any kind of thought whatsoever floating around in his brain. "You know what my business philosophy is?"

I surely do, thought Eliot. Your business philosophy is to take money from your extremely wealthy father and piss it away on moronic ideas.

"No, Bruce," he said, "what is your . . ."

"My business philosophy," said the Client From Hell, "is that there's a lot of people in the world."

To illustrate this point, the Client From Hell gestured toward the world. Several moments passed, during which Eliot waited hopefully for amplification.

"Well," Eliot said, finally, "that's certainly . . ."

"And," continued the Client From Hell, who had been waiting for Eliot to speak so he could

27

interrupt him, "all those people WANT something. You know what they want?"

"No," said Eliot. His plan was to go with short sentences.

"They want to *feel good,*" said the Client From Hell.

More moments passed.

"Ah," said Eliot.

"Do you know what I mean?" said the Client From Hell. He stared at Eliot.

"Well," said Eliot, "I . . ."

"NO YOU DON'T KNOW WHAT I MEAN!" shouted the Client From Hell, feeling better now that he was bullying a person who needed his money, which was his absolute favorite thing about being rich. "Because I gave you the *perfect concept* for Hammerhead Beer. The perfect concept! Which is *not* this piece of shit here." He made a brushing-away gesture, the kind you make at flying insects, in the direction of Eliot's concept, which Eliot had stayed up late working on. It was a board on which Eliot had mounted a close-up photograph of a hammerhead shark, its mouth gaping between its two impossibly far-apart, alien eyeballs. Underneath the photograph, in large, black type, were these words:

Ugly fish.
Good beer.

"What the hell *is* this?" the Client From Hell

demanded. "Why are you saying *ugly* here?"

"Well," said Eliot, "I'm contrasting, in a kind of humorous . . ."

"Listen," said the Client From Hell, whose idea of humor was — he had this on video, and watched it often — Joe Theisman getting the bottom half of his leg almost snapped off. "I don't want to see ugly. That is not the feeling I want. I *gave* you the concept already! I gave you the *perfect concept!*"

"Bruce, I talked to a lawyer about your concept, and he says we could get into real trouble with . . ."

" 'GET HAMMERED WITH HAMMER-HEAD!' " shouted the Client From Hell, pounding a pudgy Rolexed fist on Eliot's desk. "That's the concept!"

He stood up and spread his fat arms apart, to help Eliot visualize it. "You have a guy in a boat with a girl, she's in a bikini, she has big tits, they're on a boat, and they're getting hammered! With Hammerhead! The feeling of this ad is, somebody's gonna get laid! In the background swimming around is a shark! The girl has REALLY big tits! It's PERFECT! I give you this perfect concept, and you give me ugly! Listen, if you think I'm paying for this shit, forget it, because I'm not paying for ugly. I can get ugly for free."

You already *are* ugly, Eliot thought. What he said was: "OK, let me try to . . ."

"Don't tell me *try*. Don't *try*. I hate the word

try. Try is for *losers,*" said the Client From Hell, who got his entire philosophy of life from Nike commercials. "Lemme tell you something." He was tapping his finger on Eliot's desk (his *finger-nails* were fat). "You are *not* the only ad agency in this town."

I am the only ad agency in this town who is so far behind on his alimony that he will tolerate a moron of your magnitude, thought Eliot.

"OK, Bruce," he said.

"I wanna see it TOMORROW," said the Client From Hell.

I could get a gun by tomorrow, thought Eliot. With those hollow-point bullets.

"OK, Bruce," he said.

The phone rang. Eliot picked it up.

"Eliot Arnold," he said.

"I need to borrow your car tonight," said Matt, who was Eliot's son and seventeen years old, which meant that he was usually too busy to say hello.

"Hello, Nigel!" said Eliot. "How're things in London? Can you hold for a moment?"

"Nigel?" said Matt.

"Bruce," Eliot said to the Client From Hell, "I need to take this call from a client in London about . . ."

"I wanna see it tomorrow, and it better be *right,*" said the Client From Hell, banging open Eliot's door, walking out, not closing the door. From the hall — from right outside the next-door office of the certified public accountant

30

who complained whenever Eliot played his stereo — he shouted: "AND SHE BETTER HAVE BIG TITS!"

"Thanks for coming by, Bruce!" Eliot called to the empty doorway. "I think we're almost there!" To the phone he said: "Matt?"

"Who better have big tits?" asked Matt.

"Nobody," said Eliot.

"Who's Nigel?" asked Matt.

"Nobody," said Eliot. "I made Nigel up so my client wouldn't think I was interrupting a meeting for personal business."

"Was that the beer moron?"

"Yes."

"Whyn't you just dump him?" asked Matt.

"Matt," Eliot said, "do you have any idea where money comes . . ."

"So," said Matt, who was not about to waste valuable non-school time listening to a lecture he'd already heard, "can I borrow your car tonight?"

"What for?" asked Eliot.

"Me and Andrew have to kill a girl," said Matt.

"OK," said Eliot, "but I want the car back at my apartment by ten-thirty, and I want you to promise to drive . . ."

"OK thanks Dad," said Matt, hanging up, a busy man.

" . . . carefully," said Eliot, into the silent phone.

When she finished cleaning up after dinner,

31

Nina went back to her room — it was called the "maid's quarters," but it was just a little room with a tiny bathroom — and locked the door. She'd started locking it about three months earlier, when Mr. Herk had walked in on her. Nina was getting undressed, down to her bra and panties. Mr. Herk had not knocked; he'd just opened the door and come in.

He was holding a glass of red wine. Nina snatched her robe from the bed and held it in front of herself.

"It's OK, Nina," he said. "I just wondered if you'd like a little wine. You work so hard."

Nina knew he didn't care how hard she worked. She knew what he wanted, because of the way he looked at her sometimes, especially when he was drinking. He liked to come into the kitchen when she was there alone and stand a little too close to her, not saying anything, just looking at her.

Holding the robe close to herself, she said, "No, thank you, Mr. Herk. I am very tired."

He closed the door behind him and moved toward her. "You just need to relax," he said. He put his hand on her bare shoulder and let it slide toward her breast. His hand was wet with sweat.

Nina ducked from his hand and stepped backward, toward the bathroom.

"Mr. Herk," she said, "I don't think Mrs. Anna will like to know you are here."

His face turned hard. "She's asleep," he said. "And *I'm* not gonna tell her I was here. *You're* not gonna tell her, either, are you, Nina?"

No, she was not. He was the boss of the house, and she was the maid, and she wasn't in this country legally, and she had nowhere else to go.

"Excuse me," said Nina, and she turned and stepped into the bathroom, quickly closing the door and pressing the lock button.

The doorknob rattled as Mr. Herk tried it.

"Nina," he said, "come out."

Nina stared at the doorknob, not breathing. She could feel his sweat on her, where he had touched her.

"Nina," he said, louder, "this is *my* house, and you work for *me,* and I want you to come out *now.*"

Nina stared at the doorknob.

"Bitch," he said.

Nina heard glass breaking, then the hallway door banging open. She waited some more, then opened the bathroom door. There was a dark red stain in the middle of her white bedspread, where he had poured out the wine. He had smashed the glass on her floor. She cut her foot cleaning up.

The next day, when she served him his coffee, with Mrs. Anna there, he acted as though nothing had happened. But she still saw him looking at her. And she kept her door locked. She did not like Mr. Herk, but she needed to keep this job. She needed to make enough money to pay a lawyer so she could become legal, and then to bring her mother and her brother to the United States.

And there were things she liked about working here. The house was like a castle, and Mrs. Anna was very nice, very pretty. Nina could not understand why Mr. Herk could be so mean to such a woman. Nina had heard him yell at her, calling her bad names, making her cry. Nina thought that sometimes he hit her.

Mrs. Anna was nice to Nina. So was her daughter, Jenny, although she mostly stayed in her room, always on the phone, always listening to her music, which sounded to Nina like angry people shouting. She couldn't imagine why anybody would want to listen to shouting.

Nina listened to flute music from her country, on cassette tapes that she played on a Fisher-Price tape player that had been Jenny's when she was a little girl. At night, Nina would open her window (she didn't like air-conditioning) and lie on her bed with the lights off, letting her mind float on the music. It made her feel less lonely.

Across the yard, in his tree, listening to Nina's music, Puggy felt less lonely, too.

Matt picked up Andrew at 8:40.

"Where's the gun?" asked Andrew.

"In the trunk," said Matt. "I love this song." He cranked the volume all the way up on the stereo, which was playing "Sex Pootie," by a band called the Seminal Fluids. The lyrics were:

I want your sex pootie!
I want your sex pootie!

34

I want your sex pootie!
I want your sex pootie!
I want your sex pootie!
I want your sex pootie!
I want your sex pootie!
I want your sex pootie!

And so on.

"What's a sex pootie?" asked Andrew.

"What do you *think* it is?" asked Matt, scornfully, although in truth he wasn't sure what a sex pootie was, either. To change the subject, he said: "This sound system *sucks.*" Matt had great contempt for any sound system that was not loud enough to stun cattle.

"Why'd your dad buy a Kia?" asked Andrew.

" 'Cause he's a dork," explained Matt.

Andrew nodded understandingly. His dad was a dork, too. It seemed like *everybody's* dad was a dork. It amazed Matt and Andrew that their generation had turned out so cool.

"I just hope Jenny doesn't see this car," said Matt.

Jenny was the girl they were going to kill. Matt thought she was hot. She was in his biology class at Southeast High School, and he'd spent many classroom hours looking at her while pretending to look at diagrams of the pancreas and other organs. He'd tried to think of some way to talk to her, but he never came up with anything feasible. But now that he was going to kill her, he figured that would break the ice.

Matt had been assigned to kill Jenny by Evan Hanratty, a Southeast High student who had organized that year's edition of Killer. Killer was a game that surfaced every year at various high schools; it had been vehemently condemned and strictly banned by the school authorities, so it was very popular with the students.

There were various versions of the game, but basically it worked this way: You paid the organizer some money (at Matt's school, it was ten dollars to become a player). The organizer then gave you, in secret, the name of another person in the game; your goal was to kill that person. At the same time, you became the target of some other unknown person, who would be stalking you.

At a given time, the game officially started, and the killing began. After each round, the survivors were given new targets; the game repeated until the last surviving killer collected a cash prize from the organizer.

The killing was done with squirt guns. For the kill to be legal, you had to squirt your victim in the presence of one witness — but *only* one witness. This meant that you couldn't get your target at school or in a public place like the mall; you had to work by ambush, usually at the victim's home.

Some kids got their parents involved. A kid would get his mom to drive him over to the target's house; then he'd hide in the bushes while the mom, looking innocent, would ring the bell and ask if the target was home. When the target came to the door, the killer would leap out of the bushes, squirt gun blazing.

Matt and his friends thought it was way un-manly to use your mom to kill somebody. They preferred the night ambush, operating under the cover of darkness, when you had the element of surprise, plus the element of (you never know) possibly seeing the target naked.

Matt parked his dad's Kia two streets away from Jenny's house. He opened his trunk and got out his gun, a SquirtMaster Model 9000, top of the line, $33.95 at Toys "Я" Us. It looked like a real assault weapon and held a gallon of water; it could accurately shoot a stream of water fifty feet.

Matt and Andrew loped through the humid night to Jenny's driveway. They encountered nobody but mosquitoes; this was an expensive Coconut Grove neighborhood, whose residents stayed inside their compounds at night.

Jenny's house was big, but surrounded by trees and barely visible from the street. There was a six-foot masonry wall around the property, and the driveway was blocked by a motorized steel gate. Next to the gate was an intercom speaker.

"What's the plan?" whispered Andrew. "You wanna ring the buzzer?"

"Nah," said Matt. "What'm I gonna say? 'Hi! It's Matt Arnold, here to kill Jenny.' We gotta go over the wall."

"What if they have a dog?" asked Andrew.

"I like dogs," said Matt, thinking, *Shit, I hope they don't have a dog.*

They walked along the wall around to the back of the property. There, next to a huge tree, they found a place where the wall looked pretty easy to climb. Matt gave the SquirtMaster to Andrew and went over the wall first; Andrew then tossed the gun over and followed. Once on the ground inside, they stopped for a minute to listen for a dog, but all they heard was flute music. With Matt in the lead, they began to walk quietly toward the house.

Twenty feet above, Puggy watched the two guys with the gun disappear into the thick vegetation. He wondered what was going on. This was the *second* pair of armed people he'd seen go over this fence in the past half hour.

TWO

As it happens, the Herk household did have a dog, named Roger. Roger was the random result of generations of hasty, unplanned dog sex: Among other characteristics, he had the low-slung body of a beagle, the pointy ears of a German shepherd, the enthusiasm of a Labrador retriever, the stubby tail of a boxer, and the intelligence of celery.

On this evening, Roger was, as usual, patrolling the backyard, but he represented no threat to human intruders. Roger *loved* humans, all of them, unreservedly. Because you never knew when a human was going to, out of nowhere, like magic, produce food. And Roger *really* loved food.

What Roger hated was the toad. This was a *Bufo marinus,* a very large South American toad that had become common in South Florida since its introduction in the 1940s by well-meaning idiots who believed that *Bufo* would control sugarcane pests. The toads multiplied and thrived in the moist, fetid subtropical soil; before long, they had become the pests.

The particular toad that Roger hated, the Enemy Toad, had thrived to a weight of three pounds; it was a squat, hideous, warty, mud-brown, beady-eyed creature the size of a catcher's mitt. As far as Roger was concerned, this toad was the most evil being in the universe, because it ate his food. Each day, Nina, the maid, would fill Roger's bowl with a heaping mound of dog food and place it on the patio outside the family room. And each day, just as Roger was about to devour his food, the toad, with a startlingly quick movement, would launch its bloated body into the air and land splat in the center of Roger's dish, where it would commence to chow down on Roger's kibble.

The first time this happened, Roger, naturally, tried to eat the toad. Big mistake. In nature, you do not become a big fat toad without a defense against predators, and *Bufo marinus* had developed a dandy: Behind each eye, it had a gland that secretes a chemical called bufotenine, which is toxic. (It's also hallucinogenic; people have been known to lick these toads to get high. Sometimes, these people die. You could argue that they deserve to.)

So when Roger bit the toad, he got a mouthful of bufotenine. Fortunately for him, he spat it out rather than swallowing it, so instead of going to the Big Kennel in the Sky, he merely got very sick. Roger was not a rocket scientist, but he knew that he'd better not bite the toad again. The toad knew it, too. And so every day, for hours on end, the toad sat in Roger's dish, lei-surely eating Roger's food, while Roger sat exactly thirty inches away, growling at the toad. This activity occupied most of Roger's working day, but he made time in his schedule for other important chores such as barking at the doorbell, licking his private region, and greeting any humans who ventured into the yard, in case they had food.

When the two men climbed over the fence this night, Roger trotted happily up to them and gave them a friendly, tail-wagging welcome, which was why they elected not to shoot him. After determining that they did not have any food for him, Roger trotted back to his dish on the patio and resumed growling at his archenemy, the toad. You had to be vigilant.

A few feet away from Roger, on the other side of the sliding-glass door, Anna Herk and her daughter, Jenny, were sitting side by side on the family-room sofa, watching *Friends*, which they both liked a lot. They were laughing together, and then they stiffened together when they heard the unsteady footsteps of Arthur Herk clomp into the room behind them. He clomped over to the bar and, for the fourth time that evening, filled a tall glass with red wine. Holding the drink and swaying slightly, he stood directly behind Anna and Jenny. They were looking at the TV, but they could feel him back there.

"Why do you watch this shit?" he said.

Jenny, who rarely spoke to her stepfather, said nothing. Anna, willing her voice to be calm, said:

41

"We like this show, Arthur. If you don't like it, you don't have to watch it."

"I watch what I want to watch," said Herk. Anna was tempted to point out that this statement, in the current context, made no sense, but decided against it. For a few seconds, the three of them watched the attractive, witty, zero-body-fat *Friends* characters, who were sitting on sofas bantering.

Herk said, "Those guys are fags."

Anna and Jenny said nothing.

"Oh yeah," said Herk, "big-time fags, is what I read."

"He can *read?*" said Jenny, softly, looking straight ahead.

"What did you say?" said Herk, coming around the sofa.

Anna put her arm in front of her daughter. "Arthur," she said, "leave her alone."

"What did you say?" said Herk again, standing in front of Jenny, his head bobbing, wine sloshing from his glass.

Jenny stared straight ahead, as if looking right through Herk. She wished she could disappear into the TV set, become part of *Friends*, live with fun, nice people instead of this drunk asshole who hated her and hit her mom.

"Arthur," said Anna, knowing that she would pay for this later. "You get away from her."

Herk turned toward Anna, his head still bobbing, his eyes unfocused and red. Anna couldn't believe that she once found this man attractive.

He took a step toward her, sloshing more wine. Anna was watching his right hand, the one without the glass. He saw her looking at it, and he made his hand into a fist and jerked it toward her. Anna flinched. Herk liked that. He made her flinch again, then turned and picked up the remote control.

"Let's see what else is on," he said, and he changed the channel.

Outside in the humid darkness, at the edge of the patio, the two men — both swatting mosquitoes; one holding a rifle — were watching the Herks through the sliding-glass door. Their names were Henry and Leonard, and they were being paid $25,000 apiece, plus first-class round-trip expenses from their nice homes in suburban New Jersey, to shoot Arthur Herk with real bullets.

Henry and Leonard had been hired by a Miami company called Penultimate, Inc., where Arthur Herk was a mid-level executive. Penultimate was one of the largest engineering and construction firms in South Florida. It specialized in government contracts, and it made spectacular profits. Penultimate's formula for success was simple: aggressive management, strict employee discipline, and a relentless commitment to cheating. The company lied extravagantly about its technical qualifications, submitted absurdly unrealistic low-ball bids to get contracts, and tacked on huge add-on charges. Penultimate was able to do these things because it paid excellent bribes to government officials. Penultimate was as good at municipal corruption as it was bad at actually building things. In political circles, it was well known that Penultimate could be absolutely relied upon to do the wrong thing. In South Florida, a reputation like that is priceless.

Granted, sometimes there were problems. There was the time Penultimate won a large contract to build a prisoner-detention facility in downtown Miami. The facility was supposed to feature a state-of-the-art electronic security-door system, and the taxpayers certainly *paid for* a state-of-the-art security-door system. But what actually got *installed* was a semi-random collection of hardware that included, as a central element, garage-door openers purchased on sale at Home Depot for $99.97 apiece. The result was that, during a bad lightning storm shortly after the facility went into service, a number of key doors simply opened themselves, leaving it up to the prisoners to decide, on the honor system, whether they wished to remain in jail.

As it happened, 132 prisoners, out of a possible 137, decided that they did not wish to remain in jail. It was a huge story: a horde of criminals, some of them murderers, running loose on the streets of downtown Miami, pursued by a frantic posse of police and media. The highlight came when the capture of an escaped prisoner was shown live, nationally, on The NBC Nightly

News, and a reporter shouted to the prisoner, as he was being hustled into a police cruiser, "Who masterminded the escape?"

"Ain't nobody mastermind *shit,*" the prisoner shouted back. "The mufuh doors *opened.*"

Even by Miami standards, this was considered a major screwup. Under intense pressure from the media, Penultimate explained, through its dense firewall of high-priced attorneys, that all the blame belonged to . . . *subcontractors.* The politicians, who did not want Penultimate to get into trouble, inasmuch as almost all of them had received money from the company, pounced on this explanation like wild dogs on a pork chop: Yes! That was it! *Subcontractors* were responsible!

Unfortunately for the cause of justice, most of the key subcontractors involved either fled the country or died, generally in boating accidents. Eventually, the investigation lost steam, and the issue degenerated into a vast steaming bog of lawsuits and counter-lawsuits that would not be settled within the current geological era. Everybody lost interest, and Penultimate went back to winning contracts.

One of these was for a six-story downtown parking garage that wound up costing, what with one thing and another, just under four times the original contract figure. Each price increase was approved with virtually no discussion by key political leaders, who were invited to make speeches at the garage dedication ceremony, which fortunately was held outside the structure, which is why only two people were injured when the entire central portion of the structure collapsed *during the opening prayer.*

Once again there was outrage; once again there were statements and hearings; once again the finger of blame ultimately wound up being pointed at — it is *so* hard to get good help — those darned subcontractors. Who of course by that point were disappearing faster than weekend houseguests in an Agatha Christie story. And Penultimate continued to prosper and grow and benefit from its reputation as a company that only a fool would mess with.

As it happened, Arthur Herk, in addition to being an abusive alcoholic, was a fool. To pay off a gambling debt, he had embezzled $55,000 from Penultimate. Unbeknownst to him, his bosses, experts in the field of dishonesty and far smarter than Arthur, had discovered the theft almost immediately. They viewed embezzlement as a fairly serious violation of corporate policy, punishable by death.

And so Penultimate had hired two specialized subcontractors, Henry and Leonard, the men waiting in the humid darkness outside the sliding-glass door to the Herk family room. In whispered voices, they were discussing scheduling.

"We shoot him now," Leonard was saying, "we make the eleven-forty flight to Newark."

"I can't shoot him now," Henry said. "He's too close to the women." Henry was the man with the rifle; Leonard's main jobs were to drive and keep Henry company.

"You don't shoot him soon," Leonard said, "*I'm* dead, from these fucking mosquitoes." He slapped one on his wrist, leaving a quarter-sized blot of blood and bug parts. "Look at this thing," he said. "He's the size of that fucking *dog.*"

"She," said Henry, continuing to watch the Herk family through the window.

"She?" asked Leonard. "She *what?*"

"The mosquito," said Henry. "It's a she."

Leonard looked closely at the blot on his wrist, then back at Henry. "How the *fuck* can you tell that?" he asked.

"This show on the Discovery Channel," explained Henry. "They said only the female mosquito sucks your blood."

Leonard looked at the blot again. He said, "Bitch."

"What they didn't explain," said Henry, "is what do the male mosquitoes eat?"

"What, are you *worried* about them?"

"No, I'm not *worried* about them. I'm just . . ."

"You want I should go get a fucking *pizza* for them, set it out here in the jungle so they don't *starve?*"

"I'm just saying, what do they eat? If they don't suck blood? Is all I'm saying."

"Maybe they suck each other," said Leonard.

Henry had to smile at that, which only encouraged Leonard.

"*Oh, Bruth!*" Leonard said in a lisping mos-

47

quito whisper. *"You have a BIG thtinger!"*

Henry was quietly quaking with laughter now; his rifle barrel vibrated in the gloom.

Inside the family room, Arthur Herk was methodically, relentlessly changing channels. He was doing this partly because the instinct to change channels is embedded deep in the male genetic code, and partly because he knew his wife and stepdaughter hated it.

For a few minutes, Anna and Jenny stared at the flashing jumble of images, expressionless, not wanting to give Herk any satisfaction. Finally, Jenny sighed and stood. Addressing Anna, she said, "I'm gonna go to my room, where it's not so, I don't know . . . *stupid.* Good night, Mom."

Herk kept changing channels.

Anna said, "I think I'll let Roger in and go to bed, too."

Herk stopped changing channels and looked at her. She recognized the look. She hoped he'd pass out in the family room tonight. She hoped he would not make it to the bedroom. She rose from the sofa.

Outside, Henry whispered, "They're leaving."

"They're leaving," whispered Matt. He and Andrew, having received a warm but brief welcome from Roger, had moved to an observation point next to a large potted plant at the edge of the patio, about thirty feet from Henry and Leonard.

"Whadda we do?" asked Andrew.

"I think she's gonna let the dog in," said Matt. "When she opens the door, we run up, and I shoot her, and you witness it."

"I'm gonna witness it from here," said Andrew, "in case her father shoots us."

"With *what?*" said Matt. "The remote control? You gotta come with me so Jenny sees that you witnessed it."

"He has a gun *somewhere*," Andrew said. "This is Miami."

Matt could not argue with that. Sounding braver than he felt, he whispered, "Come on," and started across the patio toward the sliding-glass door. Andrew followed, reluctantly, a few feet behind.

Henry and Leonard did not see the boys immediately; they were both intently watching Anna Herk as she moved toward the door from the other side.

"Fine-looking woman," Leonard observed.

"Shut up," Henry observed. He raised his rifle and trained the sight on Arthur Herk, thinking about how he was going to do this. If Herk stayed in the room, sitting in front of the TV, it would be easy. But Henry had to be ready in case Herk got up and followed the women out. Henry didn't want to shoot with the women still in the room, but he would if he had to.

Anna Herk reached the patio door, unlatched it, slid it open, and called, "Roger, c'mon, boy." At this point, a number of things happened in extremely quick succession:

— Roger, calculating with his nine functioning brain cells that the chances were better of getting food inside the house with the humans than outside with the Enemy Toad, left his surveillance post and shot, a low-flying, furry missile, through the door opening into the family room.

— Right behind him came Matt, rushing toward the opening, holding his realistic SquirtMaster Model 9000. He had planned to yell, "HEY, JENNY!" but he was very nervous, so it came out more like, "HENNY!"

— Anna, seeing a shape rushing out of the night toward her yelling unintelligibly, screamed.

— Two steps behind, Jenny, hearing her mom scream, then seeing the shape, screamed.

— Arthur Herk, hearing both women screaming, dropped the remote control. Roger immediately went over to see if it was food.

— Outside in the gloom, Leonard said, "What the *fuck?*"

— In about the same time that it took for Leonard to come to that conclusion, Henry, who had a gift for processing information and making decisions very rapidly, which is why he was the one with the rifle, decided that, whatever this other shooter was there to do, he, Henry, was there to shoot Arthur Herk, and he had better do it right now.

— As Henry was deciding, Matt burst through the door opening past the screaming Anna Herk

50

and aimed his SquirtMaster Model 9000 at the screaming Jenny.

— Arthur Herk, seeing a gunman come through the door, dove forward off the sofa to the floor in front of the television, which was fortunate for Arthur, because . . .

— maybe a tenth of a second later, a bullet from Henry's rifle passed directly through the middle of the airspace where Arthur's head had been and into the thirty-five-inch diagonal screen of the Herk family TV set, which imploded with a brief, brutal "POP," shattering, in a bright bluish flash, the image of the president of the Hair Club for Men.

— Arthur Herk, hearing the explosion, scrabbled frantically at the floor with his hands and knees and shot forward, alligator-like, out of the family room and into the hallway leading to Nina's room.

— Anna Herk, a mother instinctively and fearlessly protecting her baby, jumped on Matt's back, causing him to stagger forward into Jenny, such that the three of them collapsed to the floor in a human sandwich, with Matt in the middle and both women pounding him and screaming.

— Down the hall, Nina, hearing screams, an explosion, then more screams, opened her door and saw Arthur coming out of a crouch and hurtling down the hall toward her with the face of a crazed animal. She slammed the door, which came violently open again as Arthur burst through it. Convinced she was about to be raped, Nina leaped onto her bed and slithered out the open window, dropped onto the lawn, and, wearing only a blue nightgown, sprinted, barefoot and terrified, into the night.

— At the edge of the patio, Leonard and Henry heard a siren and, without exchanging words, began quickly and professionally to get the hell out of there.

— Thirty feet to the right, Andrew, less professionally but just as quickly, did the same.

— In Roger's dish, the toad, which did not achieve its current station in life by being easily distracted, continued to eat Roger's kibble.

Nina reached the wall first; in fact, in the darkness beneath the huge ficus tree she ran *into* the wall. Emitting a sharp, high-pitched cry of pain, she stumbled backward, directly in the path of Leonard, who emerged from a thicket moving at top middle-aged-guy speed and slammed into her, causing her to cry out again as they both went down, with Leonard tripping over her and hitting the wall headfirst, hard.

Three seconds later, Henry, puffing, burst through the thicket and stopped as he saw two entangled shapes on the ground by the wall, both moaning. Crouching, Henry approached the shapes, turning the rifle around in his hands so he could use it as a club.

"Leonard?" he said. *"Leonard?"*

One of the moaning shapes began, slowly, to

sit up. It was not Leonard. Henry raised his rifle and braced himself, ready to strike. He was in that pose when Puggy landed on his head. Henry crumpled to the ground and dropped the rifle, which Puggy, bouncing quickly to his feet, snatched up.

Puggy had never shot a rifle; he had never even touched a rifle. He held this one the way he had seen people hold rifles on TV, kind of looking down the barrel with one eye. He stepped back a few feet and pointed the rifle in the general direction of Henry.

If there had been more light, and if Henry hadn't had searing blasts of pain stabbing his neck and right shoulder, he might have noticed that whoever this stocky little man holding his rifle was, he still had the safety on, and he didn't have his finger inside the trigger guard. If he had been his usual self, Henry might have made a play on this guy — kick his feet out, roll sideways, come up moving, going for the gun he kept in an ankle holster.

But Henry was not his usual self, and he knew it, and could hear that the sirens were very close now, and as much as he wanted to know what was going on here, he figured his best play was to continue getting the hell out of there. Keeping his eye on Puggy, moving slowly, keeping his hands in view, he got his knees under himself, then his feet, then stood up. Puggy watched him.

"I don't want any trouble," Henry said.

"Me neither," said Puggy. Puggy never wanted trouble.

"I'm gonna get my friend here," Henry said.

"Don't touch the girl," Puggy said.

Henry thought, *Girl?* But he said, "No, no, I'm just gonna get my friend, OK?" He moved slowly to the wall and . . . shit, there *was* a girl. What was going *on* here? He grabbed Leonard's shoulder and shook it.

"C'mon," he said. "Come *on,* dammit!"

Leonard sat up a little, his eyes starting to focus. First he saw Henry, right over him; then he saw a girl in a nightgown, on the ground next to him; then he saw a guy with a rifle. His head hurt and there was blood in his eyes and he could hear sirens really loud.

He said: "What the *fuck?*"

"Come *on,*" said Henry, yanking Leonard up, feeling a nauseating stab of pain in his shoulder. He looked one more time at the stocky man, who was still pointing the rifle vaguely in his direction. Henry knew this guy was not a pro. Henry was pretty sure he could get the rifle back — he did *not* want to leave the rifle — but Leonard was very shaky, and the siren had stopped, which meant the cops were here.

Henry pushed Leonard over to the wall, got his shoulder under Leonard's ass — another stab of pain — and shoved him over the wall; then he followed. He herded Leonard as quickly as he could to the rental car and shoved him into the backseat. He climbed gingerly in the front and drove out of the neighborhood, watching the rearview, thinking about how he was going to word the phone call.

THREE

If you asked the average seventeen-year-old male whether he would enjoy lying on the floor pressed between two attractive women, he would say, Heck yes. But it was not proving to be a sensual experience for Matt. The problem, basically, was that although *he* knew that he was just a fun-loving high-school student engaged in a harmless game, neither Anna Herk nor Jenny knew this. And so while he didn't want to do anything to hurt *them*, they had no qualms what-soever about beating the shit out of *him*.

Behind him, Anna Herk, who worked out regularly at the health club, was clinging to Matt like a psychotic lamprey. She had both legs wrapped tightly around him, pinning his arms to his side; her right arm was around his throat, pretty much cutting off his air supply. She was using her left fist to pound the back of his head, and she was screaming into his left ear, and although she was not by nature an aggressive or hostile person, she was trying desperately to sound like one.

"YOU LET HER GO YOU SON OF A BITCH!" were her exact words.

Matt would have liked nothing more than to let Jenny go, because Jenny was kneeing his groin and scratching at him with fingernails that felt like X-Acto knives. But Matt could not move, because Mrs. Herk was right on top of him, pressing him down on her writhing, scratching, screaming daughter, slamming his face into the hard tile floor every time Anna pounded the back of his head; blood was spurting from his nose. He tried to explain himself, but the only sound he could force out through his constricted throat was an ambiguous "Gack." Through the darkening haze of his diminishing consciousness, Matt felt a new, hairy presence next to his right cheek. It was Roger, who, having sized up the situation and decided what needed to be done, was licking up Matt's blood.

On the street outside, Miami police officer Monica Ramirez, who heard a minimum of three Monica Lewinsky jokes per day from her endlessly self-amused male colleagues, stopped her police cruiser in front of the Herk address, which had been phoned to 911 by a neighbor. She rolled down her window and heard what sounded like a woman's screaming. Turning the cruiser into the driveway, she nosed the front bumper up against the steel security gate and pressed the accelerator gently; the security gate, as most of them did, immediately popped open.

Monica pulled into the driveway and got out

of the car, as did her partner, Officer Walter Kramitz. They had been partners for two months now, and Monica could tell he was getting ready to ask her for a date, which meant she had been thinking about how she was going to gently tell him no, the truth being that he was a little too fascinated by his own arm muscles. Plus he was married.

Kramitz tried the front door, which was locked, then pushed the buzzer, then pounded on the door, yelling, "Police!"

Monica didn't expect anybody to open the door. She said, "I'm going around back," and took off running around the left side of the house.

When she rounded the back corner, she heard the screams coming louder from the direction of the patio. As she approached the open sliding-glass door, Monica unholstered her revolver. Through the glass, she first saw a tangle of feet; then she saw people struggling on the floor, blood, and a rifle.

Pivoting in through the door opening, she raised her revolver and shouted: "Police! Everybody hold it!" (Monica never yelled "Freeze!" She thought it was trite.) The people struggling on the floor did not appear to hear her, although Roger immediately trotted over and, in the universal gesture of dog friendship, thrust his snout into Monica's crotch.

"STOP IT!" shouted Monica. This statement was aimed at Roger, but Anna Herk heard it and,

58

with her arm still around Matt's throat, turning to see a police officer aiming a gun her way, froze.

"Get off them," said Monica.

"I live here," said Anna.

"Get off them anyway," said Monica.

Anna rolled off Matt. Matt, free at last, rolled off Jenny and put his hands up to his bleeding nose. Jenny, weeping, crawled over to her mom.

"Are you OK, honey?" asked Anna. Jenny nodded.

Monica, lowering the gun but keeping it unholstered, said to Anna, "OK, I want you to tell me what's going on."

Anna pointed to Matt and said, "This person tried to . . ."

"FREEZE!" shouted Officer Kramitz, coming through the patio doorway with his gun drawn. He had given up on the front door.

"It's OK," said Monica. "Everything's cool."

"OK," said Officer Kramitz, disappointed. "What happened?"

"This lady was just starting to tell me," said Monica. "Go ahead."

"This person tried to kill us," said Anna.

Everybody looked at Matt.

"No!" he said. "It's me! Matt Arnold." He took his hand away from his bleeding nose so they could see who it was.

"I was just trying to kill Jenny," he explained.

"You SEE?" said Anna.

"No, no," said Matt, "I don't mean *kill* her, I

mean, it's a *game*, Killer. From *school*. I'm in her *biology class*. Jenny, tell them it's me."

Everybody looked at Jenny, who was looking at Matt and realizing that, underneath the blood, he was, in fact, a guy from her biology class. She had seen him looking at her, although, like all pretty girls, she had learned to appear as though she never noticed when boys were look-ing at her, although of course she always did.

"What are you doing in my house?" Jenny asked.

"I'm supposed to kill you," said Matt.

"You *see?*" said Anna again.

"With a squirt gun," said Matt. "It's a *squirt gun.*"

Everybody looked at the rifle. Officer Kramitz went over and picked it up.

"It's a squirt gun," he said, really disappointed now.

"Oh *shit*," said Jenny. "Is THAT what this is? That stupid *game?*"

"Yes!" said Matt. "The game!"

"Oh Jesus," said Jenny. To her mom, she said: "We have this game at school where you get somebody's name, and you're supposed to squirt them."

"In their *house?*" asked Anna. "At *night?* What kind of game is that?"

"I'm sorry," said Matt. "I didn't think it . . ."

"It's about TIME you people got here," said Arthur Herk, emerging from the hallway. He had been in Nina's room, with the door locked,

60

until he was sure the danger had passed. Roger trotted over to see if Arthur was bringing food, but veered away when Arthur kicked at him.

"And you are . . ." said Monica.

"I *own* this house," said Arthur.

"Good for you," said Monica. "And your name is?"

"Arthur Herk. I know the mayor, and I want to know what took you people so fucking long."

"Sir," said Monica, "first, we came as soon as we got the call. Second, don't use that language with me."

"That's right, *sir*," said Officer Kramitz, who was hoping that Arthur would become disorderly so he could restrain him.

"What're you gonna do about this?" demanded Arthur, pointing at Matt. "Guy comes in here with a fucking gun! Trying to kill us!"

"Arthur," said Anna, "It's a squirt gun."

Arthur looked at the gun in Officer Kramitz's hand. Officer Kramitz pulled the trigger, sending a stream of water onto the floor. Roger trotted over to lick it.

"Good thing you ran away, Arthur," said Jenny. "You might have got squirted."

Officer Kramitz snorted. Arthur whirled to face Jenny and said, "Shut up, you little bitch."

There was a moment of silence while everybody in the room, except for Arthur and Roger, reflected on what an asshole Arthur was.

"OK," said Monica, "let's all just settle down and . . ."

"MY TV!" said Arthur. "HE BROKE MY FUCKING TV!"

Everybody looked at the TV, now a mute black box with a gaping hole and glass littering the floor in front of it.

"I didn't do that," said Matt.

"YOU'RE GONNA PAY FOR THAT AND YOU'RE GONNA GO TO JAIL YOU LITTLE FUCK," said Arthur.

"I didn't *do* it," said Matt. "It's a *squirt gun.*"

"He's more upset about the TV than about us," said Jenny.

"I TOLD YOU TO SHUT THE FUCK UP," said Arthur.

"Sir," said Monica, who was wondering how come she always got these domestic disputes instead of nice, simple homicides, "I'm asking you to please calm down so we can . . ."

"THIS IS MY FUCKING HOUSE," said Arthur.

"Yes, sir," said Monica. "And these right here are my handcuffs, and if you don't calm down, you are gonna be wearing them."

"That's right, *sir,*" said Officer Kramitz, wishing he had thought of the handcuff line first.

"OK," said Monica, "I wanna hear, from the beginning, one at a time, what happened, starting with Mr. Killer over here." She nodded to Matt.

"Well," Matt said, "me and Andrew were outside with the squirt gun, and . . ."

"Who's Andrew?" asked Monica.

Matt, realizing he was in danger of committing the mortal schoolboy sin of ratting on a friend, said, "Nobody."

"Andrew is nobody?" said Monica. "You were out there with a squirt gun and an imaginary friend?"

"Yes," said Matt. "I mean, no."

Monica started to rub her temple, then realized she still had her gun in her hand. She holstered it and said, "OK, so you and nobody are outside. Then what?"

"OK," said Matt, "so Jenny's mom opened the door, and I came running up to squirt Jenny, and . . ."

A buzzer sounded.

"That's the front door," said Anna.

"Officer Kramitz," said Monica, "could you please go see who it is?"

Officer Kramitz, giving Arthur a look, left the family room.

"So," said Monica to Matt, "you ran up for a squirt, and . . ."

"And Mrs. Herk jumped me, and I went down on Jenny," said Matt. "I mean, *fell* down on Jenny." Matt and Jenny both turned red.

"I'm sorry," said Anna. "I thought you were . . . I didn't realize. Are you OK?"

"Yeah, it's just a bloody nose," said Matt. "Do you work out or something?"

Anna said, "I'll get you a washcloth."

Jenny said, "I'll get it." The truth was, she

thought Matt was cute.

"You're not getting him *shit,*" said Arthur. "He broke into this house, and he broke my fucking TV, and I'm suing and I'm pressing charges."

Officer Kramitz reentered the room and said, "This guy says his son is here."

Behind him, wearing gym shorts and a Miami Fusion T-shirt and looking very anxious as he brushed Roger away from his groin, was Eliot Arnold. Eliot went straight to Matt.

"Matt," he said, "you OK?"

"Yeah," said Matt. "It's just a bloody nose. I'm sorry, Dad. I never thought, I mean . . . I'm really sorry."

"This is your son?" asked Monica.

"Yes," said Eliot. "I'm Eliot Arnold. I got a call from Andrew, Matt's friend, he said there was trouble here, so I took a cab."

"Ah," said Monica. "The imaginary friend."

"What?" said Eliot.

"Never mind," said Monica.

Arthur Herk walked over to Eliot and, standing too close, said, "You got a lawyer?"

"What?" said Eliot.

"You better have a good fucking lawyer," Arthur told Eliot. "Your son broke my TV. It was a Sony, thirty-nine inches diagonal."

"Thirty-five inches," said Jenny, returning with a washcloth.

"Bitch," said Arthur.

"Could somebody please tell me what happened?" asked Eliot.

"I was trying to kill Jenny," said Matt, "and her mom jumped me."

"Hi," said Anna, giving Eliot a little wave. "I'm Anna Herk. I didn't mean to hurt him."

"Hi," said Eliot, waving back. "Listen, I'm really sorry about this. I thought it was, I mean, the way Matt described it, it was just supposed to be a game."

"Hey," said Anna, making a what-can-you-do gesture. "Kids."

"Yeah," agreed Eliot. "Kids." Eliot was noticing that Anna had extremely green eyes.

"Your kid's going to jail," said Arthur Herk, heading for the bar.

"Monica?" said Officer Kramitz.

"What?" said Monica.

"Take a look at this," said Officer Kramitz, feeling very happy about this case again. He was crouched by the TV set, pointing at something inside the gaping opening where the picture tube had been. Monica went over and saw that he was pointing at a small, perfectly round hole in the back of the plastic cabinet. Looking behind the TV, she saw a matching hole in the wall. She went around to the other side of the wall, which was the dining room; there was a hole in the wall, and another hole in the wall on the opposite side of the room.

"Jesus," she said. She went back into the family room.

"OK," she said, "Let's go over what happened

again, and this time, let's include the part about who shot the TV set."

Arthur Herk, pouring a drink, jerked his head up.

"*Shot* it?" said Anna. "Nobody shot it."

"It's a *squirt gun,*" said Matt.

"Listen," said Monica. "There's a bullet hole in the wall there, and I want to know, right now, how . . . Wait a minute."

Monica turned and went over to the window next to the sliding-glass door and stood for a moment, staring. Eliot, Matt, Anna, Jenny, and Officer Kramitz moved closer to see what she was looking at. What she was looking at was a neat, round hole in the glass.

"Oh my *God,*" said Jenny.

"Is that a *bullet* hole?" asked Eliot.

"Looks like," said Monica.

"So," said Matt, "like, a bullet came *through this room?* With us *here?*"

"Oh my *God,*" said Jenny, again. Anna hugged her.

At the bar, Arthur Herk went pale.

"Matt," said Monica, "when you and your imaginary friend were outside, did you see anybody else?"

"No," said Matt.

"Mrs. Herk," said Monica, "does anybody live here besides you and your daughter and your husband?"

"Well," said Anna, "there's . . . My god, *where's Nina?*"

Nina could smell beer. It wasn't a bad smell; in fact, it reminded her of her father, when he came home late from work on Friday and sometimes she would sit on his lap and he would sing her songs, and on his breath was the sweet smell of the *cerveza*.

She could smell it now, but it wasn't her father; it was somebody with a different voice, a higher voice, and he was saying, "You OK? Lady? Lady? You OK?"

Nina opened her eyes, and she saw a man, but she didn't scream, because she was not afraid of this man. He had a beard and sad brown eyes, kind of like Roger the dog's, and she could see in them that he had a sad brown soul, and that he would not hurt her.

Puggy thought that Nina was beautiful. Just beautiful, like an angel in a blue nightgown, or a woman on the TV. He could not believe that a woman as beautiful as this was in his tree. He knew — he was sure — that she was the reason for the flute music, because that music was as beautiful as this woman was. He had never really loved a woman, or even really talked to one, but he believed that he loved this woman very much.

"You OK?" he said again.

"*Sí*," said Nina. "Yes."

Spanish, thought Puggy. He would die for this woman.

"What happen to me?" she asked, tentatively

67

touching her forehead, discovering a large and tender lump.

"That guy ran into you," said Puggy.

"Señor Herk," said Nina. "He chase me."

Whoever Señor Herk was, Puggy hated him.

"I got the gun," said Puggy.

"Gun?" said Nina. She pronounced it "gon." Puggy thought it was a beautiful way to pronounce it. He wanted this woman to stay in his tree forever, pronouncing things.

"The gun the other guy had," said Puggy. "I got it."

"There was another?" asked Nina.

"There was two guys," said Puggy. "They're gone, though."

Nina looked around her. She was lying on something hard and flat, like wood, but she was outside, with branches all around.

"Where is this?" she asked.

"This is my tree," Puggy said.

Nina sat up a little bit, and saw that she was in a tree.

"Well," said Puggy, "it's not *my* tree. But I live here."

"How do I come here?" asked Nina.

"I picked you up," said Puggy, remembering how warm her body felt over his shoulder. "I hope I didn't . . . I mean, I wasn't . . ."

"No, no," said Nina. "Is OK. You help me. *Muchas gracias.* Thank you." She smiled at him. She had very white teeth.

Puggy had never been happier in his entire life,

never, not even the time when he was little and his dad, who was still around then, took him to the volunteer firemen's carnival and let him ride the bumper cars over and over, his dad drinking beers and laughing and handing the bumper-car guy some bills and saying, "Let'm go again!" That was the best time he'd ever had, and this was better, to have this TV-beautiful angel smiling at him.

"Nina!" called a voice through the darkness, from the direction of house.

"*Ay Dios,*" said Nina. "*La señora!*"

Nina, thought Puggy.

"I must go," said Nina.

"Nina!" called the voice.

"Nina," said Puggy, trying it out.

Nina liked the way he said it. "What is your name?" she asked.

"Puggy."

"Puggy," she said. She pronounced it "Pogey." Puggy thought he was going to float out of the tree.

"NINA!" called the voice, sounding a little frantic, and a little closer.

"I must go," Nina said again.

"OK," said Puggy. He was used to people having to go. He held out his hand, and Nina took it, and he pulled her up, and she could feel that he was strong. She hoped her hand did not feel too rough to him. She had working hands.

But Puggy liked the way her hand felt, and he loved the way she gripped his hand, a firm grip, as he eased her down onto a lower branch, and then, following behind, eased her to the ground. He dropped down beside her, and they stood looking at each other. They were exactly the same height.

"NINA!" called the voice, now definitely coming this way.

"I don't think they know I live in their tree," said Puggy.

"OK," said Nina. She would not tell.

"Nina," said Puggy, trying to figure out a way to tell her that he loved her.

"Yes?" she said.

"I'm usually here," he said.

"OK," she said. She touched his arm, leaving her hand there a second. Then she turned and walked, a little unsteadily, toward the calling voice, leaving Puggy watching her, still feeling her hand on his arm.

Henry didn't want to make the call from his cell phone. The first pay phone he found was on Grand Avenue in Coconut Grove. This was not the world's safest place for middle-aged white guys wearing Rolex watches, which Henry was.

Leonard, still woozy and seriously hurting in the head, stayed in the car, lying across the backseat. Henry got out, fed a quarter and a dime into the phone, and dialed a number from a piece of paper. Watching him, from a vacant lot across the four-lane avenue, were three young men.

The phone rang once.

"Tell me," said a voice on the other end.

"There was another shooter," said Henry.

There was a pause, then the voice said: "What do you mean?"

The three young men started walking across Grand Avenue, very casually, toward Henry.

"I mean there was another shooter, is what I mean," said Henry.

"Who?" said the voice.

"I was thinking maybe you would know," said Henry.

Halfway across the avenue, the three young men fanned out, with one moving to Henry's left, one to his right, and one coming directly toward him. They were still moving casually.

The phone voice said: "Whoever it was, it wasn't us." Then: "Did you take care of the job?"

"No," said Henry.

"Did the other shooter take care of it?"

"No."

"So you're saying there's *two* shooters, and our guy just walks away?"

The three young men had stopped about eight feet from Henry, forming a triangle around him.

"Hang on a second," Henry said. He dropped the piece of paper with the telephone number on it, then bent down as if to pick it up. Instead, he pulled the gun out of his ankle holster, straightened, and pointed the gun at the one of the three young men, who Henry figured was the leader, on the grounds that he was the nearest, plus he was wearing the biggest pants. Henry arched his eyebrows at him, letting him know, hey, *not right now*, OK?

The leader nodded approvingly at the gun, at the general coolness of Henry's move. He pivoted and walked casually back across Grand Avenue, followed by the other two young men.

"Hello?" said the voice on the phone.

"Our guy didn't *walk* away," said Henry. "He more *crawled* away when this other shooter comes running up like he's Geronimo, and then Geronimo gets jumped by the wife, and then the cops come." Henry decided to leave out, for now anyway, the part where he lost his rifle to the guy from the tree.

The phone was silent for a moment.

"We need to talk," said the voice.

"You got *that* right," said Henry.

A police detective named Harvey Baker came and asked the Herks, several different ways, if they could think of any reason why anybody would want to shoot them. Anna had no idea. Arthur speculated that it was probably some fucking kids, because these fucking kids today, they all have fucking guns. Detective Baker did not believe that Arthur was telling him everything. He pointed out that the police could not protect people if the people didn't cooperate. Arthur stated that he didn't think the police could protect their own dicks with both hands.

Detective Baker found himself developing a strong emotional bond with whoever had taken the shot.

Nina was not helpful, either. Detective Baker, with Monica translating, made it clear that he was not interested in the legality of her residence in the United States, but she wanted no part of any police business. All she would say is that when she heard noise, she jumped out the window, ran across the yard, and hit the wall. She did not see anything; she did not hear anything. *Nada.*

Detective Baker decided that this was probably going to be one of those cases where somebody shoots a gun and nobody ever finds out who or why, which is a fairly common type of case in Miami. To make Anna Herk feel better, he poked around the backyard a bit, aided by Roger, but he didn't find, nor did he expect to find, any clues. He told the Herks that he would continue to investigate the shooting, which everybody understood to mean that he would not continue to investigate the shooting.

Detective Baker decided not to arrest Matt, thanks in part to the pleading of Anna Herk, who felt really bad about having pounded Matt's face into the floor. Detective Baker did, however, point out that creeping around people's backyards at night in Miami with what looked like a real gun was, no offense, dumber than dog shit. Matt assured the detective that he had learned this lesson.

As soon as the police left, Arthur turned to Eliot and said: "Now you and your punk kid can get the fuck out of here and never come back."

"It's been a pleasure meeting *you,* too," said Eliot.

"I'll walk you out," Anna told Eliot. They headed for the foyer, with Matt, Jenny, and Roger trailing behind.

Outside, Matt said, "I'll go get the car." To Jenny, he said, "Did you ever want to experience the thrill of riding in a genuine Kia?"

"It's only a lifelong dream," said Jenny, and they set off toward the gate, followed by Roger, in case they were going to get food.

"Sarcasm," said Eliot. "I don't know where they get it."

"*Certainly* not from their parents," said Anna.

"Listen," said Eliot. "I am *really* sorry about . . ."

"No," said Anna. "*I'm* sorry, for hurting Matt, and I'm sorry my husband is such an idiot."

"Well," said Eliot, "he's probably really upset about the bullet."

"No," said Anna. "He's an idiot."

Eliot just looked at her for a moment, because the truth was, he agreed with her that Arthur was an idiot. Also, she had *amazing* eyes.

"Well, listen," he finally said, "if there's ever anything that I can . . . I mean, not about your husband of course, I mean, the bullet, if I can . . ."

"I married him when Jenny was little," Anna

said, "and my first husband left me with no money, and I had to move to a horrible apartment and I had no job. Arthur didn't drink so much then, and he seemed . . . stable, I guess, and I just . . . I was *desperate.*"

"Geez," said Eliot.

"I don't know why I'm telling you this," she said.

"It's OK," said Eliot. He was glad she was telling him this.

"I keep looking up divorce lawyers in the phone book," she said. "Sometimes I even call, but when they answer, I hang up, because . . . I mean, I *want* to do it, and I know I *have* to do it, but I also know Arthur, and he's going to be just as big a prick as he possibly can. He's going to want to hurt me and Jenny. And I keep seeing us back in that horrible apartment."

"Geez," said Eliot. He was wondering what she would think of his apartment.

"Does that mean I'm pathetic?" she said.

"No!" said Eliot.

"I'm sorry," she said. "I'll stop dumping on you, I promise."

"Hey," he said. "Anytime."

"Thanks," she said. She touched his forearm. *Whoa.*

They stood there for a moment, both of them a little bit uncomfortable, but neither of them wanting to break the spell, and then . . .

I want your sex pootie!

75

The sound of the thudding bass preceded the Kia, which pulled into the driveway going too fast, as it always did when Matt was at the wheel. It jerked to a stop. Jenny got out, and Matt followed, holding a CD.

"You want to borrow it?" he said.

"Sure, thanks," Jenny said. "I love the Seminal Fluids." In fact, she already had this particular CD; she was borrowing it so she could return it, and thus talk to Matt again. When she took the CD, their hands touched. *Whoa.*

"I'll drive," said Eliot, and Matt did not argue, which indicated to Eliot that Matt was either falling in love or suffering from a concussion.

The four of them stood by the car for a second or two.

"Well," said Eliot, to Anna, "bye."

"Bye," said Anna, to Eliot.

"Bye," said Jenny, to Matt.

"Bye," said Matt, to Jenny.

"Get down," said Jenny, to Roger, who was checking to see if the CD was food.

As they drove away, Eliot, going into Parental Lecture Mode, said, "Listen, Matt, you . . ."

"I know," said Matt.

"Well," said Eliot, "you better not . . ."

"I *know*," said Matt.

"Well, OK," said Eliot, "but your mother . . ."

"Dad, I said I *know,"* said Matt.

"OK, then," said Eliot.

76

They lapsed into silence, each drifting off into jumbled recollections of the evening. At the Herk home, Anna, Jenny, and Nina were doing the same, as was Puggy in his tree. In each case, the recollections were surprisingly pleasant, considering that the evening had begun with somebody apparently trying to kill somebody.

Arthur Herk was pretty sure he knew who both somebodys were, and his thoughts were not pleasant. He had been thinking about the situation, and he had decided what he was going to do. After pouring himself another drink, he dialed a number from the phone on the family-room bar.

"It's me," he told the person at the other end. "Yeah." He took a swallow of his drink and looked over at the bullet hole.

"Listen," he said. "I need a missile."

FOUR

"She should be leaning over more," said the Big Fat Stupid Client From Hell, "so you can see more gazombas."

"Good point, more gazombas," said Eliot, pretending to make a note of it. He was way too tired to argue this morning. It had been a long night: He'd driven Matt home at 2 A.M., and then he'd spent forty-five minutes getting berated by his ex-wife, Patty. Patty was not the berating kind, but she recognized a stupid parental decision when she saw one.

"You *knew* about this?" Patty had said. "You *knew* he was going to be creeping around a stranger's yard with a *gun,* in *Miami,* and you *let* him?"

"It was a *squirt gun,*" said Eliot, causing Patty to roll her eyes so hard he thought they would pop out and bounce across the kitchen floor. Patty had always been way better at being a grown-up than Eliot; this was one key reason why they were no longer married.

Eliot said little after that. He just stood there and took his berating, because he knew Patty was right: He was an incompetent moron parent who had let his son get into a dangerous situation. He was also (Patty had reminded him quietly, outside of Matt's hearing) five months behind on his alimony and child support.

"I'm sorry," Eliot had said, as he left. "I'm working as hard as I can."

"I know," Patty had said. "That's what has me worried."

Driving home, Eliot pondered his situation: He was a failure as a husband and as a parent; his business was a joke; he had no prospects; he was driving a Kia. Willing his brain, against every instinct, to think practically, he tried to devise a logical, workable plan for straightening his life out, and his brain came up with: suicide. He would write a farewell letter — it would be funny, yet deeply moving — then he would put on some clean underwear and launch himself off the tiny balcony of his tiny apartment, hurtle toward the parking lot, maybe aiming for the 1987 Trans Am belonging to the asshole in unit 238 who played his Death Star stereo loud all night, and, splat, just like that, his troubles would be over. His life insurance would pay for Matt's college education. At his funeral, people would recall specific feature stories that he had written and describe him as "troubled" but "brilliant."

These thoughts comforted Eliot until he realized that he was way too scared of heights to jump from his balcony. He couldn't even look over the railing when he was out there cooking hot dogs on his Wal-Mart grill. Plus, he did not have any life insurance. So he decided to continue failing at everything.

He got back to his apartment after 3 A.M. and spent the next four hours drinking black coffee and putting together his Hammerhead Beer presentation, which he would be presenting that very morning. He had planned to come up with an idea so original, so imaginative, so creative, and so compelling that even the Big Fat Stupid Client From Hell would see its brilliance. But because it was very late and he was very tired, he decided to go with: big tits.

"I'm a whore, OK?" he said to himself several dozen times as he worked. "You got a problem with that?"

And thus it was that the next morning, when the Big Fat Stupid Client From Hell walked into Eliot's office, forty-five minutes late, without knocking or closing the door behind him, he saw, on an easel, in large type, the words

GET HAMMERED WITH HAMMERHEAD!

Under these words was an illustration that Eliot had created on his computer by manipulating various photographs that he had basically stolen off the Internet. The illustration consisted of an oily, muscular, smirking male model on a motorboat being offered a Hammerhead Beer by a female model wearing a string bikini about the size of a DNA strand, out of which were falling two flagrantly artificial, volleyball-shaped breasts.

The images in the illustration were not in scale with each other, because Eliot didn't really know how to work the computer program, and he couldn't read the manual because he couldn't find his reading glasses. Thus the male model looked, relative to the woman, comically small, like an oily, muscular, smirking weasel; any given one of the female model's breasts was larger than his head. The beer bottle appeared to be the size of a fire hydrant. It was a stunningly bad piece of graphic art, so of course the Client From Hell, except for wanting more gazomba exposure, thought it was great.

"You see?" he told Eliot. "You see the difference?"

"Well," said Eliot, "I . . ."

"You got TITS! Instead of a FISH!" pointed out the Client From Hell. "You know? You hear what I'm telling you?"

"Well," said Eliot, "it . . ."

"Ask a guy what he wants, tits or a fish, see what he tells you," said the Client From Hell, his voice starting to rise.

"I suppose that . . ."

"HE TELLS YOU TITS!" said the Client From Hell.

The certified public accountant from next door appeared in Eliot's doorway, glared at Eliot for a full five seconds, then slammed Eliot's door.

"OK, then," said Eliot, "if we're agreed on the

81

concept, we need to talk about placement, but first . . ."

"Is she from around here?" said the Client From Hell, pointing his fat finger at the gazomba woman.

"No," said Eliot, quickly. "She's . . . she lives in, ah . . . Uruguay."

"Uruguay?" said the Client From Hell. "They got tits like that in Uruguay?"

"Oh yeah, they're known for it," said Eliot. "People call it 'Uruguay: Bosom Capital of the World.' Listen, I think we need to talk about your, I mean, my fee, because . . ."

"How far is Uruguay?" said the Client From Hell. "Is that in, whaddyacallit, Europe?"

"No," said Eliot, "it's in Latin America. The thing is, I sent you several statements, but . . ."

"Latin *America?*" said the Client From Hell, looking at the gazomba woman with renewed interest. "You're telling me this is a *spic?*"

"Listen," said Eliot. "We really need to talk about your . . ."

"How much?" asked the Client From Hell, still looking at the gazomba woman.

"Well," said Eliot, "there was no retainer, I mean, there *was* a retainer, well, I mean, I sent a *statement* for a retainer, but you never, I mean, unless it's in the mail, but . . ."

"How much?" said the Client From Hell, turning to Eliot.

"Here," said Eliot, handing him a statement.
The Client From Hell looked at it.

82

"Twelve hundred dollars?" he said.

"Well," said Eliot, "bear in mind . . ."

"Twelve hundred fucking dollars?' said the Client From Hell. He spent more than twelve hundred dollars every month getting his back hair waxed. But he truly enjoyed watching people need his money. It was almost sexual, with him.

"Well," said Eliot, "it's a very reasonable, I mean, if you look at what most . . ."

Eliot stopped talking without even being interrupted, because, to his amazement, the Client From Hell was taking out his checkbook, then his pen. It was a fat pen. The Client From Hell, sensing Eliot's desperate hope, wrote the check exquisitely slowly; then he tore it out slowly and tapped it against his fat hand a few times, watching Eliot, before he handed it over.

Eliot looked at it.

"This is for four hundred dollars," he said.

"Lemme ask you something," said the Client From Hell. "Whose idea was this?" He waved his fat arm at the beer ad.

"Well," said Eliot, "we're talking about a certain investment of time that . . ."

"WHO THOUGHT UP THE IDEA OF TITS?" said the Client From Hell. In the hall outside, a door slammed; Eliot knew this was the certified public accountant exiting his office to search for the building manager.

"You did," said Eliot.

"Do you see a fish in this picture?" asked the Client From Hell.

"No," said Eliot.

"The way I see it," said the Client From Hell, "I came up with the concept. This is MY concept."

Eliot looked at the check, then at the grotesque beer ad, then at the check again. He looked at the check for several seconds. When he finally spoke, he did not look up.

"OK," he said.

The Client From Hell smirked fatly and turned back to the ad.

"Tits like that," he said, shaking his head. "On a *spic*." Then, without saying good-bye or closing the door, he walked out.

Eliot was still looking at the check.

"I'm a whore," he announced, to his office.

The phone rang, and Eliot considered not answering it, because it was probably the building manager calling to tell him that (a) he was disturbing other tenants, and (b) he was two months behind on his rent. But it also might be Matt. So he picked up the receiver.

"Eliot Arnold," he said, warily.

"Hi," said a woman's voice, and Eliot's heart jumped. "This is Anna Herk. The woman who beat up your son."

"Hi!" said Eliot, thinking about her eyes.

"How is Matt?" asked Anna. "Is he OK?"

"Oh, he's fine," said Eliot. "He's a teenager."

"I'm sorry," said Anna.

"That's OK," said Eliot. "He'll grow out of it, if nobody shoots him."

"No," said Anna, laughing, "I mean, I'm sorry about jumping on him. And I'm really sorry about dumping on you last night. I had no business doing that."

"You did the right thing," said Eliot. "He had no business being there."

"Well, anyway," said Anna, "the reason I called, besides to say I'm sorry again, is, did you lose some reading glasses?"

"As a matter of fact," he said, "I did."

"Horn-rims?" she asked.

"Yup."

"Made in Taiwan?"

"Four ninety-nine at Eckerd Drug."

"Well," Anna said, "I haven't seen them."

Eliot laughed.

"No, really," she said, "I found them in the family room, and I wanted to return them to you."

"You don't have to do that," said Eliot. "I mean they're just cheap . . ."

"Really," she said, "I want to."

Whoa.

"OK," Eliot said.

"You're in the Grove, right?" she said.

"Yes."

"Well, I'm running some errands around there this afternoon, and I thought maybe I could stop by."

Eliot looked around his small, grimy, unsuccessful-looking office, the most impressive aspect of which was the gazomba woman.

"Well," he said, "how about, I mean, if you haven't eaten, we could, I mean, we could maybe get something?"

"Are you asking me to lunch?"

"I don't mean to, I mean, if you'd rather . . ."

"Lunch sounds great."

Whoa.

"Do you know the Taurus?" he asked.

"Sure."

"Is one o'clock OK?"

"One o'clock's perfect."

"Great! Well, see you then."

"OK, bye."

"Bye."

Eliot hung up and looked at the phone, thinking: *A date!*

Kind of!

Then he thought: *She's a married woman, and she is simply returning your glasses, and you are a loser.*

But that did not stop him from feeling absurdly happy as he locked his door and — taking the back stairs, so as to avoid the building manager — headed for the bank to cash the Client From Hell's check, so he could buy lunch.

Henry and Leonard met with their Penultimate, Inc. contact at a pricey Brickell Avenue restaurant called Dunley's, which was decorated to look like an exclusive men's club, with lots of oak and fake old paintings. It was popular with business people who wished to impress clients by buying them steaks the size of Shetland ponies.

The Penultimate contact was a man named Luis Rojas, whose title was director of special operations. They sat in a corner, next to a table of four lawyers who were talking loud about golf clubs. Henry and Luis Rojas spoke quietly; Leonard, still woozy from running into the wall, mainly chewed.

"My employer is concerned," Rojas said to Henry.

"Is that right?" said Henry, cutting off a piece of steak.

"Yes," said Rojas. "He is very concerned, and he wants to know when you intend to finish this job."

"I want to know some things, too," said Henry. "For instance, who is this guy running around with a rifle, and who is this guy jumping on me out of a tree?"

"What guy in a tree?" asked Rojas.

"That's what I'm wondering," said Henry. "You bring us down here, tell us this is a simple job, just like the other times. In and out, you tell us. No security, you tell us. Next thing I know, I got Geronimo running into the house, and I got Tarzan landing on my head."

"Plus the woman," said Leonard, between chews.

"The woman?" asked Rojas.

"Outside, by the wall with Tarzan," said Leonard. "A woman."

Rojas thought for a moment.

"Listen," he said. "Like I told you, my employer is very concerned that you should finish this job. But he is also concerned about who these other people are, why somebody else wants to . . . be involved. So we would like to know anything that you can find out, in addition to doing the job."

At the next table, the four lawyers were drinking cognac and lighting cigars.

"OK," said Henry, cutting another piece of steak. "We can do the job, and we can see what we find out about Geronimo and Tarzan. But you tell your employer that, number one, we are gonna need some time, looking around, checking in the trees, you understand? And number two, the price goes up."

The lawyers were puffing vigorously; a dense cloud of smoke billowed outward from their table.

"How much?" asked Rojas.

"Excuse me," said Henry, putting down his fork. He rose from his chair, walked over to the next table, and stood there, waiting, until all four lawyers had stopped talking and were looking at him.

"Gentlemen," said Henry. "Would you mind putting your cigars out?"

The lawyer to Henry's immediate left, Lawyer A, cocked his head and assumed an exaggeratedly quizzical expression, as if he hadn't heard correctly.

"I beg your pardon?" he said.

"I asked you," said Henry, "if you would mind putting your cigars out."

"As a matter of fact, I *would* mind," said Lawyer A. This got smiles from Lawyers B, C, and D.

"The reason I ask," said Henry, "is, maybe you never thought of this, but when you light those things, everybody else has to smell your smoke. I got a nice New York strip over there, cost me twenty-seven-fifty, and it tastes like I'm eating a cigar."

"Listen, Ace," said Lawyer B. "Number one, there's no rule against smoking in this restaurant. And number two, you are *way* outta line."

"OK," said Henry, "Number one, my name is not Ace. Number two, I'm not talking about rules, here. I'm talking about *manners*. There's no rule says I can't come over here and fart on your entrée, but I don't do it, because it's bad *manners*. It detracts from your dining experience, you know? I'm just saying, I don't stink up your lunch, you don't need to stink up everybody else's lunch. So, one more time, I'm asking nice, please put out the cigars, OK?"

"Are you serious?" said Lawyer C, across the table.

"Oh yes," said Henry.

"Un-fucking-believable," said Lawyer C, to his colleagues. "Do you *believe* this fucking guy?"

"Listen, *Ace*," said Lawyer D, to Henry.

"We're paying customers here, and we happen to like cigars, and if you don't like it, tough shit."

"That's right, *Ace,*" said Lawyer A. He sucked on his cigar, then, holding the cigar between his thumb and forefinger, turned his mouth toward Henry and blew a long, thick stream of smoke into Henry's face. Henry did not move.

When he was done blowing, Lawyer A said, "So listen, Ace, why don't you *uhhh . . .*"

Lawyer A was unable to finish telling Henry what he should do, because Henry had put his hand on Lawyer A's shoulder and squeezed it. He did not appear to be exerting himself, but Lawyer A had gone rigid.

"*Uhhh,*" he said, again.

With his other hand, Henry took Lawyer A's cigar and put it out in his cognac. The other lawyers shifted in their seats, as if preparing to get up and do something, but Henry met their eyes in alphabetical order — B, C, D — and they stayed where they were.

Releasing Lawyer A, who grabbed his shoulder and moaned, Henry walked partway around the table to Lawyer B, who flinched violently as Henry gently but firmly relieved him of his cigar and dropped it into his cognac. At that point, Lawyers C and D put out their cigars unassisted.

"Thank you, gentlemen," said Henry.

Lawyer D, who was the farthest away, said, "You realize that you have committed assault."

"I know," said Henry, shaking his head. "Time was, you really had to hit somebody."

Then he went back to his table, sat down, and resumed cutting his steak. "Tell your employer," he said to Rojas, "it's going to be another ten. Apiece."

Rojas pretended to think about this, although it was pretty much the figure he already had in mind.

"OK," he said. "Just keep in mind that my employer wants this finished as soon as possible."

"Believe me," said Henry, "we don't wanna stay in this town any longer than we have to."

"You got *that* right," said Leonard, between chews.

Puggy awoke to the sound of the angel's voice.

"Puggy," the voice was calling, softly. *Pogey.*

Puggy rolled onto his stomach and stuck his face over the edge of his platform. There she was, in a blue uniform, looking up. She smiled when she saw his face. She was beautiful. Even from the tree, Puggy could see she had all her teeth.

"I bring you some lunch," she said. *I breen you son lonch.*

Puggy started down the tree, then, as Nina giggled, he scooted back onto the platform and wriggled into his pants. He started down again.

"Hey," he said, when he reached the ground. He wished he owned a toothbrush.

"For you," she said, giving him a paper plate with a sandwich on it.

It was turkey on white bread with mayonnaise,

lettuce, and sliced tomato. It was the most elaborate meal anybody had ever made for Puggy.

"Thank you for help me," Nina said.

Puggy looked at the wonderful sandwich — it also had a *folded napkin* — then at Nina.

"Listen," he said. "I love you."

"So what you're telling me," Evan Hanratty, organizer of the Killer game, said to Matt, "is that her *mom* beat you up? Her *mom?*"

They were in the Southeast High School gymnasium, which, from 11:15 A.M. through 1:35 P.M., became the Southeast High School auxiliary cafeteria, which meant that the food tasted even more like unlaundered jockstraps than it would have ordinarily.

"She jumped me from behind," said Matt. "And there were two of them. And I wasn't gonna hit *women.*"

"Looks like they hit *you* pretty good," said Evan, studying Matt's lower lip.

"Well, I got a *lot* of help from my backup man," said Matt.

"Hey," said Andrew, "call me crazy, but when somebody starts shooting, I leave."

"Are you guys *sure* there was a gunshot?" asked Evan.

"You should have seen the TV," said Matt. "It was, like, a bunch of TV molecules."

"Shit," said Evan.

They all reflected on that thought for a moment.

92

"So," said Matt, "this doesn't count as killing Jenny?"

"Nope," said Evan. "You gotta squirt her. That's the rules. If we start letting people get points for rolling around on the floor, we'd have anarchy."

"Speaking of rolling around," said Andrew, "how was it?"

"Yeah," said Evan. "How *was* it? I mean, if Jenny's mom looks anywhere near as good as Jenny . . ."

"Which she does," noted Andrew.

"So, how was it?" said Evan.

"Shut up," said Matt.

"Hey, I'm just *asking*," said Evan. "You don't have to . . ."

"I mean, shut up, here comes Jenny," said Matt.

Sure enough, Jenny was approaching. This was unusual, because Matt, Andrew, and Evan were sitting in the section of the bleachers traditionally occupied by Guys Who Were Smart but Didn't Participate in School Activities and Tended to Be Wiseasses. Jenny sat in the section for Pretty and Very Popular Girls; generally, a girl from that section would not be seen in any other section except the one for Guys Who Played Sports and/or Held Class Office.

"Hey," Jenny said, to Matt.

"Hey," said Matt.

"Does that hurt?" she asked, pointing to Matt's lip.

"Not really," said Matt.

"Maybe," said Evan, "if you kissed it, it would feel better."

"Shut up," said Matt. To Jenny, he said, "Is everything OK at your house?"

"Well, my mom's still pretty upset about the bullet," said Jenny. "But the police guy thinks it was just some crackhead who was gonna rob us, and you scared him off."

"My hero," said Andrew, in falsetto, swooning.

"Shut up," said Matt.

"So listen," said Jenny. "I wanted to tell you three things. First, thank you. And second, thanks again for the Fluids CD. I really like it."

"You gave her your *Fluids CD?*" said Evan.

"No question," said Andrew, "he wants her sex pootie."

"Shut up," said Matt.

"And third," said Jenny, "I feel really, really bad about what happened last . . ."

"No," said Matt, "it's OK, really, it's . . ."

". . . so I just wanted you to know," said Jenny, "that if you want to squirt me, I'll be at CocoWalk tonight, around eight, outside the Gap. OK?"

"OK," said Matt.

"See you," she said, turning and heading back to the section for Pretty and Very Popular Girls.

All three boys watched her go.

"Whoa," said Andrew.

" 'If you want to squirt me'?" said Evan. " '*If*

you want to squirt me'?"

"Shut up," said Matt.

Eliot waited for Anna on the patio in front of the Taurus, a venerable, mellow Grove hangout popular with older, pudgier residents escaping the predatory flatbelly young-singles scene that swirled around the glitz bars at the other end of Main Highway.

Eliot passed the time by watching two veteran Taurus patrons, each with a line of empty beer bottles testifying to a Friday well spent, play the ring game. There had been, as long as anybody could remember, a metal ring hanging by a string from a tree on the Taurus patio; the object of the game was to pull the ring back and let it go in such a way that it swung up to, and encircled, a nail sticking up from the edge of the Taurus roof. The two veteran patrons had been doing this for an over an hour, with the intensity and concentration of brain surgeons. They got the nail on almost every try. They acted like it was no big deal.

"I could never do that," said Anna, from behind Eliot.

"Hey!" he said, turning around. "Me neither. I think the secret is large amounts of beer."

"So," she said, "you hang out here much?"

"Oh yes," said Eliot. "I've even competed in the Taurus blowgun league."

"They have a *blowgun league?*"

"Every other Monday night," said Eliot.

95

Anna laughed, causing one of the ring-game contestants, who was at a crucial point in his pullback, to look over and frown. Lowering her voice, Anna asked, "They shoot blowguns in the *bar?*"

"No, that would be foolhardy," said Eliot. "They shoot them right here, on the patio, while drinking heavily, attempting to hit targets set up only a few feet from the sidewalk, where innocent civilians are walking."

"Better safe than sorry," Anna said. "How'd you do?"

"Well, I never hit the targets, but I never hit any civilians either, as far as I know. Of course it was pretty dark. But I never heard screams. You wanna get some lunch?"

"Sure."

They went inside and sat at a table near the window. Anna gave Eliot back his glasses so he could see the menu. They both ordered fish sandwiches and iced tea.

"So," said Eliot, "did the police come up with anything?"

"No," said Anna, "and I don't think they're going to, either. I guess I'm kind of naive; I pictured them going around with magnifying glasses, you know? Looking for clues!"

"Dusting for prints!" said Eliot. "Analyzing fibers!"

"Yeah," said Anna. "But they're like, 'So somebody took a shot at you. So what's the problem?' "

"Geez, it has to be scary, not knowing who did it."

"Or if they're coming back."

"You think they will?"

"I don't know. But I get the feeling my husband knows something he's not telling me. He's been acting weird, even for him. He left last night and he wasn't back this morning. Which is actually fine with me, although I promise I'm not gonna start dwelling on that subject again."

"It's OK," said Eliot. "Dwell away." He kind of liked it when she dwelled on that subject.

"No," she said, "no more talk about me. Let's talk about you. What do you do?"

"Advertising."

"What kind of advertising?"

"Well, today I did a gazomba ad."

"A *what* kind of ad?"

"Gazomba. As in, Get a load of those gazombas."

"Ah."

"Maybe we should go back to dwelling on your marriage."

"No, I want to know about the gazomba ad."

And so he told her about Hammerhead Beer, and the Big Fat Stupid Client From Hell. He told her about the CPA next door who hated him. He told her about the rise and sudden fall of his journalism career. He told her about how he and Patty met in college and fell in love and went dancing all the time, and then Matt was born and that was wonderful, but they didn't dance as much, but they swore they would, one of these days, when Matt got a little older, but they never did, and after a while they stopped talking about going dancing, in fact they stopped talking about pretty much everything, and they made love only when neither of them could immediately think of an excuse not to, which happened very rarely, because any excuse would do, starting with "I'm kinda tired tonight," which they both were, every night. He talked about the slow, agonizing slide down the slope of divorce, and how guilty he felt, and how understanding Matt had been, and how that made him feel guiltier. He told her that he drove a Kia.

"Now you," he said.

She told him that she had been married twice, the first time to the guy she dated for her last two years at the University of Florida, who was captain of the tennis team and came from a very wealthy family and was so incredibly handsome that everybody, particularly her mother, drilled into her brain that she would be crazy *not* to marry him, because they made such a Beautiful Couple.

"We had a really great marriage, no problems at all," she said, "until maybe the second hour of the wedding reception, which is when my maid of honor told me in the ladies' room that my new husband had just put his tongue into her mouth all the way down to her tonsils. This guy just could *not* keep his weewee in his pants.

He was like Bill Clinton, but without any domestic policies."

But she stuck with him, she said, because her mother told her that you have to Make the Marriage Work.

"The thing was," she said, "while I was trying to make the marriage work, he was trying to make every woman in Dade and Broward Counties, and generally succeeding. Never marry an incredibly handsome man."

"I won't," Eliot promised.

"So," she said, "after Jenny was born, maybe the fiftieth time it took him three hours to get back from taking the baby-sitter home, I filed for a divorce. That was when I found out that his family became very wealthy by not letting anybody, ever, get a *nickel*."

"Didn't you have a lawyer?" asked Eliot.

"Oh, sure, I had a lawyer. But my ex-husband had like the entire Supreme *Court*. So he got basically all the money, and I got Jennifer. Which is why we ended up living in a dump of an apartment, which is why Arthur looked good to me, which I promise I am not going to start dwelling on again."

The lunch lasted for four iced teas. On the way out of the Taurus, Eliot and Anna were accosted by two disabled homeless Vietnam veterans. Except they weren't really disabled homeless Vietnam veterans; they were Eddie and Snake, who were ages nine and six, respectively, when the Vietnam War ended. Snake's ankle injury had given them the idea of being disabled vets; they hobbled around the Grove, hassling people for money, and on some days it was more lucrative than helping people park. Eddie saw it as a potentially important career move.

"Hey, man," he said to Eliot, "can you help out a disabled veteran?"

"No," said Eliot, who recognized Eddie from around the Grove.

"Fuck you," said Eddie. "How about you, pretty lady?" he said to Anna. "You wanna give me something?"

Snake grabbed his crotch and said, "Hey, *I'll* give you something."

Anna and Eliot kept walking. She said, "And people have the nerve to say romance is dead."

When they reached Anna's car, she said, "Thanks for lunch."

"Hey, my pleasure," Eliot said. "You want to keep my reading glasses, so we could do this again?"

Anna laughed, but didn't answer. She started looking in her purse for her car keys.

Eliot said, "Do you think I'm incredibly handsome?"

She looked up from her purse and studied his face for a moment.

"No," she said.

"Whew," he said.

She laughed, then studied his face some more. She had the *greenest* eyes.

"Just so you know," she said, "I *love* to dance."

"Man," said Eddie, watching Eliot and Anna walk away. "I can't believe the way some people treat veterans, after what we done for this country."

"We didn't do shit," Snake pointed out. "We ain't veterans."

"*They* don't know that," said Eddie. "And I bet I *would* of been a vet, if I was old enough."

"I think you have to graduate from at least, like, eighth grade," said Snake.

"Well, that ain't the point," said Eddie. "Point is, these people are some ungrateful fucks." He spat a wad of brownish glop on the sidewalk. "We ain't made but three dollars today."

"Speaking of which," said Snake. "Somethin' I wanna do."

Eddie waited.

"You know that little punk at the Jackal?" Snake said. "Who did my ankle?"

"Yeah."

"I heard he works there now, sometimes."

"So?"

"So I wanna pay him a visit."

"I dunno, man. I don't wanna fuck with that bartender again. Him and his baseball bat."

"His bat don't mean shit if we got a gun."

"We ain't got a gun."

"I know a guy can get us one."

Eddie thought about it. "I dunno," he said. "Why don't we just jump the punk outside?"

"Because the cash register is inside."

Eddie looked at Snake.

"So this ain't really about the punk," he said.

"Oh, it's about the punk," said Snake. "And the bartender. And the cash register. Three birds with one stone."

Eddie thought about it.

"I don't know nothin' about no guns," he said.

"Time you learned," said Snake. "Bein' a veteran and all."

FIVE

When the guy walked into the Jolly Jackal, Puggy was sitting at the bar, watching a rebroadcast of *The Jerry Springer Show.* The topic was husbands who wanted their wives to shave the fuzz off their upper lips. The position of the wives was that fuzz is natural; the position of the husbands was, OK, maybe it's *natural,* but it's also *ugly.* The wives were now arguing that if the husbands wanted to see *ugly,* they might look at their own selves in the mirror, because they were not exactly a threat to Brad Pitt. Nobody on either side of this debate weighed under 250 pounds. So far, there had not been any punching, but Puggy could tell, from the way Jerry Springer was edging away from the stage into the audience, that there soon would be.

The guy who walked into the Jolly Jackal was carrying a briefcase, so Puggy figured he was going to go to the back to talk to the bearded guy, John. That's what the guys with briefcases usually did.

Puggy was not the sharpest quill on the porcupine, but he had figured out that the Jolly Jackal was not a regular bar. There were few drinking patrons: The best customer, as measured in total beers consumed, was, by a large margin, Puggy, who did not pay. The real action at the Jolly Jackal, Puggy noted, took place in the back, at the table where John sat. A couple of times a day, a guy, or maybe several guys, would come in to talk to John. Every few days, Leo the bartender would call Puggy back to the locked room with the crates, and they'd grunt and shove and heave a crate or two into, or out of, the Mercedes, or some van, or sometimes a U-Haul.

Puggy still didn't know what was in the crates. If he had to guess, he'd say it was drugs, although it seemed kind of heavy to be drugs. But basically his position was, as long as they let him watch TV and drink beer, it didn't concern him what was in the crates, or who John and Leo were.

In point of fact, John and Leo — whose real names were Ivan Chukov and Leonid Yudanski — were Russians. They had met in 1986, when they'd both served as maintenance technicians in a Soviet army division whose mission was to protect and defend — which meant occupy and, if necessary, stomp on — the Soviet Socialist Republic of Grzkjistan.

This was not a plum assignment. The Soviet Socialist Republic of Grzkjistan was a remote, harsh, mountainous, extremely tribal nation whose economy was based primarily on revenge. The Grzkjistanis spent their adult lives thinking up and carrying out elaborate plots to kill and maim each other in connection with bitter, centuries-old grudges, many of them involving goats.

The only group that the Grzkjistanis hated more than each other was outsiders, which meant that the Russian soldiers were as popular as ringworm. Fraternization between the two cultures was officially banned, but every now and then a soldier would try to hook up with one of the Grzkjistani women. This required a breathtaking level of horniness, because after centuries of inbreeding, the average Grzkjistani was, in terms of physical attractiveness, on a par with the average Grzkjistani goat.

Nevertheless, such liaisons did occasionally take place, and when they were discovered, as they inevitably were, the army had learned that it was wise to get the soldier involved out of the country immediately, because otherwise, sooner or later, he would be found tied naked to a rock with his genitals nowhere near the rest of his body.

And thus most of the soldiers assigned to protect the Republic of Grzkjistan wisely elected to perform their mission by staying in their barracks and getting as drunk as humanly possible. Ivan and Leonid were in an excellent position to facilitate this mission, because, as maintenance technicians, they had access to large metal drums full of solvents and fluids that could, taken internally, put a real buzz in a person's brain. Unfortunately, some of these chemicals could also permanently shut down a person's central nervous system; the trick was to know exactly what was safe to consume, and in what quantities. Ivan and Leonid had developed considerable expertise in this branch of maintenance, and pretty soon they built up a nice little franchise, supplying recreational beverages to their comrades in exchange for money, cigarettes, *Debbie Does Dallas* videos, et cetera. Ivan was the brains, good at organizing and negotiating; Leonid was the muscle, good at keeping customers in line, if necessary by fracturing their skulls. As their business grew, word got around that if you needed something — and not just something to drink — Ivan and Leonid were the guys to see.

One day in 1989, a man came all the way from Moscow to visit Ivan and Leonid. He wore nice clothes that actually fit, and he identified himself as a businessman, which Ivan and Leonid correctly understood to mean that he was a criminal. The man had an attractive proposition: He was willing to give Ivan and Leonid cash American dollars, and all he wanted in return was some machine guns that — while not technically the property of Ivan and Leonid — were basically just sitting around.

And thus Ivan and Leonid moved up the career ladder from bootleggers to arms merchants. The timing was perfect: The Soviet Union was imploding, and Moscow was having trouble feeding, let alone paying, its far-flung troops. At remote outposts such as Grzkjistan, discipline and morale — not to mention inventory controls — were virtually nonexistent. Ivan and Leonid found that if you were paying American dollars, you could have just about any piece of military hardware you wanted. You need machine guns? Right over here! A tank? Pick one out, comrade!

Ivan and Leonid had a knack for procuring and selling army property, and their new business grew rapidly. When their terms of enlistment expired, they left the army, but they maintained their network of contacts throughout the vast and increasingly chaotic Soviet military complex. They expanded their customer base, sometimes traveling abroad; soon they were dealing with foreign governments, terrorists, revolutionaries, paramilitary organizations, religious leaders, and random wackos in places all over the world, such as Idaho.

In the marketplace of international arms sales, Ivan and Leonid developed a reputation for flexibility and customer service. Unlike their larger competitors in the arms trade, particularly the American government, Ivan and Leonid didn't put you through a lot of red tape, and they would go the extra mile to locate that hard-to-find item. For example, when a Jamaican Marxist group called the People's United Front was looking to trade a large quantity of high-grade marijuana for an attack submarine, Ivan was able to broker a complex deal involving — in addition to the Soviet navy — the government of Paraguay, a Chicago street gang named the

Cruds, and the Church of Scientology. The deal culminated, six months later, in the delivery of a semi-reconditioned World War II–era Russian sub, the *Vrmsk*, which the People's United Front renamed the *Mighty Sea Lion*. As it turned out, the People's United Front had considerably more zeal than nautical expertise, and the *Mighty Sea Lion*, while attempting a dive on its first revolutionary mission — an attack outside Kingston Harbor on the new Disney-built luxury cruise ship *Goofy* — sank like an anvil. But this did not reflect badly on Ivan and Leonid. They were in sales, not training.

By the late 1990s, with the Russian economy melting down, Ivan and Leonid decided to move their operation abroad, and they settled on South Florida. They had visited the area when they had worked on the submarine deal, and they liked the warm weather. They also liked the seaport and airport, which were very hospitable to the international businessperson; if you dealt with the right people, you could bring in almost anything, including probably live human slaves, without having to answer a bunch of pesky questions from Customs. Guns were easy. Ivan and Leonid always got a kick out of going through the airport security checkpoint, seeing surly personnel in bad-fitting blazers grimly scrutinizing the Toshiba laptops of certified public accountants, while, in the cargo tunnels a few feet below, crates containing weapons that could bring down a building were whizzing past like shit through a goose.

So Ivan and Leonid, now calling themselves John and Leo, became the proprietors of the Jolly Jackal. They found it amusing to be, once again, in the field of recreational beverages. And the bar was good cover for their real business: Random people could come and go at all hours, and nobody official cared what was going on, as long as John and Leo paid off the various municipal inspectors. The only downside to owning a bar, they found, was that people sometimes came in and actually wanted to buy drinks. But Leo was able to keep that to a minimum via a combination of poor service and occasionally hitting patrons with his bat.

Miami turned out to be a great market: It seemed as if everybody here wanted things that went bang. You had your professional drug-cartel muscle people, who needed guns that shot thousands of rounds per minute to compensate for the fact that their aim was terrible. You had your basic local criminals, who wanted guns that would scare the hell out of civilians; and your civilians, trying to keep up with your local criminals. You had your hunters, who, to judge from the rifles they bought, were after deer that traveled inside armored personnel carriers. You had your "collectors" and your "enthusiasts," who lived in three-thousand-dollar trailers furnished with seven-thousand-dollar grenade launchers. You had an endless stream of shady characters representing a bewildering variety of revolutionary, counterrevolutionary, counter-counterrevolutionary and counter-counter-counterrevolutionary movements all over the Caribbean and Central and South America, who almost always wanted guns on credit.

But their best local customer, by far, was a local outfit that was always in the market for serious, big-ticket weapons, the kind of weapons real armies fight real wars with. John and Leo had no idea why anybody in Miami would need so much firepower, nor did they care. The important thing, as far as they were concerned, was that when they got hold of a serious weapon, this outfit would usually buy it, no haggling, for cash.

The man who delivered the cash was the man who walked into the Jolly Jackal with the briefcase while Puggy was watching the couples argue about lip fuzz on *Jerry Springer*. Leo, standing at the cash register, nodded as the man walked past. John rose from his table and quietly greeted the customer by name.

"Hello, Mr. Herk," he said.

It was, indeed, Arthur Herk, spouse abuser, embezzler, and legal owner of Puggy's tree. Arthur's employer, Penultimate, Inc., builder of faulty buildings, was John and Leo's big local customer. The reason Penultimate was buying weapons — in fact the whole reason Penultimate existed in the first place — was that it was planning to take over Cuba once Fidel was dead. Quite a few organizations in South Florida, not to mention Cuba, were planning to do this. One thing you could say for sure about post-Castro Cuba: It would not lack for leadership.

Arthur was the bag man for Penultimate. That was pretty much his entire mid-level-executive job: delivering bribes and other illegal payments. He had done this job reasonably well until a few months before, when his gambling problem had begun to get out of hand. He'd come out of work one day and found two men waiting for him in the parking lot; they'd informed him that, unless he came up with a very specific amount of money within twenty-four hours, they would have no choice but to remove one of his fingers without benefit of anesthetic. They'd taken Arthur around to the back of their car, opened the trunk, and made him look inside. On the floor of the trunk was a pair of pruning shears. Arthur peed his pants.

So Arthur began skimming cash from the bribes, just enough to keep all his digits through the next week. He hoped, with the irrational hope of the true loser, that somehow the money would not be missed, or that its loss would be blamed on somebody else. But of course it was missed. Arthur's superiors said nothing to him; they didn't want to spook him into running to the police. They let him continue his bribe deliveries while they quietly brought Henry and Leonard down from New Jersey to take care of the situation. Their intention was that it would look like a gambling-related mob hit, nothing to do with Penultimate.

When Arthur's thirty-five-inch Sony TV got assassinated, he had figured out that he was meant to be the victim, and that whoever fired the shot had been hired by Penultimate. But when Arthur walked into the Jolly Jackal, John and Leo did not know anything about this. As far as they were concerned, Arthur was connected to a valued customer, and so they treated him courteously, although like everybody else who dealt with him, they thought he was an asshole.

"Do you want something to drink?" asked John.

"Vodka," said Arthur, who always wanted something to drink.

John said something in Russian to Leo, who brought over a glass of vodka. Arthur grabbed it, gulped the contents, set the glass down, and leaned in toward John. His eyes were red; his voice raspy.

"Like I told you on the phone," he said, "I need a missile."

"I see," said John. "This is for you? This is personal missile?"

"What the fuck do you care?" said Arthur.

It was a good point. John did not really care. He was just curious, because Arthur had never before mentioned, let alone taken delivery of, a weapon. He always just dropped off the money.

"It must be missile?" John asked.

"Is that a problem?" Arthur asked.

"Unfortunately," said John, "right now we do not have missile. Missile is very hard to get." It

112

was true. The market for missiles was tight; somebody was snapping them all up. Rumor was that it was either Iraq or Microsoft.

"Well," said Arthur, "I want you to try very fucking hard to come up with something for me." Arthur mocked John's pronunciation of "very," so it sounded like "wary."

John, hearing the mockery, considered having Leo escort Arthur out. But John was a business-man, and a customer was a customer.

"How are you wanting to use this weapon?" he asked.

"Never mind how I am vonting to use this veppon," mimicked Arthur. "Just gimme a serious veppon."

Arthur did not plan to use the weapon as a weapon. He knew nothing about weapons. The whole reason he wanted one was that he was planning to save his butt by going to the feds and telling them what he knew about Penultimate — the contracts, the bribes, the Jolly Jackal, and anything else he could think up or make up. In his panicked, alcohol-impaired mental state, he had concluded that the surest way he could get the feds' attention would be to show up with an actual Russian missile.

"How much you pay?" asked John.

Arthur pushed the briefcase across the table. "Ten thousand," he said. "You can count it." Arthur himself had counted the briefcase contents earlier. At that time, there had been $15,000, in packages of twenties, but Arthur had taken $5,000 for himself, stuffing $500 in his wallet and the rest into his pants pockets. He was supposed to have delivered the $15,000 two days earlier to a Dade County commissioner, who was then supposed to cast the deciding vote to award Penultimate a contract to build fourteen bus shelters, every single one of which would, what with one thing and another, wind up costing the taxpayers of Dade Country as much as a luxury two-bedroom condominium on Key Biscayne.

John opened the briefcase, glanced inside, then closed the lid. He continued looking at the briefcase as he considered the situation. On the one hand, this whole transaction stank. This idiot across from him was clearly way out of his league here. On the other hand, cash was cash. And if the idiot really didn't care what he was buying, John saw a way not only to make a little money, but also to solve a problem that had been bothering him.

"OK," he said. "Maybe I have item for you."

He led Arthur down the hallway to the back room, unlocked the door, and opened it. He went to a back corner room and grabbed the handle of what looked like a high-tech suitcase, a little bigger than a rolling carry-on bag, made out of a silver-gray metal. He dragged it toward the door, laid it on its side, undid the four heavy-duty latches, and lifted the lid. The inside of the case was lined with yellow foam padding; inside of that was a black metal box with some kind of foreign writing on it and a bank of electrical switches. Next to the box, connected to it by some electrical cables, was a steel cylinder that looked a little like a garbage disposal.

"What the fuck is that?" asked Arthur.

"Bomb," said John.

"It looks like a fucking garbage disposal," said Arthur.

"Is bomb," said John.

"How does it work?" asked Arthur.

"Follow instructions," said John, pointing at the foreign writing.

"That supposed to be funny?" asked Arthur.

"No," said John.

"How do I know this is a bomb?" asked Arthur. "How do I know I'm not paying ten grand for a garbage disposal?"

"Take a look," said John, deadpan.

Arthur, compelled by masculine instinct, leaned over and frowned at the contents of the case, exactly the way countless males have frowned at household appliances, plumbing, car engines, and all manner of other mechanical objects that they did not begin to understand. After a few seconds, as if he had seen something that satisfied his hard-nosed masculine skepticism, he straightened up and said, "OK."

John nodded solemnly. He closed the case, relatched it, and called for Puggy to come carry it out to Arthur's car.

John was pleased. At one time or another, he and Leo had kept some very dangerous things in the back room, and none of them had ever bothered him. But this particular thing was different. This was the first thing they'd had back there that made him nervous. He was very glad to see it go.

At 7:45 P.M., Matt was standing outside the Gap at CocoWalk in downtown Coconut Grove, waiting for Jenny to show up so he could kill her. His witness, Andrew, was across the street at Johnny Rockets, buying a milk shake. Matt was too excited about the prospect of seeing Jenny to be hungry.

Not wanting to draw attention to himself in the bustling open-air shopping complex, Matt had left his rifle-sized Squirtmaster Model 9000 at home, and instead was packing the handgun-style JetBlast Junior. It had nowhere near the water capacity or range, but it would do the job. Periodically, Matt pulled the black plastic water pistol partway from his pocket to check it for leakage, because he didn't want to look like he'd peed his pants.

Matt did not notice that he was being observed by a stocky, balding man sitting one level above him, in an outdoor bar called Fat Tuesday that served slushy, garish-colored alcoholic drinks from a row of clear plastic dispensers, each labeled with a wacky name such as You Gotta Colada. The man's name was Jack Pendick. He had just that afternoon lost his job as a salesclerk at a Sunglass Hut, after one too

116

many women customers had complained about his flagrant attempts to look down their blouses when they leaned over to examine the display case.

Jack had not been happy in retail anyway. His dream was to pursue a career in law enforcement. He had twice applied to the Metro-Dade police department, but was rejected both times because his psychological profile indicated that he was, to put it in layperson's terms, stupid. But he remained obsessed with the idea of being a crime fighter, and, as he sucked down the last slurp of his third drink, an iridescent green concoction called the Vulcan Mind Melter, his attention was focused, laserlike, on the suspicious young man just below him.

Jack had watched many real-video police shows on TV, and he believed that he had a sixth sense for when a crime was about to go down. That sense was tingling now. This punk below him was acting nervous, and he'd been checking something in his pocket, something that Jack, through surveillance, had concluded was — there it was again! — a gun.

The punk was getting ready to pull something. Jack *knew* it.

In his mind, Jack started to hear the song. It was Jack's personal law-enforcement theme song; he'd first heard it in his all-time favorite episode of his all-time favorite show, *Miami Vice*. It was echoing in his brain now, the voice of Phil Collins, singing . . .

*I can feel it comin' in the air tonight.
Oh lawd . . .*

And Jack, as he observed this perpetrator getting ready to commit some felony, could feel it
comin', too — his chance, finally, to step up to
the plate; to prove that he was not a loser; to be a
hero; to show the world, especially the management of Sunglass Hut, what kind of a man he
was. With his right hand, he reached into his
pocket and felt the smooth, cold, reassuring
hardness of the pistol he'd purchased a week earlier at the Coconut Grove Gun and Knife Show.
With his left hand, he signaled to the waitress for
another Vulcan Mind Melter.

Nine blocks away, Henry and Leonard were
sitting in their rental car, a few car lengths down
the dark street from the entrance to the Jolly
Jackal. They had tailed Arthur Herk there, and
were waiting for him to emerge so they could
continue tailing him. They were listening to a
sports talk show on the radio. The host was talking.

*Where are the Gator fans now? All you Gators call
when you WIN, but now that you LOSE, you don't
have the guts.*

"What the fuck are Gators?" asked Leonard.

"Football," said Henry. "College."

"Morons," said Leonard, who could not imagine engaging in a violent activity unless he was
getting paid.

118

The radio host took a call.

I'm a Gator fan. And I'm calling.

And what do you have to say?

You said we didn't have the guts to call, so I'm calling.

Yeah, OK, and so what do you have to say?

I'm saying, here I am. I'm calling.

That's it? You're calling to say you're calling?

You said we didn't have the guts.

Because you DON'T have the guts. All week I had all these Gator fans on here, talking trash, and now they run and hide.

Well, I'M calling.

OK, so what's your point?

My point is, you said we didn't have the guts to call, so I'm . . .

Henry, shaking his head, turned off the radio.

"This country," he said.

"No shit," agreed Leonard.

They sat in silence for a few minutes, both of them looking at the Jolly Jackal's crippled, grime-encrusted neon sign, beaming "ACKAL" into the night.

"Why'd he come here?" asked Leonard. "Guy like him, nice house, good job, plenty of cheese, what's he doing in a shithole like this?"

"Good question," said Henry.

"How about we just bring him out here and find out?" asked Leonard.

Henry shook his head. "Not yet," he said. "I wanna see what he does."

"Too bad," said Leonard. "Because, you give

me two minutes with him and this" — he pulled the car cigarette lighter out of its socket — "and he tells us whatever we want to know. He sings like whatshisname, Luciano Calamari."

"Pavarotti," said Henry.

"Whatever. He sings, we whack him, boom, we're onna plane back to Newark. No more mosquitos, no more guys in trees, no more Gators, no more . . ."

"Shut up," said Henry.

Leonard followed Henry's gaze, and saw two men, one of them limping, approach the door of the Jolly Jackal. In the purple-red light of the ACKAL sign, Henry and Leonard could see that both men were wearing what looked like women's stockings over their faces. The limping one was holding a gun.

"Looks like it's happy hour," said Leonard.

Andrew, sucking hard on a straw inserted into a thick chocolate shake, rejoined Matt outside the Gap. From the low-fidelity speakers of the Johnny Rockets across the street came the voice of young Elvis:

I'm proud to say she's my buttercup
I'm in love . . . I'm all shook up!

Andrew, reluctantly parting his lips from his straw, said, "Can you imagine being *proud* to say that somebody was your buttercup?"

Matt thought about it.

"Like," said Andrew, "you're introducing her to people, and you go, 'This here is MY BUTTERCUP!' Hey, did you pee your pants?"

"Shit," said Matt, looking down at his khakis, which, as was mandatory for seventeen-year-old boys, were six waist sizes too large and covered only the lower butt area. The JetBlast Junior had indeed leaked, forming a large, darkish wet splotch on the right side of Matt's crotch.

"Shit," said Matt, again.

"Here comes Jenny," said Andrew.

"*Shit,*" said Matt. He violently untucked his white T-shirt and tried to tug it down over the splotch.

"Hi," said Jenny.

"Hi," said Matt, twisting his lower body sideways, trying to aim his splotch away from her.

"Is that a squirt gun in your pocket," asked Jenny, "or are you just glad to see me?"

Andrew barked in laughter, spitting a milk shake mouthful onto the sidewalk. Matt tried to punch him, but missed.

"So," said Jenny, "where are we gonna do this? There can only be one witness, right? So it's like *way* too crowded here."

"I was thinking, we could go that way," said Matt, gesturing toward Grand Avenue. "There's a parking lot behind the five-and-dime store."

"OK," said Jenny.

"Listen," said Matt, "I was wondering if, after I kill you, if you're not doing anything, I mean . . ."

"What he means," said Andrew, backstepping quickly to avoid Matt's second punch attempt, "is he's proud to say you're his buttercup."

"Matt," said Jenny, solemnly, "I would be *honored* to be your buttercup."

Whoa.

"OK," said Matt, just as solemnly. "But I gotta kill you first."

They set off toward the five-and-dime, Matt making an effort to keep his splotch on the side away from Jenny, but otherwise feeling good and natural, walking next to her. As they left the noise and bright lights of CocoWalk, the three teenagers did not notice the stocky figure of Jack Pendick, Crime Fighter, following unsteadily twenty-five feet behind them, his hand in his pistol pocket, the nasal wail of Phil Collins filling his melted mind as he steeled himself for whatever was coming in the air tonight.

SIX

"I can't see out this thing," said Eddie.

"Well, *try*, goddammit," said Snake.

They were standing at the entrance to the Jolly Jackal, wearing panty hose on their heads. Snake had pulled the left leg of his panty hose over his face; the right leg was dangling down his chest. Eddie had pulled the pelvic region of his panty hose over his face, so that both of the legs were hanging down his back, making him look like a large, frightened rabbit.

"I'm just saying," said Eddie, "we should of got a lighter shade."

"We got what we got," said Snake.

They had obtained the panty hose from the five-and-dime in Coconut Grove. They had not had time to examine their selections carefully, because Snake had shoplifted them while Eddie had distracted the store employees by pretending to have a seizure. Snake had grabbed the first panty hose he saw. They turned out to be Hanes Control Top, for the full-figured woman, in jet black.

"Might as well have a bucket over my head," said Eddie.

"You just do like I tole you," said Snake. "You got the sack?"

"I got the damn sack," said Eddie, patting a rolled-up Winn-Dixie grocery bag tucked into the waistband of his shorts. The plan was, while Snake held the gun on the bartender, Eddie was going to fill the sack with money from the cash register, starting with the large bills, then the small bills, then, time permitting, the coins.

"OK," said Snake, taking a deep breath. "Remember, don't say nothin' in there. 'Specially don't say my name. And don't do nothin' stupid."

"Far as I'm concerned," said Eddie, "this whole fuckin' idea is stupid."

"We'll see who's stupid," said Snake, gripping his gun and pushing open the door.

"So," said Matt, "where do you want to be shot?" He, Jenny, and Andrew had walked through the alley from Grand Avenue and were in the dimly lit parking lot behind the five-and-dime, which contained a couple dozen cars, and, at the moment, no other people.

"Whyn't you shoot her in the crotch?" said Andrew. "You could be, like, a couple."

"Shut up," said Matt. To Jenny, he said, "How about I just shoot you on your hand?"

"OK," she said. She liked that Matt was considerate about where he shot her.

"OK, then," said Matt. "Andrew, get ready to witness this."

"Yes, SIR!" said Andrew, leaning forward and scrunching his face into a major frown to indicate how seriously he was taking this responsibility.

Jenny held out her right arm, turning the palm toward Matt, offering her hand to him. He could not believe how beautiful she looked. He raised the JetBlast Junior, holding it with both hands, straight out, like on the TV cop shows. He aimed at Jenny's hand and began to squeeze the trigger.

"FREEZE!" came the hoarse shout from the alley. The three teenagers turned to see a stocky shape lumbering toward them. "FREEZE!" the shape yelled again, even though so far nobody had moved. Then the shape emitted a pop, and the windshield of the car next to Matt fractured into a craze of cracks.

"Holy shit, he's *shooting,*" said Andrew.

"Come *on,*" said Matt. He grabbed Jenny's arm and, pulling her with him, started running toward the far end of the parking lot. "Andrew!" he yelled back over his shoulder. "C'MON!"

Andrew started running after Matt and Jenny.

"FREEZE!" yelled the shape again. There was another pop.

Matt kept running, still towing Jenny, who was whispering "JesusJesusJesusJesus" as she ran, one Jesus per step. There was another pop and an instantaneous *THUNK* as a bullet struck near Andrew, who dove sideways behind a car. Matt and Jenny reached the edge of the parking lot, burst through a thick hedge, and found themselves in the waist-high weeds of an unlit, trash-strewn backyard. They stumbled straight ahead, blindly, into the dark.

Back in the parking lot, Andrew, crouching, fear-frozen, behind the car, heard the shape lumbering toward him. It was breathing hard.

"FREEZE!" it gasped. "FRUNHHHMPH."

The shape, having tripped on a low concrete barrier, went down like a two-hundred-pound sack of suet. The pistol went clattering ahead, coming to rest directly in front of the crouching Andrew. Andrew, not thinking at all, just doing, grabbed the pistol, jumped up, and sprinted toward the alley leading back to Grand Avenue, past the sprawled, moaning mass of Jack Pendick, Crime Fighter.

When Snake pushed open the door of the Jolly Jackal, it banged hard into Leo, who had been on the other side, starting to pull the door open for Puggy, who was straining under the weight of the suitcase containing Arthur's bomb. Behind Puggy was Arthur, feeling in his pocket for his car keys so he could open the trunk of his Lexus. Behind Arthur was John, holding the briefcase.

The force of the opening door knocked Leo into Puggy, who staggered back and dropped the suitcase on Arthur's toe. Arthur screamed and lurched hard into John, who fell backward over a chair, landing on the floor, dropping the briefcase.

Snake, surprised to see so many people right

there, jerked his gun up and waved it vaguely around. He said, "Don't nobody *unh.*"

Snake stumbled forward a step. Eddie, right behind him, had walked into his back.

"Watch *out,* goddammit," Snake said.

"I can't see *shit,*" whispered Eddie.

"Just *shut up,*" Snake said. To Leo, Puggy, John, and Arthur, he said, "Stick 'em up."

They stuck 'em up, except for John, who was lying on the floor next to the briefcase, and who stuck 'em more or less horizontally.

On the TV screen, two hefty women with lip fuzz were beating on a man with long greasy hair and maybe 60 percent of his original teeth.

Snake said, "OK, first thing." He moved close to Puggy, who started to back away, watching the gun. Snake — using his left foot, the one Puggy had not broken — kicked Puggy hard in the balls. Soundlessly, Puggy fell to the floor, putting his hands between his legs. Snake kicked him in the face. Puggy moved his hands up to cover his face and curled away from Snake. Snake kicked him in the back, twice, then stepped away.

"I ain't done with you yet," he said. He pointed the gun at Leo and said, "Open the cash register. Keep your hands where I can see 'em. You reach for that fuckin' baseball bat and I blow your fuckin' head off."

Leo, keeping his hands up and his eyes on the gun, backed around the bar and over to the cash register. Keeping his left hand in the air, he pressed a touchpad on the register. The cash drawer slid open.

"OK," said Snake, elbowing Eddie. "Go get it."

Eddie, holding his hands out in front of him like Boris Karloff in *The Mummy*, inched forward until he felt the bar. He then began to feel his way along it.

"Jesus CHRIST, will you hurry UP?" said Snake.

"Next time, *I* hold the gun," said Eddie. With his right hand, he pulled the waistband of the panty hose away from the bottom of his face, so he could see the floor right in front of him. He shuffled around the end of the bar and over to the cash register. He looked in the cash drawer.

"I'll be goddamn," he said.

"Get the big bills first," said Snake.

"*Which* big bill?" said Eddie. "The one? Or the other one?"

"What the *fuck* are you talkin' about?" asked Snake.

"I'm talkin' about, there's two bills in here, and they're both ones."

"There's gotta be more," said Snake.

"Oh yeah, there's more," said Eddie. "There's, looks like, prolly a buck fifty in change in here."

Snake pondered this.

"You want me to put it all in the sack?" asked Eddie, holding up the Winn-Dixie grocery bag.

Snake pointed the gun at Leo and said, "Where's the money?"

Leo shrugged. "Business very bad," he said, pronouncing it "wary bod."

"You got the money *somewhere*," said Snake. "You wanna get shot?"

"No," said Leo.

"You don't gimme the money," said Snake, "you're *gonna* get shot."

On the TV screen, the greasy-haired man had yanked down the front of one of the lip-fuzzed women's tank tops, exposing a pair of massive flopping breasts. The nipples were electronically blotted out, in accordance with the rules of network-TV decency.

From the floor, John said, "I have money."

Snake looked at him. "Where?" he asked.

"Wallet," said John. "In my pants. I give to you."

Snake pointed the gun straight at John's head. He said, "It better be a wallet you pull outta them pants."

John, moving slowly, put his right hand in his pants pocket, pulled out a cheap cloth wallet, and tossed it across the floor to Snake. Snake picked it up with his non–gun hand and counted the contents with his thumb. This did not take long, because the wallet contained one ten, one five and three singles.

"Eighteen fucking *dollars?*" he said. "What kinda bar *is* this?"

"Business very bad," repeated Leo.

"Is bad location," pointed out John.

"You want the sack to hold the eighteen dollars?" asked Eddie.

"You don't shut up," said Snake, "I'm gonna shoot *you.*"

Snake pondered some more. He figured there was something going on here . . . these four guys all standing by the door . . . he just couldn't figure out *what.* He looked at the guys more carefully. His gaze rested on Arthur. He noticed that Arthur was wearing nice clothes and a gold watch.

"You," said Snake, gesturing at Arthur with the gun. "Gimme your watch."

Arthur took off his watch and tossed it to Snake, who caught it and held it up to his panty hose for a closer look. It looked like real gold. Snake perked up.

"Now gimme your wallet," said.

Arthur extracted his wallet from his back pocket and tossed it to Snake, who thumbed it open and saw a wad of twenties. Stuffing the wallet in his pocket, he looked at Arthur. Snake was putting the clues together . . . a guy in nice clothes, with a wad of cash, in a shithole like this . . . no question about it, this guy was a drug dealer. Maybe even a *kingpin.* Which meant that . . .

"What's in there?" he asked Arthur, pointing to the suitcase.

"A bomb," said Arthur.

"Yeah, right," said Snake.

"Really!" said Arthur, who had been a world-class snitch in junior high. "It's a bomb! These guys are Russians, and they sell bombs!"

130

Snake looked at John. John rolled his eyes to indicate what a ridiculous idea this was.

"Bombs," he said, snorting. *"Pfft!* No bombs! Is bar."

"Is bar," agreed Leo.

Snake looked at the suitcase. On the TV, Jerry Springer was saying that, in a relationship, people need to compromise.

"Eddie," said Snake. "Open the suitcase."

"Dammit, Snake," said Eddie, "you said my name!"

"Well, you just said *my* name, you moron," said Snake.

"Snake ain't a name," said Eddie. "Snake is a *nick*name."

"Before we criticize others," Jerry Springer was saying, "we need to take a look in the mirror at . . ."

Snake shot Jerry Springer, who disappeared in a violent implosion of glass shards. Everybody, Snake included, flinched at the gunshot; Arthur made a whimpering sound. It was Snake's first real effort to shoot anything, and he was pretty surprised to have hit the target, which was now a smoking hole in the plastic TV cabinet. It made him feel good; he took it as an indication that he was well suited to this new line of work.

"Now," said Snake to Eddie, *"open the damn suitcase."*

Muttering, Eddie pulled the panty hose waist off of the lower part of his face and shuffled back around the bar to the suitcase, which was lying on its side. He fumbled with the latches and finally got them unfastened. With his hand on the lid, he looked up at Snake.

"What if it *is* a bomb?" he asked.

"Open it," said Snake.

Gingerly, Eddie opened the lid and looked inside.

"What is it?" said Snake.

"Beats the shit gutta me," said Eddie. "It ain't money, tell you that."

Snake stepped closer and looked at the contents of the suitcase. He couldn't tell what it was, either. It looked kind of like a garbage disposal. But he knew it had to be something important. That much he knew. Maybe it was some kind of drug container. Or maybe emeralds were in there; somebody told Snake once that drug kingpins always had emeralds. Whatever it was, Snake saw this as an opportunity, after a lifetime of being a low-life scum, to show some initiative, to *do* something with his sorry self, to move up the ladder to the level of big-time scum. But how should he handle it? He knew he needed to think, and think hard. He aimed the gun at Leo, behind the bar.

"Gimme a drink," he said.

Leo poured a vodka and set it on the bar. Snake picked it up and attempted to slug it down, but, because he was wearing panty hose on his head, much of it dribbled down the front of his T-shirt.

On the floor, John snorted. Snake whirled and

pointed the gun at him.

"You think that's funny?" he said.

"No," said John.

"All right," said Snake. "Here's what we're gonna do. You got a car?" He was looking at Arthur.

Arthur nodded.

"Outside here?"

Arthur nodded again.

"Gimme your car keys."

Arthur tossed Snake the keys.

"OK," said Snake. "Eddie, I want you . . ."

"Stop sayin' my name!" said Eddie.

"OK, *whoever* you are, latch up the suitcase." said Snake, "We're goin' for a ride. You're goin' with us." He pointed the gun at Arthur.

"You don't want me!" said Arthur. "You want these other guys! They're Russians! They sell missiles! There's ten thousand dollars in that briefcase there!"

"Yeah, *right*," said Puggy. These drug kingpins would try to tell you anything.

"No!" said Arthur. "I'm *telling* you, there's ten thou—"

"Shut up, asshole," said Snake, aiming the gun at Arthur.

Arthur shut up.

"OK, Ed . . . *you*," said Snake. "Pick up the suitcase."

Eddie grabbed the handle and heaved. The suitcase barely moved.

"It's too heavy," said Eddie.

"Do I gotta do *everything?*" asked Snake. He stepped over and yanked on the suitcase handle and *damn* that thing was heavy. Snake pondered for a moment, then remembered who was carrying the suitcase when he came in.

He kicked Puggy, who was still curled fetally on the floor, hoping to be forgotten.

"Pick up the suitcase," said Snake.

Slowly, Puggy stood up. His nose had bled a streak down the side of his cheek. He picked up the suitcase with one hand and stood holding it.

Snake turned to Leo. "You," he said. "Get back around here and go sit next to your friend."

Warily, Leo came around the bar. As he passed Snake, Snake slugged him on the back of the head with the barrel of the gun. Snake thought this would cause him to collapse to the ground, unconscious, because that's what always happened to people on TV when they got slugged on the head with guns. Instead, the gun went off, shooting a bullet into the ceiling, and Leo lurched forward, clasping his hand to his head and going "OW!"

Snake, trying to act as though this was exactly what he had wanted to happen, said, "That'll teach you to hit people with bats. Now siddown with your friend there."

Leo sat on the floor next to John.

Snake, in his most menacing voice, told them, "If you assholes try to call the cops after we leave, next bullet goes through your head."

This threat did not make logical sense, but

134

John and Leo chose not to point this out.

Eddie shuffled over and put his head close to Snake's so that they could have a confidential conference, panty hose to panty hose. Eddie whispered, "Where the *fuck*'re we goin'?"

"That guy's house," whispered Snake, indicating Arthur.

"Why the *fuck*'re we doin' that?" whispered Eddie.

"Because," said Snake, "this here is a drug kingpin, and we got 'im by the *balls*, and he has somethin' good in that suitcase, which we are gonna find out what it is, and I bet he got a lot more good stuff at his house." Snake knew, from *Miami Vice*, that drug kingpins lived in big, modern houses with stashes of valuable drugs and cash money. Also fine-looking women who were attracted to powerful lawless men with guns.

"Snake," whispered Eddie, "we got the guy's wallet, we got the other guy's eighteen dollars. Let's just get the fuck *out* of here."

"No way, man," hissed Snake. "This is our *chance*. We're *not* gonna blow this. And you are *not* gonna punk out on me now."

"Oh, man," said Eddie, shaking his head, so that his panty hose legs flopped back and forth.

Snake grabbed the door handle and pulled the door open. He pointed the gun at Puggy and Arthur.

"Move," he said.

Arthur said, "Listen, you don't want me, you

want these guys here, they're Russians and they have ten th . . ."

Arthur flinched backward violently as Snake stepped toward him, raising the gun.

"I tole you to shut *up,* asshole," said Snake. You had to be tough with these kingpins; it was the only way they'd respect you. "OK, let's go *now.*"

And so they exited the Jolly Jackal — first Arthur, limping on the toe that Puggy had dropped the bomb on; then Puggy, lugging the suitcase; then Snake, holding the gun; then Eddie, still wagging his sad rabbit ears.

After the door closed behind them, there was a moment of silence in the Jolly Jackal. Finally, John, sitting on the floor next to the briefcase containing ten thousand dollars in cash, said to Leo, *"Kakimi chertyami oni viigrali holodnuyu voinu?"*

This translates roughly to: "How the *hell* did these people win the Cold War?"

Eliot was on his sofa watching a rerun of *Buffy the Vampire Slayer* and eating Cheez-Its from the box when the phone rang.

"Hello?" he said.

"Hey," said Anna, "it's Anna. Are you busy?"

"As a matter of fact," said Eliot, "I'm working on a six-figure ad campaign for a very important client."

"Oh, gosh, I'm sorry," said Anna, "I'll . . ."

"Not really," said Eliot. "I'm watching a rerun

of *Buffy the Vampire Slayer* and eating Cheez-Its from the box."

"Wow. I've heard about you swinging bachelors."

"And that's not all. After *Buffy*, I'm gonna log on to America Online and see if I received any email from total strangers wanting to make me rich or send me pictures of themselves naked."

"Well, I won't keep you . . ."

"No! Keep me! Keep me!"

"Well, I wanted to say, first, thanks again for lunch."

"Hey, any time. In fact, right now! You wanna get lunch again right now?"

Anna laughed. "I'd love to, but right now I'm trying to be a good mother, which is the other reason I called. I'm trying to track down Jenny. She was meeting your son at CocoWalk for that stupid Killer game, and she was gonna call me and let me know when to pick her up, but I haven't heard from her, and I was wondering if Matt called you."

"Of *course* not. Matt only calls when he needs the car. Which he did earlier tonight, to go kill Jenny. He's supposed to be back" — Eliot looked at his watch — "any minute now."

"Well, could you let me know when you hear from him?"

"Sure," said Eliot. He was thrilled to have an excuse to call her.

"I hate to be a hovering mother," said Anna, "but I'm a little worried, what with the stuff that's happened lately. Jenny's usually good about calling."

"Well," said Eliot, "it's a mother's job to hover. But I'm sure the kids're OK. I mean, they're at CocoWalk, there's lots of people around. How much trouble can they get into?"

"JESUSJESUSJESUS . . ."

Jenny panted her prayer as Matt, stumbling in the darkness of the vacant lot, pulled her by the arm through the weeds, away from the sound of the popping gun. They came to a sidewalk along a narrow back street. Matt stopped and looked back.

"Where's Andrew?" he said.

"I don't know," said Jenny. "Oh God, what if they shot him?"

"Jesus," said Matt. "Maybe we should go back."

"Matt," said Jenny, "there's a guy back there shooting. With a *gun.* We need to call the cops."

A car was coming toward them. Matt jumped into the street and waved his arms over his head.

"Stop!" he yelled at the driver. "Hey, please STOP!"

The driver did what most Miami residents would do when confronted with a shouting person in the middle of the road: honked and accelerated. Matt leaped aside as the car brushed past. He landed back on the sidewalk on his hands and knees.

"Thanks," he said to the receding car.

"Are you OK?" asked Jenny.

"Yeah," said Matt, getting up. "Listen, let's go to my car. I parked right up there on Tiger Tail, and if we don't see a phone on the way, we can drive to one."

"OK, as long as we get out of here," said Jenny, looking back toward the parking lot.

They half ran, half jogged the three blocks to the Kia, not passing any phones. As they got into the car, Matt said, "Do you know where the police station is around here?"

Jenny said, "Could we just go to my house? My mom'll be worried by now, and we can call the police from there." Jenny wanted her mom.

"OK," said Matt. "We gotta call Andrew's mom, too." He started the engine.

I want your sex pootie!
I want your sex pootie!

"Sorry," said Matt, stabbing the stereo power button. He put the Kia into drive, and the two teenagers set off toward Jenny's house, both of them shaken, both of them looking forward to turning this scary situation over to responsible grown-ups.

In the rental car outside the entrance to the Jolly Jackal, Henry and Leonard were waiting for the armed robbery, which they viewed as none of their business, to be completed, so they could continue tailing Arthur Herk. Leonard was attempting to tell Henry a joke about a lady being examined by a doctor with a thick Japanese accent.

". . . so the doctor says to the lady, 'Rady, I see your probrem.' And the lady says, 'What is it, doctor?' And the doctor says, 'You have Ed Zachary disease.' And the lady says, 'Oh no! Ed Zachary disease! Is that serious?' And the doctor says, 'Oh yes, Ed Zachary disease very serious.' And the lady says, 'What does it mean?' And the doctor says, 'It mean your face rook Ed Zachary rike your ass.' "

Henry sighed.

"Get it?" said Leonard. "Your face rook Ed Zachary rike your ass! Whoo. Who thinks this shit up?"

Henry turned the radio back on.

. . . *point is that all these Gators ever do is talk trash, and then when they lose, you don't hear a peep out of 'em.*

Well, I'M a Gator, OK? I'm a Gator, and I'm talkin' to you right now, so what's your problem?

My problem is that you weren't calling until I SAID no Gators were calling. THEN all of a sudden there's all these Gators calling.

I would of called before. I'm not afraid to call.

But you DIDN'T call. You're calling now, but before I SAID there were no Gators calling, there were no Gators calling, including you.

OK, but I'm calling, OK? You hear me on the phone now, right? I'm a Gator, and I'm . . .

Henry turned the radio back off.

"Those guys need a hobby," he said.

"Maybe they should jack off more," said Leonard. "If that's possible."

"Seriously," said Henry, "do you think any of those guys could name the vice president of the United States?"

"Hah," said Leonard, who in fact was not certain that he could name the vice president, either. He knew it was a guy in a suit, but he wasn't sure which one. The car was silent for a moment, then Leonard, who did not handle silence well, said, "Your face rook Ed Zachary rike your . . ."

"Shut up," said Henry.

The door to the Jolly Jackal had opened. Arthur Herk was coming out.

"There's our boy," said Henry. "Looks like he developed a limp."

Puggy came out next, lugging the suitcase.

"Who's that?" said Leonard.

"I believe that's Tarzan," said Henry, sitting up.

"Who?" said Leonard.

"Guy who jumped on me from the tree at our boy's house," said Henry.

"What the fuck's *he* doin' here?" asked Leonard. "And what's in the suitcase?"

"We are definitely gonna find that out," said Henry.

Snake limped out, holding the gun, followed by Eddie.

"Great idea, panty hose on your head," said Henry. "Whyn't they just wear a big sign that says 'Armed Robber.' "

The four men went to Arthur's Lexus. Puggy, with Snake directing, put the suitcase into the trunk. Then they got into the car — Arthur driving, with Snake next to him; Puggy and Eddie in the back, with Puggy behind Arthur, where Snake could watch him. There was a moment of discussion, and the car started moving. Five seconds later, Henry put the rental in gear and followed.

"Where you think they're going?" asked Leonard. "Our boy's house?"

"Ed Zachary," said Henry.

SEVEN

Miami police officer Monica Ramirez could feel
the pout vibes radiating from her partner, Walter
Kramitz, as they patrolled westbound on Grand
Avenue in their police cruiser. Walter was pouting
because of what had happened forty-five minutes
earlier, when they were eating dinner at the Burger King on 27th Avenue.

What happened was, Walter finally made his
move. Monica knew he was getting ready, because he'd been displaying his biceps even more
than usual, which was a lot. Walter had very
large biceps; he kept them inflated by doing hundreds of curls per day. He rolled up the already
short sleeves of his uniform shirt so their whole
studly bulging masculine vastness was on display. At the Burger King, he was giving Monica a
good view of them, flexing them when he raised
his Whopper to his mouth, as though it weighed
fifty pounds.

"So," he said, with elaborate casualness, "I
was thinking maybe you and me could get together sometime?"

"Walter," she said, "we're together *all the time*.
We're together *now*."

143

"You know what I mean," he said.

Of course she knew what he meant. He meant *let's have sex*. Monica had discovered that's what guys always meant when they said, *Maybe we could get together*. Their other favorite way of putting it was, *Maybe we could get to know each other better*. What they'd like to get to know was how you looked with no clothes on. But they could never just say it, just come right out and say, *Hey, let's have sex*.

"No," said Monica, "I don't know what you mean. What do you mean?"

"I mean, we're, like, in the car all the time, and I been thinkin' maybe we could get to know each other better."

Monica sighed. "Walter," she said, "do you want to have sex with me?"

Walter stopped in mid-chew and stared at Monica, trying to figure out if this was really happening, if Monica was going to let him take the shortcut straight to paradise, if he had somehow found the wormhole in the universe that guys had been seeking for aeons, the wormhole that would enable him to bypass all the talking talking talking and just *do* it. He thought hard about exactly how he would phrase his response to Monica's question.

Finally, he said, "Yeah."

"Well," said Monica, "I don't want to have sex with you."

Walter stared at her. It had been a trick!

"It's not personal," Monica said. "You're a

good partner, a good police officer. But you're married."

"The thing is, me and my wife . . ."

"Walter, I don't want to hear about you and your wife. I don't care if you and your wife are having problems. I don't care if she doesn't understand you. I don't care if you've been thinking seriously about a separation. All I care about is, you're married, and I'm not going to get involved with you." Monica was glad Walter was married, so she didn't have to go into any of the other reasons she didn't want to get involved with him, such as the fact that he had the intellectual depth of mayonnaise.

"You know," said Walter, "there's plenty a women think I look pretty good." It was true. A police officer like him, good shape, tight uniform, big arms, did not have trouble finding women willing to meet him somewhere at the end of the shift; or, if he had an understanding partner, during the shift.

"I know that, Walter," said Monica. "You're an attractive man" — *even though your head is shaped like an anvil and you wear enough Brut to kill small birds* — "but with you being married, and us having to work together professionally, I just think it's a bad idea. But we're still partners, right? And we can be friends, OK?"

"OK," said Walter, though in fact this was devastating news. Walter had spent over two months in the cruiser next to this woman, who he could tell had an excellent body, which he

145

wanted desperately to see without a uniform on it. That possibility, that vision, had given him a sense of purpose, a goal, a reason to look forward to the working day. And now it was gone. Yet he was still going to be in the car with this woman hour after hour, day after day. What was he supposed to do now? Just *talk* to her? Get to *know* her? Jesus, what a waste.

So it was not a happy cruiser that was patrolling westbound on Grand Avenue. Neither Monica nor Walter had said a word since they'd left the Burger King.

It was Monica, at the wheel, who spotted Andrew up ahead, running out of the alley next to the five-and-dime, carrying a pistol.

"Man with a gun, your side," Monica said, stomping the accelerator. "Call it in." As the cruiser surged forward, Walter grabbed the radio microphone. Ahead, Andrew raced straight out of the alley, across the sidewalk and into Grand Avenue. He turned left, heading directly toward the cruiser. Monica slammed on the brakes, jammed the gearshift into park, opened her door and slid out onto the street, crouching behind the door as she unholstered her Glock 40 semiautomatic pistol. Walter, having radioed for backup, slid out on his side. Both officers rose up partway behind their doors with their guns aimed at Andrew.

"Police!" shouted Monica. "Stop and put down the gun *right now*."

"FREEZE!" shouted Walter.

Andrew stopped, blinking into the cruiser headlights.

"FREEZE!" shouted Walter, again.

"Put down the gun," said Monica.

"It's not my gun," said Andrew. "Some guy was . . ."

"Put down the gun," said Monica.

Andrew bent down and set the pistol on the street, then stood. By the time he'd straightened up, Walter was on him, pulling his arms behind him and slamming his face onto the hood of the cruiser. Monica carefully picked up the pistol — a cheap .38 revolver; a classic Saturday night special — and put it inside the patrol car. She radioed in that the subject was in custody.

Walter unclipped the handcuffs from his belt. He yanked Andrew's arms up high behind the back.

"Ow!" said Andrew. "Listen, please! I'm not the . . ."

"Shut up, punk," said Walter, yanking Andrew's arms higher.

"Ow!" said Andrew. "Please, I'm not . . ."

"I TOLD YOU SHUT UP," said Walter.

Andrew shut up. He was wearing khaki pants and a knit polo shirt. His nose was bleeding, and he was obviously terrified. To Monica, he looked about as menacing as Kermit the Frog.

"Officer Kramitz," she said, "maybe we don't need to cuff him right now, OK?"

Walter looked at Monica. "We're supposed to cuff him," he said. He was dying to try out his handcuffs. In his apartment, when his wife was out, he sometimes practiced handcuffing a chair to the dinette table, but he had never cuffed anybody for real.

"Let me just talk to him for a minute, OK?" Monica said.

Walter thought about arguing with her. He was feeling much less inclined to agree with her on police procedure, now that he knew he wasn't going to get to see her naked. Reluctantly, he said, "OK."

With Walter standing close, ready to pounce if necessary, Monica advised Andrew of his rights and asked him if he understood them. Andrew nodded. Monica asked him his name.

"Andrew Ryan," he said.

"OK, Andrew," said Monica. "What were you doing with the gun?"

"I picked it up back there," Andrew said, gesturing toward the alley. "Some guy was shooting at us, and he dropped it, and I picked it up and ran."

Walter snorted, to indicate that he, for one, was not buying this load of bullshit.

"Who was shooting at you, Andrew?" asked Monica.

"I don't know. Some weird fat guy, he kept yelling *'Freeze'* and shooting at us."

"Who was with you?"

"My friends Matt and Jenny."

A synapse fired in Monica's brain. *Andrew, Matt, and Jenny.* She couldn't quite remember

148

where she'd heard those names, but she knew she had.

"What were you doing back there?"

"Matt was gonna kill Jenny," said Andrew.

"He was gonna *what?*"

"With a *squirt gun,*" said Andrew. "It's just a *game.*"

"Oh Jesus," said Monica, remembering now who Andrew, Matt, and Jenny were. "Are you talking about that, whaddyacallit, Killer?"

"Yeah!" said Andrew. "That's it! Killer!"

Monica sighed, wondering why these kids couldn't settle for the innocent diversions of her youth, such as drinking beer and groping each other.

A backup police cruiser arrived, siren yelping. Monica took Walter aside and said, "Let's leave the kid with these officers and check behind the five-and-dime, see if there's a shooter back there."

Walter snorted again. "You *believe* this punk?" he asked.

"I just wanna look, OK?" said Monica.

"OK," said Walter, "but all you're gonna find back there is . . ."

"POLICE! HELP POLICE!"

The hoarse shout came from the thick figure of Jack Pendick, Crime Fighter, stumbling out of the alley. Seeing the police cruiser, he lurched toward it.

"POLICE!" he shouted. "POLICE!" He kept shouting it as he approached, until he was shouting it directly into Monica's face, thus giving her a strong whiff of rum fumes.

"POLICE!" he shouted, yet again.

"That's correct," said Monica, putting her hand on his chest and gently pushing him back a step, which nearly caused him to fall down. "We are the police. And who might you be?"

"They were gonna shoot her!" said Pendick.

"Who was?" asked Monica.

"Perpetrators!" explained Pendick. "They took her back there with a gun and . . . Hey! That's one a them!"

Pendick was squinting at Andrew.

"That's one a the perpetrators!" he said.

"It was a *squirt gun,* dork," said Andrew.

"And so you . . . what's your name, please?" said Monica.

"Jack Pendick," he said.

"So, Mr. Pendick," said Monica, "you saw these people with the gun, and then what?"

"I tailed 'em," said Pendick, proudly. "I was gonna be in lawn forcement."

"Good for you," said Monica. "Did you have a gun with you?"

"I got a gun," said Pendick. "Need it for my line a work."

"And that is?" asked Monica.

"Sunglasses," said Pendick.

"Sunglasses?" asked Monica.

"I got fired," explained Pendick.

"I see," said Monica, rubbing her temple. "And where is your gun now?"

150

"I lost it back there," said Pendick, gesturing toward the alley and almost falling down as a result.

Monica got the .38 out of the cruiser and showed it to him.

"Is this your gun?" she asked.

Pendick squinted at it.

" 'At's it!" he said. "Can I have it back? I need it for my line a work."

"Not right now," said Monica. "So, so you followed the perpetrators into the alley, and then what?"

"He was gonna shoot her!" said Pendick. "The perpetrooter! He was pointin' his gun at her!"

"His *squirt gun,*" said Andrew.

"An' so I, I yelled, 'FREEZE!' " said Pendick.

"And then what?" asked Monica.

"And then . . ." Pendick paused. For the first time, in his small, alcohol-drenched brain, he began to sense that perhaps he should be careful about what he said.

"And then what?" asked Monica.

"I don't remember," Pendick said.

"You *don't remember?*" asked Monica.

"No," said Pendick, shaking his head hard enough to make himself stagger. "No no no no."

A dozen or so tourists, lured by the flashing lights of the police cruiser, had drifted over from CocoWalk to watch the action. One was shooting video. Cops, criminals, guns — *this* was the Miami they had heard so much about. *This*

151

would be something to tell them about, back home.

A Human Barbie Doll with long legs, tight shorts, and a tiny halter top being overwhelmed by exuberant, 94 percent silicone breasts came up to Walter and said, "Officer, what's going on?"

"We had a little shooting," said Walter, in a tone of voice intended to convey that he could not count the number of times he had been around shootings. "But we got it under control."

"Is that the one who did it?" the Human Barbie Doll asked, pointing to Pendick.

"We're trying to ascertain that now," said Walter. He made his biceps as big as possible without audibly grunting. The Human Barbie Doll gave him a look that clearly indicated that she understood and appreciated the effort he was making. She thrust her twin balloons at him. Love was in the air.

"Officer Kramitz," said Monica.

"What?" he said, reluctantly tearing his eyeballs away from the HBD.

"Do you think you can keep things under control here while I take a look in the alley?" asked Monica.

"I can handle it," said Walter, his eyes back on the balloons.

Monica and two other officers went through the alley and spent ten minutes looking around the parking lot. They found one fractured car windshield with a bullet-sized hole in it; they found another car with what looked like a bullet hole in the door panel. They found no people.

By the time they returned to Grand Avenue, the tourist crowd had grown to around one hundred. A dozen Hare Krishnas had shown up and were expressing their spirituality by beating drums and jumping up and down. The HBD was still standing close to Walter, whose face had reddened from the effort of keeping his biceps at full flex for such an extended period. Several more police cruisers had arrived. So had Miami police detective Harvey Baker, for whom Monica summarized the situation.

"So," said Baker, "what you're saying is, for the second time, these three kids are playing this squirt-gun game, and for the second time, a real shooter shows up?"

"That's what it looks like," said Monica. "Except this shooter" — she nodded toward Pendick — "couldn't hit the planet he's standing on."

"Still," said Baker, "it's quite a coincidence, don't you think? A real shooter showing up both times?"

"This is Miami," noted Monica.

"Good point," agreed Baker. "OK, here's what we're gonna do. I'm gonna take him" — he pointed at Pendick — "and him" — he pointed at Andrew — "downtown to get this straightened out."

"Can I call my mom?" asked Andrew.

"Yes," said Baker.

"I wanna call whashisname," said Pendick, picturing a lawyer he'd seen on a local TV commercial, standing in front of a shelf full of law books and basically suggesting that anybody who had ever fallen down was entitled to compensation.

"Who?" asked Baker.

"I don't remember," said Pendick.

"Absolutely, you can call him," said Baker.

"Good," said Pendick, " 'cause I got rights."

"You surely do," agreed Baker. To Andrew, he said, "I also want to talk to your two friends. Any idea where they are?"

"They ran when he started shooting," said Andrew.

"Any idea where they ran to?"

Andrew thought about it. "Probably they got Matt's car and went to . . . I guess either his dad's apartment or Jenny's house."

"Jenny's house," said Monica. "That's where somebody shot the TV, right? And you were in the backyard, with Matt?"

"Yeah," said Andrew. "I mean, no."

"The imaginary friend," said Monica, nodding. To Detective Baker, she said, "How about I swing over to Jenny's house, see if the kids went there?"

"Sounds good," said Baker.

Monica looked over at Walter, who was in Deep Lust Eyeball Lock with the HBD.

"Officer Kramitz," she said, "you ready to roll?"

"Yeah," said Walter. He told the HBD, "We gotta take care of somethin'. See you in a while." Walter had determined, through investigative techniques, that the HBD was staying in the Doubletree Hotel, room 312, and that she had two girlfriends with her, but they would not be a problem because they planned to spend the evening at a South Beach nightclub called Orgasm.

"Be careful," said the HBD, resting her hand on his forearm.

"Don't worry," he said, shifting his flex effort from biceps to triceps. "We're professionals." He turned and strode in a professional manner toward the cruiser. As he reached Monica, he whispered, *"Lemme drive, OK?"*

Monica, rolling her eyes, handed him the keys and got into the passenger seat. Walter gave the HBD one last view of his arm muscles, swung into the driver's seat, started the cruiser, and gunned the engine. He fired up the siren and, with a totally unnecessary squeal of the tires, roared off down Grand Avenue.

After a minute, Monica said, "Walter, turn off the damn siren."

Glancing into the rearview to make sure they were far enough from the HBD, he switched it off. "Hey," he said, "where're we goin'?"

"The house over on Garbanzo Street that we went to the other night, where the kid had the squirt gun and somebody shot the TV."

"Why the hell're we going *there?*" he asked.

"To see if the other two kids are there, Matt

155

and Jenny," said Monica. "The detective wants to talk to them."

"What, we're a *school bus* now?" said Walter. "Jesus."

Walter could not believe he was being pulled away from an actual crime scene, featuring a hot babe, to be sent on this lame errand. Walter did not get into police work to fart around with kids and squirt guns. Walter wanted *action*.

Matt punched in the code Jenny had given him, and the electronic gate blocking the Herk driveway — which had just been repaired after having been broken open by the police — slid open. Matt pulled into the parking area in front of the garage, and he and Jenny got out and went to the front door. Jenny, who had held it together pretty well on the ride over, was shaking badly now, fumbling with her key. She finally got the lock open and burst into the foyer.

"Mom!" she shouted. "Mom where are you?"

"Jenny?" Anna's voice came from the living room. "Are you OK, honey?"

"Mom!" said Jenny, running to Anna. "Somebody shot at us! He kept shooting and shooting!" She wrapped her arms around Anna, sobbing violently.

"Who?" said Anna, hugging her. "Who was shooting at you, honey? Where?"

Jenny was sobbing too hard into Anna's shoulder to answer. Matt entered the living room.

"What happened?" Anna asked him. "What's going on?"

"We were in the Grove?" said Matt, "Playing Killer? And I was gonna shoot Jenny? But somebody started shooting at us."

"You mean with a squirt gun?" asked Anna.

"No," said Matt. "It was a *gun* gun. With bullets."

"Oh my God!" said Anna, horrified. *"Who?"*

"We don't know," said Matt. "He was, like, this *crazy* person."

"Oh my God!" said Anna, hugging Jenny tighter.

"So we ran away, and we don't know where Andrew is," said Matt. "We came here to call the police."

"OK, right," said Anna, fighting to calm herself. "We'll call the police."

"Can I call my dad first?" asked Matt.

"Right," said Anna, "call your dad, let him know you're here, then we'll call the police."

"Mom," sobbed Jenny, "I was *so scared.*"

"It's OK, honey," said Anna, stroking her daughter's hair. "It's OK. You're home now. You're safe here."

On the street outside, in the backseat of the Lexus, Snake looked in Arthur Herk's wallet to make sure the address on the driver's license — 238 Garbanzo — was the house Herk had driven to.

Satisfied, he said, "OK, open it."

157

Herk punched in the code and the driveway gate slid open.

From the backseat, Snake said, "OK, chief, who're we gonna find at home?"

"Nobody," said Arthur. "I mean, just my wife and her kid."

"That's all? Just women?" Snake knew that a lot of these drug kingpins had henchmen around.

"Far as I know," said Arthur.

"Well, you better be right," said Snake, " 'cause when we go in, I'm gonna have this gun pointin' right at your head. Anybody tries to fuck with me, your brains is spaghetti on the fuckin' wall."

"Look," said Arthur, "you don't need to shoot me. You can have whatever you want, OK? Just take it. *Anything.*"

Snake thought about that.

"Your wife," he said. "She good-lookin'?"

Arthur turned and looked right at Snake.

"Very," he said. "And so is her kid."

Buffy moved cautiously through the dark and dripping underground passageway, gripping a wooden stake, knowing she had to destroy the hideous creature before it destroyed her. The creature was close by; she could feel it.

Eliot could feel it, too. In the excruciating tension of the moment, he had suspended, temporarily, the chewing of his Cheez-It. The small damp orange square rested uneasily on his tongue.

Buffy saw an opening just ahead to her right, a low, dark hole in the wall. She stopped in front of the opening, peering inside, her eyes unable to penetrate the gloom. But she knew the thing was in there. And she knew she had to go in there after it. Crouching, holding the stake in front of her, she began to edge forward into the darkness, when suddenly . . .

BRINNNGG!

Eliot started, spewing a Cheez-It glob onto his shorts.

"Damn," he said, reaching for the phone. "Hello?"

"Dad, somebody shot at us and we gotta call the police," said Matt.

"Matt?" said Eliot. "Are you OK?"

"Yeah but we gotta call the police."

"Where are you?"

"Jenny's house. We drove the Kia here."

"What do you mean, somebody shot at you? You mean with a squirt gun?"

"No! With a gun!"

"Who?"

"Some guy. Andrew ran away and we don't know where he is and I gotta hang up and call the police."

"OK, you call the police and I'll get a cab over there right now."

Eliot hung up, grabbed his wallet, stuck his feet into his flip-flops, and ran out the door, not taking the time to turn off the TV.

The creature lunged out of the darkness and sent Buffy sprawling backward onto the ground. The stake flew from her hand, landing just out of her reach. The creature stood over her, snarling, its gaping, fanged mouth twisted into a grotesque grin of triumph. Things looked very bad for Buffy.

Matt hung up the phone and looked over at Anna and Jenny, who were sitting on the sofa. Anna had her arm around Jenny, who was still crying, but calming down.

"My dad's on his way over," Matt said. "I'll call the police now."

Anna nodded. Matt picked up the phone to dial 911. He had pressed 9 when the front door opened hard, whacking into the wall, the sudden noise causing Jenny to scream. Matt put down the phone to go see who it was.

EIGHT

At the Jolly Jackal, Leo was sweeping up the shattered remains of the TV picture tube, while John was thinking about whether he should call his contact at Penultimate to report what had happened to Arthur Herk. He had just decided the hell with it — why go looking for trouble? — when the door opened and two men came in, one tall and one short, both wearing suits. The tall one held out a wallet, flipped open to show a badge.

"FBI," he said. "I'm agent Pat Greer, and this is Agent Alan Seitz."

John shot a quick glance at Leo. They were both thinking the same thing, which was that, the way this evening was turning out, maybe they'd been better off back in Grzkjistan, drinking solvents from barrels.

To Agent Greer, John said, "How I can help FBI?"

"You can tell FBI where the suitcase is," said Greer. He paused a beat, then added, "Ivan."

John stared at him. "My name is John," he said.

"Sure it is," said Greer. "Your name is John, and you're just a hardworking, law-abiding, immigrant small-business man, running this little shithole bar where you got no customers."

"Yes," said John.

"Yes indeed," said Greer. "Then you surely will not mind if we take a look in the back room. The one with all the locks."

"You have warrant?" said John.

Greer looked at Seitz and shook his head. "Isn't it heartwarming," he said, "the way a person can come here from another country, with nothing but the shirt on his back and maybe a couple hundred grand he got from selling military weapons he doesn't own, and in just a short time in America, he has embraced our way of life to the point where he wants to know if we got a warrant? Doesn't that just warm the cockles of your heart, Agent Seitz?"

"It warms the shit out of my cockles," said Agent Seitz. "My cockles are burnin' up."

Ivan frowned and looked at Leo, who shrugged to indicate that he didn't know what cockles were, either.

Greer turned back to John. "Listen, *Ivan*," he said. "Number one, we already got you. You have not been careful about who you do business with. We got you so good that, if we want, by the time you get out of federal prison, there will be glaciers in Key West, OK? That's number one. Number two is, we don't need a warrant. We're operating under . . . what's that thing that we're operating under called again, Agent Seitz?"

162

"Special Executive Order 768 dash 4," said Seitz.

"That's right," said Greer, "Special Executive Order 768 dash 4, which basically means that, if it's a matter of national security, which this is, we can search wherever we want, and we don't need a warrant. We can send a search party and a Doberman pinscher up your ass if we want, *Ivan.*"

John glanced at Leo, then turned back to Greer. He said, "I want lawyer."

"Did you hear that, Agent Seitz?" said Greer. "He wants a lawyer! As is his right, under our constitution! Which we hold sacred!"

"You want me to shoot him in the forehead?" asked Agent Seitz, producing a pistol from his shoulder holster.

"Not right now," replied Greer. To John, he said, "My partner would like to shoot you in the forehead, which I have absolutely no doubt he could legally do, under Special Executive Order 768 dash 4. Me, I'm thinking it would be better, for all concerned, if you just got out your keys and showed me around that back room, OK?"

John stood still for a moment, then reached for his pocket.

"Easy," said Seitz, not aiming the gun directly at John, but raising it a little.

Slowly, John pulled out a ring of keys.

"Excellent!" said Greer. "That's the spirit of Special Executive Order 768 dash 4! Now let's you and I go see what you got back there. Agent

Seitz will stay out here and be ready to render assistance to Leonid, in case the customer load gets to be too much for him to handle."

Greer and John went down the hallway to the back room. Seitz walked over to the bar, slung one leg over a stool, and pointed his chin in the direction of the shattered TV.

"What happened?" he asked Leo.

"Jerry Springer," said Leo.

"About time," said Seitz.

"What do you think?" said Leonard. "We go in the front?"

He and Henry had followed Arthur Herk's Lexus to 238 Garbanzo. They had watched it go in through the gate; they had pulled over to the curb just past the driveway.

"No," said Henry. "I think we wanna go around the back again."

"With the fuckin' *mosquitoes?*" said Leonard. "Chrissakes, *why?* I mean, we could just go in there, pop our boy, bingbing, we're onna plane to Newark. We ain't gonna have a problem with the guys wearin' the *panty hose,* for chrissakes."

"I wanna see what they're doin'," said Henry. "I wanna know what's in that suitcase. And I wanna make sure we don't have any surprises. Like somebody up a tree." He put the car in gear and started driving around to the side of the property.

Leonard sighed. "We don't shoot somebody soon," he said, "I'm gonna forget how."

The first person Matt saw, when he reached the foyer, was Arthur Herk, standing in the doorway. Matt was going to say hello, but the look on Arthur's face — a very unpleasant look, even for Arthur — stopped him.

"Who is it, Matt?" It was Anna's voice, from the living room.

Matt started to answer, but stopped, because he had just noticed, behind Arthur, a short, wide, bearded man lugging a suitcase. Behind him was . . . *ohmigod* . . .

"Who *is* it?" came Anna's voice again, now rising.

Matt backed around the corner, followed by Arthur and Puggy. Anna, seeing them, said, "Arthur! Who's . . ." She caught her breath, and Jenny screamed, as the panty hose-distorted face of Snake came into view.

"SHUDDUP, 'less you wanna get shot," said Snake, brandishing the gun at Anna and Jenny. They quieted, both staring, horrified, at the hole in the end of the gun. Snake liked that. He liked holding a gun, having this magical thing in his hand that he could just point at people, like a wand, and they did whatever he said.

He studied the two women on the sofa, the kingpin's women. He was pretty sure he'd seen the older one somewhere around the Grove . . . . Yeah, that was her; she'd walked past him like he was a piece of shit. Tonight would be different.

Snake moved closer to Anna and Jenny; they

shrank back on the sofa.

"Lessee what we got here," said Snake. "Mmm-*mmm*. These are some *fine*-lookin' women, here. *Fine*-lookin'." He glanced back at Arthur. "Just like you promised."

Anna looked at Arthur. He would not meet her eyes.

Snake said to Anna, "We gonna have some fun tonight." With his non-gun hand, he reached down and slowly, deliberately, stroked his crotch.

"If you touch my daughter," said Anna, "I swear to God I'll cut your balls off."

"Your daughter, huh?" said Snake, looking at Jenny, his hand still rubbing between his legs. "That right? She's a young thing? Can't leave her momma?" He raised the gun and aimed it right at Anna's face, and he could see in the way she looked at it that, despite her tough talk, he owned her. As long as he had the magic wand, he owned everything.

"I touch what I wanna touch," he said. He took his hand from his crotch and reached it toward Jenny, who whimpered and shrank back.

Matt said, "Drop the gun right now or I'll shoot you."

Snake, still aiming at Anna, turned his head and saw the boy aiming a gun at him. It was the JetBlast Junior squirt gun, but it looked real to Snake.

"Don't fuck with me, kid," he said.

"I swear I'll shoot you, mister," said Matt.

166

"You shoot me," said Snake, "I shoot your girlfriend." He moved his gun slightly, so it was pointing at Jenny. He was not letting go of his wand.

They stood that way for five seconds, Matt aiming at Snake, Snake aiming at Jenny, nobody with a clue what to do next. The silence ended with a crash from the foyer, which was the sound of Eddie, blinded by his panty hose, falling over an umbrella stand. The sound startled everybody, especially Matt, who squeezed the trigger of his JetBlast Junior, squirting a stream of water onto Snake.

"Whoops," said Matt.

Snake, in two steps, was next to Matt, slashing sideways with his gun barrel.

"Unnnh," said Matt, going down, his hands grabbing his face. Snake knelt and pressed the gun barrel against Matt's ear.

"You fuckin' *punk*," he said. "Before I kill you, I'm gonna let you *watch* what I do to your girlfriend, you hear me? *You hear me?*" He forced the gun barrel hard into Matt's ear.

"Yes!" said Matt. "OW YES!"

"You better hear me, punk," said Snake. "Eddie! Get in here!"

"Dammit, Snake," said Eddie, from the foyer, "you keep sayin' my name!"

"Never mind that," said Snake. "Get in here and take that thing off your head."

"They'll see us," said Eddie, feeling his way into the living room.

"Don't matter anymore," said Snake, ripping the panty hose off his head. He was thinking like a kingpin now; he had a plan.

Eddie took off his panty hose, brushed some greasy strands of hair out of his eyes, and blinked at the scene in the living room. On the sofa were two women, one he'd hassled for money earlier that day in the Grove, the other very young, both way out of Eddie's league. In the corner were the two guys they had brought from the bar, the kingpin and the little strong guy that Snake had kicked. On the floor was some kid, holding his face.

Eddie went over to Snake and whispered, "Snake, what the fuck're you doin'?"

"What *we're* doin'," Snake whispered back, "is we're gonna tie up these assholes" — he nodded toward Arthur, Puggy, and Matt — "and then we're gonna have us some pussy" — he nodded toward Anna and Jenny — "and then we're gonna find out what's inna suitcase, and where this guy keeps his real money, and then we're gonna tidy up in here, and then we're gonna go to the Bahamas and we ain't never gonna have to work again."

"The *Bahamas?*" said Eddie. "Snake, we don't know nothing about no Bahamas."

"We're gonna find out," said Snake. He'd heard they went pretty easy on kingpins in the Bahamas.

"What do you mean, tidy up in here?" said Eddie.

"I mean get rid of the loose ends," said Snake. "Now go find us some rope."

Agent Greer, with John preceding him, came out of the back room of the Jolly Jackal, shaking his head.

"It's not there," he said to Agent Seitz. "They got enough stuff back there to fight a war with North Korea, but no suitcase. Ivan here says he doesn't know what suitcase I'm talking about."

"Is that right, Ivan?" asked Seitz.

John nodded.

"Are you maybe thinking that you could use the suitcase as, like, a bargaining chip?" said Seitz. "Like, we want it so bad that we work out some kind of deal with you, like you tell us where it is, and we go easy on you? Maybe even just deport you back to Russia? Is that what you're maybe thinking?"

John said nothing. But that was, in fact, exactly what he had been thinking.

"Hmmm," said Seitz, frowning. "What do you think, Agent Greer?"

"Hmmm," said Greer, also frowning. "What do *you* think, Agent Seitz?"

"I think," said Seitz, pausing a moment, "nah." Without moving from the bar stool, he shot John in the foot. He was an excellent shot.

John fell to the floor screaming. He grabbed his shoe, which was oozing blood from holes on both the top and the bottom.

"Don't be a baby, Ivan," said Greer, looking

169

down. "It's just your foot."

"It's what we at the Bureau call an 'extremity shot,' " explained Seitz. "Generally, the victim survives. They don't do so good with what we call a 'torso shot.' "

Greer, bending down to the writhing figure on the floor, said, "What do you think, Ivan? You want to experience a torso shot?"

John, through gritted teeth, said, "I tell you who has suitcase."

Greer looked at Seitz and said, "I love Special Executive Order 768 dash 4."

Roger the dog crouched on the patio, his nose thirty inches from the Enemy Toad. The toad was sitting in Roger's dish, munching on Roger's kibble, and Roger was growling at it. This had been going on for more than two hours, but Roger was not bored. Growling at the toad was a big part of his day.

Roger's head snapped up when he heard the sound of something scraping against the fence at the far end of the yard. The sound meant that there was an intruder, and to Roger, that meant only one thing: *There might be food.* In an instant he had left the toad and was hurtling through the underbrush, a hungry, hairy bullet.

Eddie couldn't find any rope, so, at Snake's instruction, he went around the living room, dining room, family room, and kitchen and ripped out the cords to the telephones, which

Snake didn't want working anyway. He brought the cords into the living room, where Snake had Anna and Jenny still on the couch, and Puggy and Arthur sitting on the floor next to Matt, whose face was red and whose nose was bleeding about as much as the last time he'd been over to the Herk household, when Anna had punched him out.

"OK," said Snake, gesturing at the three men on the floor. "Tie 'em up."

Eddie, looking uncertain, went over and stood behind Matt.

"What kinda knot?" he asked Snake.

"Whaddya mean, what kinda knot?" said Snake. "Just tie 'em the fuck *up.*"

"OK," said Eddie, "but I ain't no damn Boy Scout. All's I know is the square knot and the whaddyacallit, the bowman. Which one you want?"

"JUST TIE 'EM UP," said Snake. He had decided that, once he got established as a kingpin in the Bahamas, he was definitely going to get a better class of henchman.

Leonard, definitely feeling the second order of spaghetti and sausage he'd had for dinner, grunted as he heaved his body over the wall at the back of the Herk property. He dropped to the ground next to Henry, who was peering up into the big tree.

"You lookin' for Tarzan?" asked Leonard. "He's inna house, right?"

"I'm thinking maybe my rifle is up there," said Henry. "Looks like there's some kind of platform up there, where he jumped from."

Leonard looked up into the tree and said, "Why the fuck would he — *OOOM!*"

Roger had just given Leonard a traditional hearty dog welcome, which consisted of rocketing headfirst into Leonard's groin, knocking him backward and down.

"Get *away* from me, dammit!" said Leonard, unsuccessfully trying to fend off Roger, who had detected several residual atoms of marinara sauce on Leonard's chin and was frantically trying to lick them off before some rival dog found them. "Henry, get him *off* me!"

Henry grabbed Roger by the collar and lifted him off Leonard. This did not cause Roger any physical discomfort, as Roger was basically a large fur-covered muscle controlled by a brain the size of a Raisinet. In fact, Roger was delighted: *Another* person was here! Maybe *this* one had food!

"Get *down*, dammit," said Henry, trying to push the dog away, wondering if maybe he would have to shoot it. Suddenly, Roger's head snapped up. He had detected something that Henry and Leonard could not hear at this distance: the intercom buzzer! Roger knew that sound; it meant *somebody was here.* And whoever it was *might have food.* As suddenly as he had appeared, Roger went rocketing back toward the house.

Henry said, "I'm gonna take a look up in the tree."

From the ground, Leonard said, "I'm never gonna leave New Jersey again."

Eddie, wrapping the phone cord around Matt's wrists, had tied one knot — he thought it was a square, but it was actually a granny — when the intercom unit in the foyer buzzed.

Everybody looked at Snake. The intercom buzzed again, longer this time.

"OK," said Snake, grabbing Anna by the arm and yanking her roughly to her feet. "You go tell whoever that is to go away. You don't say nothin' stupid or you get shot." He followed Anna partway into the foyer, standing where he could see her and the living room. The intercom buzzed again. Anna pushed the talk button.

"Who is it?" she asked.

"Miami Police," said a male voice.

"Shit," whispered Snake.

The intercom voice said, "This is Officer Kramitz and Officer Ramirez. Can we come in, please?"

Anna looked at Snake, who was pointing the gun at her. "Ask 'em what they want," he whispered.

"What do you want?" Anna said.

"We need to talk to Jenny Herk," said the voice.

Snake whispered, "Tell 'em she ain't here."

"She's not here," said Anna.

There was a pause, then the voice said, "Well, can we come in and speak to you for a moment, ma'am?"

Anna looked at Snake, who again whispered, *"Shit,"* and then, "OK, open the gate and let 'em come to the front door."

"I'm opening the gate," said Anna, punching in the code.

"Sounded to me like somebody was telling her what to say," said Walter, as the gate slid open.

"Yeah, I heard that, too," said Monica. "I'm wondering if it was the husband."

"He's the asshole, right?" said Walter.

"That's him," said Monica. "I'm wondering if Jenny told them what happened at the five-and-dime, and they're just telling us she's not here to keep her out of it."

"They don't wanna get involved," said Walter.

"Right," said Monica.

"Well," said Walter, stopping the cruiser in the Herk driveway, "they're *gonna* get involved."

He and Monica got out of the car and went to the front door. Walter knocked and said, "It's the police."

The door opened just wide enough for Anna to show her face.

"Yes, officers?" she said. "Can I help you?"

Her jaw was clenched; her eyes were too wide. Even Walter could tell there was something wrong. Both he and Monica assumed that the

174

asshole husband had told her what to say, and was listening to her.

"Mrs. Herk," said Monica, "we want to talk to Jenny about a . . . about something that happened in the Grove. We think she and her friend Matt were witnesses. Your daughter's not in trouble, but it's important that we talk to her."

"I told you Jenny's not here," Anna said.

"Mrs. Herk," said Monica, "Do you mind if we come in for a minute?"

"I . . . I . . . No," Anna said. "I mean *yes,* I mind. Please don't come in."

"Mrs. Herk, is something wrong?" asked Monica.

"No," said Anna, her voice tight. "No."

Monica and Walter looked at each other. They both knew that, without a warrant, they could not legally enter this house by force.

"OK, then, Mrs. Herk," said Monica. "I'm gonna give you a card, and when Jenny gets here, I'd appreciate it if you'd give us a call, OK?"

"Yes," said Anna, taking the card, her hand shaking, and Monica saw something in her eyes, and before she could talk herself out of it, she put her shoulder to the door, pushed it open, and stepped inside.

"Do you think you could go a little faster?" Eliot asked the cab driver. The driver looked up into the rearview and studied Eliot for a few seconds, which was not really a dangerous maneuver, because he was going only about eight miles

175

per hour. Over the years, Eliot had noticed that in Miami, in contrast to other cities, where cab drivers tended to go faster than everybody else, they generally traveled at the speed of diseased livestock. Eliot suspected that this driver was stoned on something.

"What's the big hurry?" the driver asked, still looking at Eliot, as opposed to the road.

"This is an emergency," said Eliot.

"Huh," said the driver, not going any faster. In fact, he appeared to actually slow down, while he thought about it.

After a few seconds, he said, "Which one is Caramba Street?"

"It's not Caramba Street," said Eliot. "It's *Garbanzo* Street. *Garbanzo.*"

This new information caused the cab driver to slow still more.

"I thought you tole me Caramba Street," he said.

"No," said Eliot, starting to lose it, *"Garbanzo."*

The cab driver thought about that. They were now going slower than Eliot normally walked.

"Tell you the truth," said the cab driver, "I never even heard of no Caramba Street."

"Look," said Eliot, "could you just . . ."

"I ain't sayin' there ain't no Caramba Street," said the driver. "I'm just sayin' I never *heard* of it."

"Could you please go to Garbanzo as fast as possible?" said Eliot.

"What's the big hurry?" asked the driver.

"THIS IS A FUCKING EMERGENCY," said Eliot.

"OK, OK, OK," said the driver, taking both hands off the wheel and holding them in front of him, palms out, to indicate that, sheesh, enough already. "You don't gotta yell."

When Monica shoved her way through the front door of the Herk home, Anna staggered back a step. Monica quickly brushed past her, not sure what she was looking for. Suddenly, she stopped.

Two steps behind, Walter, surprised by Monica's decision to force her way in, was saying, "Jesus, Monica, what're you . . ." Then he stopped, too, because he saw what Monica was seeing: Snake, standing just beyond Anna, at the entrance to the living room, aiming a gun at them. It looked to Walter like a .45.

"I'll kill you both," Snake said. "Swear to God, you gimme one excuse, I'll fuckin' kill you both right now."

Monica said, "We're not gonna . . ."

"Shut up!" said Snake. "Just shut up an' put up them hands. Eddie! Get in here."

Eddie came around the corner and saw the two police officers, with their hands up.

"Oh Jesus, Snake," he said.

"Shut up, goddammit," said Snake. "Just do like I say. Close the door and get their guns and bring 'em here."

Eddie closed the door, then went to Monica, unsnapped her belt holster, and took the Glock 40. It felt heavy in his hand. Next he got Walter's gun. Walter, his arms in the air, tensed his biceps and gave Eddie a hard-ass stare, but Eddie didn't meet his eyes.

Eddie, carrying the cops' Glocks as though they were rabid weasels, brought them over to Snake, who stuck one in each of his pockets. He was feeling very confident now; he had *three* magic wands. The cops had been a surprise, but he'd handled it, hadn't he? He had a new plan now, and he was feeling good about it, seeing in his mind the moves he would make.

Snake waved Anna and the two police officers toward the living room. "Everybody in here," he said.

"You're making a mistake," said Monica.

"Only mistake will be if you open your fuckin' mouth again, lady cop," said Snake. "Lady cops bleed just as good as man cops." He liked the way that came out. It sounded like something a kingpin would say.

When everybody was in the living room, Snake said, "Lady cop, I want you to take muscle boy's handcuffs and cuff him to . . . to that thing there."

He gestured toward a massive entertainment unit, eight feet high and eight feet wide, made of steel tubes. Its shelves held a stereo system, some decorative vases, and a framed picture of Anna and Jenny.

Monica took Walter's handcuffs from the case on his belt. She snapped one end around Walter's left wrist and the other to one of the vertical steel tubes on the entertainment unit.

"Make it tighter on his wrist," said Snake.

Monica, giving Walter a look that said *sorry*, made it tighter.

"Now toss me the keys," said Snake.

Monica got Walter's keys and tossed them to Snake.

"Now, lady cop," said Snake, "I want you take your cuffs and cuff this asshole here" — he gestured at Arthur — "to the other end of that thing, nice and tight." Snake had decided that the kingpin and the muscle cop were the biggest threats in the room; the rest were just punks and women.

Monica handcuffed Arthur to the other end of the entertainment unit.

"Now gimme the keys," said Snake. He liked telling the lady cop what to do.

Monica tossed the keys.

"Now," said Snake, pointing the gun straight at Monica's face, "take off your cop shirt and show me your titties."

Monica looked at the gun.

"C'mon, lady cop," Snake said. "Looks like you got a nice pair under there."

Monica forced her eyes to leave the gun and look at Snake.

"Fuck you," she said.

Snake stared at her down the gun barrel for a

long moment. Finally, he said, "Maybe later." Then, to Eddie, he said, "Finish tyin' up the punk" — he pointed at Matt — "and then tie up the lady cop and this lady." He pointed at Anna.

"What about them two?" asked Eddie, pointing to Puggy and Jenny.

"I got plans for them two," said Snake, looking at Jenny.

Eddie got the telephone cords and went to work. He really wanted some guidance on the knots, but he decided this was not the time to ask, seeing as how Snake now had three guns and had gone, as far as Eddie could tell, completely batshit. So he did the best he could, wrapping the prisoners' wrists in tangled, semi-random snarls.

When Eddie was done, Snake checked the wrists one at a time. The knots were ugly, but the cords were tight. Satisfied, he went over to Arthur and said, "Where's the money?"

"What money?" said Arthur.

With his good leg, Snake kneed Arthur hard in the balls. Arthur howled and bent over, his cuffed arm yanking the heavy entertainment unit, which would have toppled over, had not Walter, at the other end, managed to get it back upright.

"Where's the fuckin' money?" said Snake, cocking his leg again.

"In my pocket," gasped Arthur, weeping from the pain in his groin. "It's in my pocket! Don't kick me again!"

"Take it outta your pocket," said Snake.

Sniffling, Arthur reached his non-handcuffed hand awkwardly across his body and into his right pants pocket. He pulled out a fat wad consisting of $4,500 in $20 bills, the rest of the $5,000 Arthur had stolen from the Penultimate bribe money. He handed the wad to Snake, who had never seen, let alone held, this much money in his entire life. Snake was more convinced than ever that drug kingpin was the ultimate profession, a line of work where a man would be walking around with this kind of cash in his damn *pocket*.

"You got any more?" Snake asked, cocking his leg again. He didn't think there was, but he liked making the kingpin cringe.

These kingpins, you kicked them in the balls, they weren't so tough.

"NO!" said Arthur, sobbing now. "Please, just take the money, take the suitcase, take the girl, just leave me alone."

At the words *take the girl*, Anna lunged forward, struggling, despite her bound hands, to get to her feet, to get at Arthur.

"You *bastard!*" she screamed, "How *could* you?"

Snake stepped over and, with elaborate casualness, shoved Anna with his foot, forcing her down on her back. Matt struggled forward, as if to protect her; Snake kicked the boy in his already-bloody face and he fell back, groaning. Monica started up also, but Snake stopped her with a look, then pointed the gun at Walter, who was tensing as if to lunge with the entertainment unit.

"Go ahead, muscle boy," Snake said. "Try it."

Jenny crawled over and knelt by her mother. Turning away from Walter, Snake grabbed the girl by her hair, and she screamed as he yanked her back.

Holding the sobbing girl by the hair, he said to Anna, "Don't worry, momma. I'll take good care a her."

"Please," said Anna. "Please leave her. You can take me. I'll do whatever you want. Please."

Snake thought about that for a moment.

"Will you let me see your titties?" he asked.

"Oh God," said Jenny, shuddering.

Anna looked Snake in the eyes. "Yes," she said.

"Eddie," said Snake. "Open up this lady's shirt."

"Jesus, Snake," said Eddie, "I don't . . ."

"Do it," said Snake.

Eddie bent over Anna and fumbled with the buttons on her blouse. He tried to tell her, with his eyes, that he was sorry, but she didn't look at him; she was staring straight at Snake. Eddie got the buttons undone and opened the blouse, revealing a lacy white bra.

"Push it up," said Snake, licking his lips.

Gingerly, Eddie pushed up the bra, revealing Anna's full, smooth breasts.

"Oh God," whispered Jenny, at Snake's feet.

She shut her eyes, wishing this moment away. *"Oh God."*

"Shut up," said Snake, yanking her hair, but not taking his eyes off Anna's breasts. He was getting a hard-on. To Anna, he said, "You let me suck 'em?"

"Oh Jesus," said Monica. "You sick creep, you . . ."

"Yes," interrupted Anna, still looking Snake right in the eyes. "Yes. Let her go, and you can suck them."

Snake pretended to think about it, this offer from this desperate, bare-breasted woman in front of him. This was as good as it got.

"Nah," he said, giving Jenny's hair another tug, pulling her sobbing face toward his crotch. "I think this girlie's titties might be even nicer."

"NO!" screamed Anna, her eyes burning into Snake's now. She fought for calm. "If you hurt her," she said, "I swear to God I'll kill you."

"Sure you will," said Snake. "You can kill me with those big titties a yours." He licked the air with his tongue. Then he pulled the sobbing Jenny to her feet and turned to Walter.

"Muscle boy," he said, "who got the keys to the police car?"

Walter, insane with the frustration of being unable to strangle this scumbag, clenched his jaw and glared at Snake, trying to kill him with rage.

Snake pointed the gun right at Walter's face

183

and said, slowly, "Tell me right now who got the keys."

Walter breathed in and out twice through his nose. Finally, through his teeth, spacing the words out, he said, "They're in the car, scumbag."

On hearing "scumbag," Snake pulled the trigger. He intended to shoot Walter — he'd been aiming right at him — but when he pulled the trigger, he jerked the gun, and the bullet went through the wall several inches from Walter's head. Snake was surprised: He had figured himself for a natural marksman, after the effortless way he'd taken out Jerry Springer. But he felt better when he saw the big man cringing, obviously terrified. Snake decided to act as though it had been a warning shot.

"Next one's in your ugly face, *scumbag*," he said. He pointed the gun at Puggy, who had been squatting on the floor, totally still, hoping to be forgotten.

"Pick up the suitcase," he said.

Sighing, Puggy stood and picked up the suitcase.

Snake grabbed Jenny by the arm, and said to Eddie, "Let's go. We gotta plane to catch."

Eddie thought, *what* plane? But he didn't dare ask. He really didn't want to go with the new, batshit Snake. On the other hand, he figured he couldn't stay there with the cops, either. So he reluctantly followed Snake, who was pulling Jenny, and herding Puggy, toward the foyer.

Snake had considered simply shooting every-body in the living room, but he was concerned — you had to plan ahead, in this line of work — about using up bullets he might need in the Ba-hamas to establish kingpinship. Also he had heard somewhere that you could get in extra trouble if you killed a cop. The way he figured it, the prisoners were no threat: The men were handcuffed, and the women and kid were tied up. Snake had a big wad of cash money and a suitcase that — he was absolutely sure, now — contained a large amount of valuable drugs. He had three guns. He had a scared, fine-looking young thing to enjoy later on, when he had some time. He was on top of the world, is what he was. And to think: Just that morning, he'd basically been a lowlife.

As Snake opened the front door, Anna called after him, her voice now raw and desperate. *"Please,"* she said. "Oh God, *please* don't take her."

"Hey, don't worry, momma," Snake called back. "I'll show her a *good* time."

He closed the door, and for a second or two, the only sound in the house was Anna's an-guished wail.

"Did you hear a shot?" asked Leonard.

"Sounded like a pistol," said Henry. "In the house."

They were standing under Puggy's tree. Henry was catching his breath; he had spent the last ten

185

minutes struggling his way up to Puggy's platform — where he found his rifle, still loaded,
wrapped in a sheet of plastic — and then pains-
takingly climbing back down.

"You think our boy got whacked?" said Leonard. "The Panty Hose Gang beat us to the
punch?"

"Could be," said Henry, moving toward the
house. "Or, could be somebody whacked them."

"Or," said Leonard, following, "maybe somebody finally shot the dog."

Snake told Puggy to put the suitcase in the
trunk of the police cruiser. He made Puggy
climb in with it, then he slammed the lid. He put
Jenny in the backseat and got in with her.

"You drive," he told Eddie.

"I ain't never drove no police car," said Eddie.
In fact, it had been fifteen years since he had
driven any car, and that one had been stolen,
and he ended up driving it into a canal.

"It's just a fuckin' car," said Snake, who was
also very rusty in the automotive department,
which was why he had made Eddie the driver.
"Drive it."

"Where to?" said Eddie.

"Airport," said Snake.

"Which way is that?" said Eddie.

"I bet this little girlie knows," said Snake,
putting his hand on the back of Jenny's neck and
squeezing hard. "Don'tcha, little girlie?"

Jenny, whimpering from the pain, nodded.

Snake gave her neck another hard squeeze. "She's a good little girlie," he said.

"You said Garbanzo, right?" said the taxi driver.

"Yes," said Eliot. "Garbanzo. It's the next right."

The driver slowed down to process that information.

"This next right here?" he asked.

"Yes, *turn right here*," said Eliot, gripping the seat to keep from screaming.

The driver came to a complete stop at the intersection and peered up at the street sign, studying it as though it were a new constellation in the night sky. Finally, he said: "Garbanzo."

"Jesus *Christ*," said Eliot. Yanking open the cab door, he tossed a twenty-dollar bill, which was the smallest he had, onto the front seat and got out. He slammed the door and set off running toward the Herk house.

The taxi driver looked down at the twenty, then at Eliot's receding figure.

"What's the big hurry?" he said.

Eddie turned the ignition key, and the big police-cruiser V-8 rumbled to life. On the radio, staticky voices were talking in numbers, which made Eddie nervous. He turned around and looked through the back window.

"There's a gate," he said to Snake.

"I know there's a gate," said Snake. "Back up to it, and it'll open."

Gingerly, Eddie put the cruiser in reverse and pressed the gas pedal. The engine revved. The cruiser shuddered, but did not move.

"It ain't movin'," said Eddie.

Snake looked over the front seat. "You got the fuckin' brake on, asshole," he said, pointing to a lever labeled brake by Eddie's left knee.

Eddie, still revving the engine, pulled the lever. The tires squealed and the cruiser rocketed backward, smashing through the gate. As it roared into Garbanzo Street, Eddie frantically smashed his right foot onto the brake and turned the wheel; the cruiser spun in a tight, tire-smoking circle and then stopped, rocking twice on its shock absorbers.

"Jesus," said Eddie.

Suddenly he was aware of a figure on the side-walk next to the destroyed driveway gate. It was a guy in shorts, yelling at him.

"Get the *fuck* outta here," said Snake. "Now."

Eddie jammed the cruiser into drive and stomped the gas pedal. The cruiser fishtailed forward, just missing a taxi, then straightened out and shot away into the night.

NINE

"I got rights," said Crime Fighter Jack Pendick, for perhaps the fortieth time since he had been taken into police custody.

"Indeed you do, Mr. Pendick," said Detective Harvey Baker. "You have rights up the wazoo. And I'm sure you're going to exercise every single one. But first you're going to go with these officers, who are going to take you to a nice room where you can lie down and see if you can get your blood alcohol content down below that 300 percent mark, OK?"

"Do I get my gun back?" asked Pendick.

"Of course you do!" said Baker. "Just as soon as we run a couple of tests and a giant, talking marshmallow is elected president."

"OK," said Pendick, satisfied. "Because I got rights."

As Pendick was being led away, Baker called the radio room, for the third time, to find out if officers Ramirez and Kramitz had reported back. They had not. This bothered Baker. He thought about sending another cruiser out to check on them. But then he decided — he wasn't sure why — that he'd take a ride out to the Herk house himself.

As soon as she was sure that the bad man was gone, Nina came out of her bedroom. She had peeked out before, when she had heard shouting; that was when she saw the bad man at the end of the hall, by the foyer. He was wearing some kind of stocking on his head, covering his face, flattening his features, so that he looked like a snake. He was holding a gun and shouting at somebody. He did not see her. She quietly closed and locked her door. After that she heard screaming and a gunshot, and she had been very scared. She wanted to call the police, but there was no telephone in her room. So she just waited, sitting on her bed, pressing her face into her hands, until the door slammed and she no longer heard the bad man talking.

When she came out, she ran down the hall, toward the sound of Mrs. Anna's crying. Rounding the partition to the living room, she stopped and put her hand over her mouth. Mrs. Anna was lying on her back with her hands under her. Her blouse was undone and her bra was pushed up; her eyes were wild like a crazy woman's. Next to her was the lady policeman who had been there the other night; she was struggling with something behind her back. Next to her was Miss Jenny's young friend Matt, whose nose was bleeding, and who was also struggling with something behind his back. By the entertainment unit, which Nina dusted once a week, the big policeman from the other night was yanking at something and cursing. On the other side of the entertainment unit, Mr. Herk was doing the same thing.

Nina ran to Anna. "Mrs. Anna!" she said, pulling down Anna's bra.

"Nina, they took Jenny," said Anna. "They *took* her."

"Nina," said Monica, turning sideways and holding out her bound hands. "Untie me. *Desatame*."

Nina picked at the knots on Monica's wrists and had them loose in a few seconds. Nina then untied Anna, while Monica untied Matt.

"I need a car," said Monica.

"My dad's car is outside," said Matt, digging in his pocket and pulling out the keys. "It's the Kia."

"Thanks," said Monica, grabbing the keys.

"What're you doin', Monica?" asked Walter, from the entertainment unit.

"I'm going after the creep before he gets too far," said Monica.

"How do you know where he's going?" asked Walter.

"He said he had a plane to catch," said Monica. "I think he's going to MIA."

"Get me loose from this first," said Walter, yanking his cuffed arm.

"Walter," said Monica, "I don't have the handcuff keys, and I don't have time to take those shelves apart. Get yourself loose and call the station and tell them to get somebody out to the airport."

"You can't leave me stuck here!" said Walter. "How'm I gonna . . ."

"Walter," said Monica, heading for the door, "I gotta go *now*."

"SHIT," said Walter, yanking violently on the entertainment unit, sending the photo of Jenny and Anna clattering to the floor. *"SHIT!"*

Anna caught Monica in the foyer. "I'm going with you," she said.

"You stay here," said Monica, opening the door.

Anna grabbed Monica's arm with both hands, gripping it hard. "That's *my daughter*," she said, "and *I am going with you*."

Monica could see that if she wanted to leave this woman behind, she'd have to fight her.

"OK," she said, opening the door.

"I'm going, too," said Matt, entering the foyer.

Monica looked back at him.

"It's my dad's car," he pointed out.

"Jesus," said Monica, heading out the door, with Anna and Matt behind her.

On the patio, Roger the dog pawed at the sliding-glass door and barked a couple of times. Sometimes when he did this, people came and let him in and gave him food. But this time, nobody was coming. Roger could hear noises in there. He pawed at the door a couple more times. Nothing. Roger sighed and went back over to resume growling at the Enemy Toad.

Eliot, after yelling at the police car that had missed him, only because he had jumped, by maybe three-eighths of an inch, stood on the sidewalk for a few seconds, bending over, hands on knees, trying to calm down. He was definitely going to file a complaint with the police department. This *maniac* comes out of the driveway *backward,* for God's sake! Knocking down the gate!

Eliot took a couple of deep breaths, collecting himself, then stepped over the smashed gate and started walking quickly up the driveway. He had almost reached the front door when it burst open and he was almost knocked over by a lady police officer, whom he recognized, after a second, as the one he'd met here the other night. She looked very agitated. She grabbed Eliot by the front of his T-shirt.

"Which way did they go?" she said.

"The police?" said Eliot. "Those idiots damn near . . ."

"Those aren't police," said Monica. "Those are robbers."

"*What?*" said Eliot. Then he saw Anna, looking even more agitated than Monica, and Matt, who had blood on his face and shirt.

"Matt!" he said, "Are you OK?"

"They got Jenny!" said Matt. "We gotta go after her!"

"They got *Jenny?*" said Eliot. "What are they . . ."

"WHICH WAY DID THEY GO?" shouted Monica, shaking Eliot's T-shirt.

"That way," said Eliot, "straight down Garbanzo. We can follow them in my . . ."

Monica, Matt, and Anna were already running for the Kia. Eliot caught up just in time to jump into the backseat with Anna. He was closing the door when somebody pulled it back open. It was Nina.

"Nina!" said Anna. "You shouldn't . . ."

"You have to stay here," said Monica, starting the car. "*¡Quedate!*"

"No," said Nina, cramming in next to Eliot and slamming the door. She wasn't staying in this crazy house, especially not with Mr. Herk.

"Jesus," said Monica, mostly to herself, as she swung the Kia out of the driveway.

"Now what?" Snake asked Jenny. The police cruiser was headed north on Le Jeune Road.

"Just keep straight," said Jenny, her voice dull.

"Good girlie," said Snake. He stroked the back of her neck. She tried to pull away. He jerked her back close against him. His stink was strong in the closed car.

In the front seat, Eddie was gripping the wheel the way a drowning man grips a life preserver. His driving was erratic, but this was not unusual in Miami, a place where most motorists obeyed the traffic laws and customs of their individual

countries of origin. Plus, Eddie was driving a police car, so even if he ran a red light — which he
had already done, twice — nobody honked.

"Snake," he said, "there's gonna be a lotta
people at the airport, and cops."

"So?" said Snake. He was not afraid of cops.
He left cops handcuffed to entertainment units.

"So," said Eddie, trying to keep his voice
calm, "we're inna cop car here, and case you for-
got, we ain't no fuckin' cops. I'm thinkin', let's
just pull over somewhere, leave the car, leave the
girl, leave the guy in the trunk, take the money,
and get the fuck outta here."

Snake sighed. "That's a loser talkin', Eddie,"
he said. "Don't you see what we done? We *beat*
the bar assholes, we *beat* the cops, we *beat* the
drug kingpin. We're *winnin'*, Eddie. And we're
gonna *keep* winnin'." Snake could not believe he
had wasted so much of his life hassling people for
change. For fucking *dimes*. He was never going
back to that. He was moving ahead, to the bright
future that beckoned through the windshield,
beyond the tightly clenched hands of his soon-
to-be-ex-henchman.

Walter was so frustrated, he was about to tear
his arm out of its socket. His partner was in a *car
chase*. Involving *armed robbers*. This was something Walter had dreamed about ever since he'd
gotten into police work, and he was handcuffed
to an *entertainment unit*. With his *own handcuffs!*
Using the results of hundreds of grunting,

sweating hours in the weight room, Walter gave a mighty yank on the entertainment unit, causing it to topple forward hard, its weight dragging both Walter and Arthur to their knees. The massive unit crashed to the floor, the glass shelves smashing and the stereo components bouncing across the room. But the frame remained intact; the thick steel tubes were welded solidly together.

"What the fuck did you do *that* for?" shouted Arthur.

"I'm trying to break this thing," said Walter. "Don't you wanna get outta here? Don't you wanna go help your family?"

Arthur said nothing. The truthful answer was no.

"*Shit,*" said Walter, yanking at his handcuff again. To Arthur, he said, "We need a telephone."

"They ripped them all out of this part of the house," said Arthur.

"You got a phone in the bedroom?" asked Walter. "Down the hall?"

"Yeah," said Arthur, "but how're we gonna . . ."

"Help me get this thing up," said Walter, struggling to lift the frame.

"We can't move this thing that far," said Arthur.

"We're gonna try," said Walter.

"You can't make me," said Arthur.

Walter shoved the frame hard sideways; it hit

Arthur in the shoulder.

"OW!" said Arthur.

"You help me move this thing," said Walter, "or I'll shove you into that wall and crush you like a bug."

With great effort, most of it provided by Walter, they got the entertainment unit upright and began dragging and pushing it toward the hall, where Walter discovered that it was too tall for the hallway ceiling.

"SHIT!" he said. "We hafta get outside."

"What?" said Arthur.

"We hafta get outside, yell for the neighbors," said Walter.

"Outside?" said Arthur. "Attached to *this* thing? Are you outta your fucking *mind?"*

But Walter wasn't listening. He looked toward the foyer; there was no way the entertainment unit would go through the front door. So how had they gotten it into the house in the first place? He looked toward the family room, and saw the answer.

"This way," he said, giving the entertainment unit a mighty and purposeful yank.

"You see anything?" asked Leonard. He and Henry were in the dense vegetation that started at the edge of the Herk patio.

"No," said Henry. "But I'm *hearing* plenty."

"Yeah," said Leonard. "Sounds like they're breakin' furniture in there. Either that, or rap music."

"Whatever it is," said Henry, "I'm about ready to . . . Hey, look at that."

"Jesus," said Leonard, as the grunting, struggling figure of Walter Kramitz came into view, dragging the entertainment unit. "Is that a *cop?*"

"Miami PD," said Henry. "Big boy. What the *hell* is he doing?"

"Looks like he's attached to some kind of . . . I'll be goddamn," said Leonard, as Arthur came into view.

"There's our boy," said Henry. "Leads an interestin' life, don't he?"

They watched as the large, red-faced police officer dragged the even-larger entertainment unit, trailed by the reluctant Arthur Herk, relentlessly toward the very same sliding-glass door that Henry had shot a hole through just the other night. Somebody had put a piece of duct tape over the hole.

When they got to within a few feet of the door, Henry said, "I made a decision."

"Which is?" asked Leonard.

"Which is, I'm gonna take our boy out."

"Now?" asked Leonard. "While he's attached to a *cop?*"

"Yup," said Henry. "The cop can't do anything to us, cuffed to that thing. And I wanna get this job over with and get outta here. The longer we stay down here, the weirder it gets."

"You got that right," said Leonard. "This is Weirdsville Fuckin' USA, this town."

"So we're gonna do this," said Henry, raising

his rifle, "and then we're bookin' to the airport."

"Amen," said Leonard, flailing futilely at a mosquito. "Airport sounds *real* good to me."

Roger the dog was not sure what to do. On the one hand, he had the Enemy Toad to growl at. But he also had people coming toward him from inside the house, and they might have food. Plus, the other people, the ones he'd greeted earlier at the far end of the yard, had come closer. Roger recalled, somewhere in his primitive brain circuitry, that these people had tasted pretty good. Maybe he should check them out again! But what about the toad? What about the people in the house? So many decisions!

Walter tried to slide the patio door open; it was locked, with the kind of lock that requires a key to open.

"Where's the key?" he asked Arthur.

"I dunno," said Arthur. He was very unhappy. His wrist was bleeding, from where the handcuff chafed.

"OK, then," said Walter, shoving the entertainment unit so it was parallel to the patio door. "On three, we're gonna smash this through the door."

"Like fuck we are," said Arthur.

Walter braced himself. "One," he said.

"What're they doing?" asked Leonard.

"They're making an excellent target," said

Henry, sighting through the rifle scope.

"Two," said Walter.

"This is *glass*, you moron!" said Arthur. "You're gonna get us killed!"

"Three," said Walter, and with all his considerable strength he toppled the entertainment unit forward. At exactly that moment, two things happened. One was that Henry squeezed the trigger. The other was that Roger, having decided that he had just enough time in his busy schedule to check in with his new friends, ran headfirst into Henry's groin. The result was that the bullet, instead of passing through Arthur's skull, passed just over it. It could be argued that this was actually unfortunate for Arthur, in light of what happened next, which was that Arthur, dragged by the heavy steel shelf through the shattering window, was hurled forward headfirst to the patio, where he landed, dazed, facedown in Roger's dish, with his lips and nose pressed firmly against the Enemy Toad.

The toad, which was not *about* to share Roger's food, immediately emptied the glands behind its eyes, emitting two substantial, milky, highly hallucinogenic squirts of bufotenine directly into Arthur's face. Arthur moaned and yanked his head out of the dish. The toad went back to eating.

Henry and Leonard were heading for the wall, not running, but walking briskly in the dark.

"You get him?" asked Leonard.

"I think so," said Henry. "The dog ran into me, but I definitely saw our boy go down."

"Cop went down, too," said Leonard.

"Yeah," said Henry. "I think he ducked when he heard the shot."

"You got *any* idea why a cop would be helpin' our boy carry a big-ass shelf around the house?" asked Leonard.

"No," said Henry.

"Weirdsville Fuckin' USA," said Leonard.

"What kinda street name is Garbanzo?" asked Greer. He was reading the map; Seitz was driving. "Listen to these other streets they got here. Loquat. Kumquat. You believe that? *Kumquat.* Turn left here. You think they got our suitcase?"

"Sure sounds like it," said Seitz. "I mean, we been wrong before on this, but I tend to believe old Ivan was telling the truth."

"Me, too," said Greer. "He definitely did not wanna get his other shoe ventilated. That's it there, 238 Garbanzo, on the . . . What happened to the gate?"

"Somebody left in a hurry," said Seitz.

"Goin' where, I wonder," said Greer.

"Let's hope somebody inside can help us with that," said Seitz.

Walter was crouched in a pile of shattered glass, struggling to right the entertainment unit. He was getting no help from Arthur, who was still prone on the other side, moaning and rubbing his burning face with his free hand.

"Come ON," Walter said, shaking the shelving. "Get UP."

"My face!" moaned Arthur. "It got my face!"

"Well, whatever it is," said Walter, "we can get you some help if we get this thing . . ."

"GET AWAY!" Arthur screamed. "OHMIGOD GET AWAY FROM ME!"

Arthur was screaming at Roger, who was a few feet in front of him, enthusiastically snorking up a few pieces of kibble that had flown out of his dish when Arthur's face landed in it. Hearing the screams, Roger glanced up for a moment and wagged his tail to let Arthur know that he would be over to say hi just as soon as he had completed the important work at hand.

"For chrissakes," said Walter, "It's a *dog*. It's *your* dog."

Arthur turned to Walter, his face contorted by terror. "Can't you SEE?" he said. "You can't SEE her?"

"See *what?*" asked Walter. "What're you *talking* about?"

"HER!" said Arthur. "It's HER!!"

"Who?" asked Walter.

"THAT WOMAN!" said Arthur, pointing at the happily wagging Roger. "The one with the guy, you know . . . Bob Dole! His wife!"

Walter looked at Arthur, then at Roger, then back at Arthur. He said, "You think that's *Elizabeth Dole?*"

"YES!" said Arthur. "IT'S HER!" He was looking right at her, and she was definitely Elizabeth Dole, a woman he had always found vaguely scary, right in front of him, on his patio. But at the same time she was *not* Elizabeth Dole. She had Elizabeth Dole's face and highly disciplined hair, but her eyes were glowing red malevolent orbs, and she had huge, sharp teeth. Also she was eating kibble. Arthur knew — he *knew* — that she was a demon form of Elizabeth Dole, and she was here to take his soul.

"GO AWAY!" Arthur screamed at the demon Elizabeth Dole. She stared back at him, her eyes glowing, her demon tail wagging. She opened her fanged mouth and spoke to him, spoke his name in a terrible voice.

"Herk!" said Elizabeth Dole. "Herk! Herk!"

"NO!" said Arthur, jerking violently on his handcuffed arm, trying to crawl backward. "NO!"

"STOP IT!" said Walter. "That's a DOG, goddammit!" But he got no response from Arthur, who was staring at Roger, whimpering. He had also started foaming from the mouth. Walter, realizing that he was not going to get any help, grabbed the entertainment unit and started to lift it, and with it Arthur at the other end. Grunting, he raised it a foot, only to drop it again when he heard the voice behind him.

"You OK there, officer?"

Walter twisted around and saw two men, one tall and one short, both wearing suits, standing in the gaping hole that had been the sliding door.

"Who're you?" he asked.

The tall one flipped open a badge wallet.

"FBI," he said. "My name is Agent Pat Greer. This is Alan Seitz."

"Thank God," said Walter. "Listen, I need you to . . ."

"We're looking for an Arthur Herk," said Greer.

"That's him over there," said Walter, pointing toward Arthur. "But listen, I need you to . . ."

"Not now," said Greer.

"But my partner is . . ."

"I said *not now,*" said Greer.

Walter almost lost it at that point, but he decided that, what with him being handcuffed, and this being an FBI agent, he'd shut up for the moment.

Greer moved over to Arthur, who was still staring at Roger, who, having snorked up the last subatomic particles of kibble, was reverently licking the place on the patio where it had once been.

"Mr. Herk," said Greer.

Arthur slowly turned his head to look at Greer. His pupils were the size of dimes.

"Mr. Herk," said Greer, "I'm with the FBI, and I need you to tell me where the suitcase is."

Arthur opened his mouth, releasing a streamer of foamy drool, which dribbled down onto his collar.

"Mr. Herk," said Greer, "did you hear me?

This is very important."

Arthur slowly closed his mouth, then opened it again and said, "She wants my soul. Don't let her take my soul."

"Don't let *who* take your soul?" asked Greer.

"Her," said Arthur, pointing at Roger. Roger wagged his tail.

"The *dog?*" asked Greer.

"He thinks the dog is Elizabeth Dole," explained Walter.

"Jesus," said Greer, rubbing his face. To Seitz, he said, "Whaddya think?"

Seitz peered into Herk's deranged eyes. "He's gone," he said, "and I don't think he's coming back anytime soon."

Greer said to Walter, "Listen, we have reason to believe that Mr. Herk had a suitcase, probably made out of metal, very heavy. Did you see that suitcase?"

Walter thought for a moment. "Yeah," he said, "they had a suitcase. They took it."

"Who's they?" asked Greer, although he was pretty sure he knew, from what John had told him.

"Some scumbag, goes by 'Snake,' " said Walter. "Him and another scumbag was here when we got here, me and my partner. He had a gun, which is how I got . . . I mean, they surprised us. They took this guy's daughter" — he gestured toward Arthur — "and some little guy with a beard. The little guy carried the suitcase. They took our car. My partner went after 'em with this guy's wife."

"Where'd they go?" asked Greer.

"Airport," said Walter. "MIA. The scumbag said he was gonna catch a plane."

"He say where to?" asked Seitz.

"No," said Walter. "Fact is, Monica, that's my partner, was just guessin' it was MIA."

Greer and Seitz looked at each other.

"Whaddya think?" said Greer.

"I think we go to MIA," said Seitz.

"Me, too," said Greer. To Walter, he said, "Keep this man in custody for us, will you?" He turned to go.

"Hey!" said Walter. "You can't leave me here like this!"

"I'm sorry," said Greer, "but we gotta go."

"BUT I'M A POLICE OFFICER," said Walter.

"I know that," said Greer. "I know you're an *excellent* police officer, because I can't think of any other explanation for the fact that you're handcuffed to an entertainment unit that's handcuffed to a man who thinks a dog is Elizabeth Dole. But we really gotta go." With that, he and Seitz went back into the house.

"COME BACK HERE GODDAMMIT!" yelled Walter.

Arthur was still watching Roger. "She's gonna get me," he said. "I can feel it." He turned to Walter. "She's gonna get you, too."

"Herk! Herk!" said Elizabeth Dole.

"Turn right!" shouted Snake. "You can't see the fuckin' sign?"

206

The stolen police cruiser was northbound on Le Jeune, in the far left lane. Eddie, who had been too busy watching the road right in front of him to notice the Miami International Airport sign, yanked the wheel to the right, swerving across three lanes of traffic, cutting off a cab that braked, tires screaming, then spun sideways into the path of a battered 1963 Ford pickup truck carrying a large wooden crate. The truck hit the cab broadside and plowed it ahead a few feet, then came to a smoking stop. The impact caused the crate to topple out of the truck bed and onto Le Jeune, where it was sideswiped by a Toyota Tercel, breaking it open and releasing its occupants, eight goats. The goats had been destined for sale in Hialeah, for use in ritual sacrifices by practitioners of the Santeria religion, but for now they were free goats, wandering among the swerving, honking traffic.

Oblivious to the chaos he had caused behind him, Eddie veered onto the airport access road, where he was confronted by a parade of signs displaying information about parking, rental-car returns, terminals, and other matters Eddie knew nothing about.

"Which way?" he asked.

Snake, who was also not a frequent flyer, studied the signs, looking for some reference to the Bahamas, but seeing none.

"Just keep goin'," he said.

"OK," said Eddie, "but up here we gotta pick a road, Arrivals or Departures."

To Snake, it seemed like a trick question. On the one hand, he thought maybe they should go to Arrivals, because they were arriving at the airport. On the other hand, they wanted to depart from the airport, so maybe they should go to Departures. Snake thought about asking the girl, but he didn't want to admit that he didn't know, plus she looked pretty much zoned out. Finally, he decided just to take a stab at it.

"Departures," he said.

"Departures it is," said Eddie, swerving again.

When Detective Harvey Baker arrived at the Herk address, he noted that the driveway gate was lying across the sidewalk, and that the police cruiser wasn't there. He parked on the street and walked up the driveway. The front door was open. He stood on the doorstep for a moment and listened; there were footsteps coming toward him through the house. Removing his revolver from his shoulder holster, he stepped to the side of the door and waited. The two men emerged from the house, walking quickly.

"Hold it," said Baker. "Police."

The men stopped and turned to face Baker. The taller one sighed.

"We're FBI," he said.

"Can you prove that?" asked Baker.

"If you let me get out my badge, yes," said Greer.

"Very slowly," said Baker.

Greer took out the badge wallet and flipped it

208

open. Baker glanced at it and holstered his gun.

"I'm Detective Harvey Baker, Miami PD," he said.

"I'm Agent Greer," said Greer. "This is Agent Seitz. I don't want to be rude, detective, but we can't stay."

"Can you tell me what's going on here?" asked Baker.

"To be honest," said Greer, "no."

Greer and Seitz started down the driveway. Baker followed them.

"Hey, wait a minute," he said.

"We don't have a minute," said Greer, over his shoulder.

Baker grabbed Greer's arm and spun him around.

"Well, *make* a minute," Baker said.

"Detective," said Greer. "We're dealing with an extremely important federal matter here, and I'm very sorry, but we don't have time to explain it to you." He and Seitz turned and started walking again.

"Hold it right there," said Baker.

Greer and Seitz looked back. They both stopped walking, because Baker had his gun back out.

Greer said, "You're making a very big mistake, detective."

"Listen," said Baker. "I don't know why you're here. But I'm here because I got two police officers who I sent here, who have not reported in, and now I come here and find the gate busted down and the door open and you two here, and I wanna know what's going on, *now*, and if you don't tell me, I'm gonna arrest you, and you can stick your important federal matter right up your federal ass."

Greer looked at Seitz. Seitz shrugged.

"OK," said Greer. "We'll tell you. But it has to be on the way to the airport. You can ride with us."

"Are my officers at the airport?" asked Baker.

"One is," said Greer. "The one you should be worried about."

The Kia, with Monica at the wheel, rocketed north on Le Jeune at eighty miles per hour, thirty-five over the speed limit. Monica was leaning on the horn and pretty much disregarding traffic signals. Matt, next to her, his feet braced hard on the floor, was trying not to look scared. In the backseat, Nina was praying softly in Spanish. Anna was weeping, her body shaking. Eliot, not sure whether this was the right thing to do, put his arm around her shoulder.

"She's gonna be all right," he said.

"You don't know that," Anna said. "You didn't see that man, the way he . . . he . . ." Anna lost it there, thinking about Snake, with his hands on Jenny.

"They can't get far," said Eliot, feeling a little guilty about the way part of his brain was thinking how good it felt to have his arm around her.

210

"I mean, this is a city, there's police every-where."

"He's right," said Monica, veering wide to pass a bus. "My partner will report it, and those guys'll be in custody by the time we get to the airport." *I hope,* she added to herself. She was wondering if she shouldn't have made sure Walter could get loose, or taken the time to call it in herself. She was also wondering if she was right about the airport.

"Anybody got a cell phone?" she asked.

"I do, but not with me," said Anna. "Why?"

"Never mind," said Monica. "We're almost at the airport. We'll call from . . . *shit.*"

Ahead, traffic was stopped. People were getting out of their cars. One man had climbed on the roof of his car to see what the problem was. Up ahead, in the space between the lines of cars, a small, dark shape skittered sideways, into and then out of view, followed by a running man.

Matt said, "Was that a *goat?*"

The cruiser drifted slowly along with traffic on the roadway next to the Miami International Airport terminal. Snake tried to comprehend the signs announcing a bewildering array of airline names — TAM, LTU, Iberia, KLM, BWIA, Lacsa — none of which gave any hint, at least not to Snake, as to where they went.

Snake saw an empty stretch of curb to the left, next to a parking garage under construction. It was supposed to have been finished a year earlier, but it was being built by Penultimate, Inc., which was far behind schedule, and way over cost, because large pieces — Penultimate blamed incompetent subcontractors — kept falling off. The garage entrance was blocked by barricades, which were also provided by Penultimate at a cost of nearly three times per barricade what the other barricade suppliers had bid.

"Over there," Snake told Eddie, pointing to the entrance.

Eddie pulled the cruiser up to a barricade. He looked back at Snake.

"Move that thing and drive in there," said Snake.

Eddie, no longer arguing with Snake about anything, moved the barricade, drove the cruiser into the unfinished, dimly lit garage, then replaced the barricade. For a moment, standing outside, he thought about running, but he saw Snake watching him through the rear window. He got back into the cruiser.

"Now gimme your sweatshirt," said Snake.

Eddie started to say something, then took off his sweatshirt. It had once been light blue, but was now basically the color of grime. Underneath he wore a T-shirt that may once have been white, although at this point there was no way to tell. He handed the sweatshirt back to Snake, who draped it over the gun in his right hand. With his left, he gripped the back of Jenny's neck and forced her head downward, so that her eyes were a foot from the gun barrel.

"You see the gun, girlie?" he asked.

Jenny nodded.

"When we get outta this car, I'm gonna have this in my hand, pointed right at you. You do anything stupid, *anything,* and I will kill you. OK? You got that?" He squeezed her neck hard.

Jenny nodded again, grimacing.

"That's my good little girlie," said Snake.

TEN

"OK, I'm listening," said Baker. He was in the back of a rental car; Seitz and Greer were in front, with Seitz driving.

"OK," said Greer, "because you're a cop, and you got officers involved in this, I'll tell you. But then I might have to kill you."

"Ha ha," said Baker.

"Yeah, ha ha," said Greer, exchanging a look with Seitz. "Anyway, what we're looking for is a suitcase, made of metal, pretty heavy."

"What does this have to do with the Herk house?" asked Baker.

"We think the suitcase was there tonight. We think two scumbags took it from there and are now on the way to the airport, with possibly two hostages, one of which is the Herks' daughter. We think they're driving the police cruiser."

"*What?*" said Baker. "What about the officers?"

"One of them, Monica I think her name is, is heading for the airport now in a civilian car, with civilians," said Greer.

"Jesus," said Baker. "What about the other one?"

214

"He's back at the Herk house, handcuffed to a large entertainment unit, which is handcuffed to Arthur Herk."

Baker lunged forward and grabbed Greer by the shoulder. "Are you saying," he said, "that we left a police officer in trouble back there?"

"Easy," said Greer, removing Baker's hand. "He's fine. He's not *going* anywhere, but he's fine, and he's doing the federal government a favor by keeping a suspected illegal-weapons trader in custody."

"Weapons?" asked Baker. "That's what's in the suitcase?"

"We think so," said Greer.

"You mean guns?" asked Baker.

"I wish," said Seitz.

"Tell you the truth," said Greer, "we don't know, a hundred percent, what's in this particular suitcase. But we got a pretty good idea, and if we're right, you could say it's highly urgent that we get hold of it before some idiot does something stupid with it."

"Sounds like idiots got it now," said Baker.

"I realize that," said Greer, "which is why we're kinda hoping this is a different suitcase. But I don't think so."

"OK," said Baker, "so if it's the right suitcase, what's in it?"

Greer twisted around in his seat, so he was looking straight into Baker's eyes.

"It's bad," he said.

"How bad?" said Baker.

"Very, very bad," said Greer.

"What're you saying?" said Baker. "I mean, it's in a suitcase, right? How bad can it be? It's not like we're talking about a nuclear *bomb,* right?"

Greer stared at him.

"Right?" said Baker.

Greer kept staring.

"Hold it," said Baker. "You're not saying . . . This is a joke, right?" He looked at Seitz, and said, "He's kidding, right?"

"I wish," said Seitz.

Puggy was relieved when the car finally stopped moving. It had been jerking back and forth, and, crowded by the suitcase in the hot trunk, he was getting carsick. He was glad when the trunk opened, although he was less than thrilled to see Snake again.

"You see this, punk?" Snake asked, showing Puggy the gun.

Puggy nodded, thinking, this guy really likes showing people his gun.

"I'm gonna have it right under here," said Snake, draping Eddie's sweatshirt over his gun hand. "It's gonna be pointin' right at you. You don't do like I say, you know what's gonna happen to you, right?"

Puggy nodded again.

"What's gonna happen, punk? Say it. Say what's gonna happen."

"You're gonna shoot me," said Puggy.

"That's right, punk," said Snake, enjoying the sound of it. "I'm gonna shoot you. Now get the fuck outta there and pick up the suitcase."

In the front of the Kia, Matt had his eyes closed completely. In the back, Eliot had his arm around Anna, hugging her tight; Nina was looking down at her hands and praying.

They were now heading northbound in the *southbound* lanes of Le Jeune. This was not unheard of in Miami, but it was irregular, and the southbound motorists were not happy about it. Monica, her face rigid with concentration, was yanking the wheel left and right to avoid the oncoming, horn-blaring cars. Just past the crumpled corpses of the pickup truck and the taxi, where the two drivers were screaming curses at each other in two different languages, Monica spun the wheel hard right, jouncing the Kia over a low median barrier and screeching across three lanes of traffic into the airport entrance road.

"Don't ever tell anybody I did that," said Monica.

"I didn't see a thing," said Matt, truthfully.

"I don't believe this," said Henry, slapping the steering wheel. Ahead of the car, and now behind it, traffic on Le Jeune had congealed into a nonmoving mass.

"You see what the problem is?" asked Leonard, peering ahead through the windshield.

"Looks like it's jammed up way past those lights," said Henry. "Some kinda commotion up there. Maybe they got something about it on the radio." He punched the power knob.

. . . not hearing what I'm saying. What I'm saying is, when they lose — not now, tonight, but when they play a game and LOSE — then I don't hear a peep from Gator fans.

Well, you're not hearing what I'M saying. I'm saying that I'M a Gator fan, and I'm calling you now, OK? I'm talking on the phone right . . .

Sighing, Henry punched the power knob again. Behind them, horns were honking. Ahead, they heard shouting. Suddenly, a low, dark shape scooted past their car.

"Please tell me I did not see that," said Leonard. "Please tell me that I did not just see a fucking goat."

"OK, Mr. Herk," said Walter. "We gotta work together here. We're gonna carry this thing around the house to the street, OK? So we can get some help. OK? Mr. Herk?"

Arthur slowly turned his gaze from Roger to Walter. Arthur's eyes were black voids; his chin was covered with foam.

"Tell her to leave me alone," he said.

"Listen to me," said Walter. "You have to *listen* to me. That's a *dog*, OK? A *dog*. And we're gonna be here all night if you don't . . ."

"Make her leave me alone," said Arthur.

"Look," said Walter, "we need to . . ."

"TELL HER TO LEAVE ME ALONE!" screamed Arthur.

Walter began to realize that his only hope of getting Arthur's cooperation was to play along. He sighed, then shook a finger at Roger and said, "Leave him alone."

Roger perked up, in case Walter was talking about food.

"You have to call her by her name," said Arthur.

"Jesus," said Walter.

"BY HER NAME!" said Arthur.

Walter sighed again, then said to Roger, "Leave him alone, Mrs. Dole!"

Roger, thrilled at the attention, trotted over to Walter and jumped up, putting his front paws on Walter's chest.

"SHE WANTS YOUR SOUL!" screamed Arthur.

"Down!" said Walter. "Get down, Mrs. Dole!"

"A nuclear bomb in a *suitcase?*" said Harvey Baker.

"Yup," said Greer.

"I thought nuclear bombs were big," said Baker. He recalled an old newsreel showing the Hiroshima bomb, which looked like a small submarine.

"Not all of 'em," said Greer.

"Jesus," said Baker. "Where'd it come from? What the hell is it doing *here?*"

"Long story," said Greer. "Which I will try to make short. In what now passes for Russia, they got nuclear missiles left over from the Cold War, OK? A *lot* of missiles. Under a treaty, which I won't go into the details, the Russians are supposed to take a lot of these missiles out of service, which is called decommissioning. Problem is, a lot of the parts on these missiles — things like gyroscopes, position indicators, accelerators . . ."

"Accelerometers," interrupted Seitz.

"Excuse me, Wernher Fucking von Braun," said Greer. "Anyway, these parts are exactly what you need if you are a low-level international asshole like Saddam Hussein looking to get hold of some serious missiles and rise to the position of high-level international asshole. These missiles are new Corvettes in a bad neighborhood. Lotta people want 'em for parts."

"Doesn't the Russian government have, like, controls on this stuff?" asked Baker.

"Sure they do," said Greer. "Same as the city of Miami has controls to keep building inspectors from taking bribes."

"That's different," said Baker. "That's just bullshit graft. You're talking about nuclear weapons here."

Seitz snorted. "Only difference," he said, "is how much money."

"So anyway," continued Greer, "the *really* scary part of the missile, obviously, is the warhead, the part that goes bang. And the Russians actually have been pretty good about keeping track of those."

"Pretty good?" asked Baker.

"Right," said Greer. "In other words, not good enough. About two years ago, somebody got two warheads, we still don't exactly how, out of a missile dismantlement facility in a place called, um . . ."

"Sergeyev Posad," said Seitz. "Not far from Moscow. Used to be named Zagorsk. Very beautiful churches there."

"Thank you, Mr. Michelin," said Greer. "So anyway, this person gets these warheads, which disappear for a while, nobody in the world can find 'em. And then one of them shows up — guess where — the Middle East, Jordan to be exact."

"Jesus," said Baker.

"Exactly," said Greer. "Only now, the warhead's been modified, by somebody who knows his shit. Now it's in a metal suitcase. One strong man can carry it. You put it somewhere, set the detonation timer, walk away. Timer goes off, boom, wipes out your whole downtown. Makes Oklahoma City look like a cherry bomb."

"From something the size of a *suitcase?*" asked Baker.

"The actual warhead part is a lot smaller than the suitcase," said Greer. "It looks kind of like a garbage disposal. The real weight of the suitcase is a big wad of conventional explosive that sets off the warhead. The explosive is set off by a detonator with a timer, which is no big deal, like something you could get at Radio Shack. But forget about the size. This thing will blow away *all* your big buildings, bucko. This thing will fry your eyeballs at ten miles."

"And you're saying the other suitcase is here in Miami," said Baker.

"What I'm saying," said Greer, "is that when they found the one warhead, in the suitcase, it was in the hands of some people who are not real big fans of the United States. These people were taken into custody."

"By whom?" asked Baker.

"That I definitely can't tell you," said Greer, "except to say that they don't waste a lot of time advising suspects of their Miranda rights."

"The Israelis," said Baker.

Greer nodded. "Like I say, I can't tell you," he said. "Alls I can tell you is, they are *very* good at getting information from people who don't feel like talking. And the information they got is that the other suitcase was supposed to go to New York City, where it was gonna be picked up by a True Believer, who was gonna express his beliefs by turning Times Square and the surrounding area into radioactive grit."

"No great loss," said Baker.

"Hey, it's a lot nicer," said Seitz. "They fixed it up."

"Anyway," said Greer, "this point, we still don't know when or how the suitcase is going to New York. But we *do* know who the True Believer is, so we got him under surveillance. We got this guy under a *blanket*. We know if he *farts*. So when he gets in a cab and heads toward Kennedy airport, we are *on* him. Except, guess what, some dickwad Secret Agents from a federal agency that I will not identify here except by the initials C, I, and A . . .”

“Which don’t even have fucking jurisdiction,” noted Seitz.

“. . . which, as Justice Rehnquist here points out, don’t even have fucking jurisdiction,” said Greer. “These morons have *also,* without telling anybody, been watching the True Believer, who they think is about to flee the country, so on the access road to Kennedy they run the cab off the road and grab the guy in what they call a Clandestine Operation.”

“Which was as clandestine as a Super Bowl halftime show,” noted Seitz.

“So there we are,” said Greer, “we’re within sight of the fucking terminals, and we’re about to shoot these morons who are supposed to be on *our side,* and of course now the True Believer is not gonna lead us to shit. We search the international arrivals, but we don’t find the suitcase. Whoever had it, something spooked him, we’re betting the Secret Agents, so he’s outta there. We do some checking around, we think probably our guy took a cab from Kennedy to La Guardia, jumped a plane, and got the hell out of New York, we think maybe either to Atlanta or here.”

“Or Houston or New Orleans,” said Seitz.

"Or them," agreed Greer.

"Way to narrow it down," said Baker.

"Hey," said Greer, "all we got to go on is a *very* vague description. Basically, we got, 'It's a guy with a suitcase.' But we keep asking around, and we hear, various sources, that this guy is scared now. He just wants to get rid of this thing and get enough money to get the hell back to True Believerland. What we think he did, he sold it cheap to some illegal-arms dealers, guys who mainly deal in machine guns, things like that."

"Why would they want a nuclear bomb?" asked Baker.

"We think they didn't really know what it was," said Greer. "The reason we think this is, far as we been able to trace it, they sold it to some other guys, who sold it to some guy runs a place here called the Jolly Jackal."

"The *bar?*" said Baker.

"That *bar*," said Greer, "has more AK-47s than Budweisers."

"Jesus," said Baker. "This town."

"Thing is," said Greer, "we could be wrong about all of this. This could be another suitcase, unrelated. Could be drugs, could be counterfeit money. We also got guys looking in Atlanta, Houston, New Orleans, some other places. But based on the conversation we had earlier this evening with the guy who runs the Jolly Jackal . . ."

"Who will not be runnin' anywhere in the near future," noted Seitz.

"No, he won't," agreed Greer. "Anyway, based on our conversation with him, we think this is the suitcase we want, and that we think is now going to MIA with these local scumbags."

Baker sat back in the seat and looked out the window for a few moments. He leaned forward again and said, "Here's what I don't get."

"Lemme guess," said Greer. "You don't get how come, if we think there's a chance the suitcase is here, we don't tell the cops, make some kind of announcement, evacuate the public outta here. That it?"

"Basically, yeah," said Baker.

"Several reasons," said Greer. "Number one, these assholes don't know it, but we got 'em trapped at the airport."

"What do you mean?" asked Baker.

"I mean," said Greer, "just before we ran into you, I made a phone call." He held up what looked to Baker like a cell phone, except it was on the thick side, and it had a short, fat antenna. "Until we say otherwise, no plane is takin' off from MIA. There won't be any announcements; the planes'll be boarded as usual, but they won't get clearance to push back from the gates."

"You can do that?" asked Baker.

"You'd be surprised," said Greer. "Point is, we got these assholes bottled up."

"Then why don't you evacuate the area around the airport?" asked Baker.

"That's the second reason," said Greer. "Think about it. If word gets out, which it would, there's a nuclear bomb practically in fucking downtown, what do you think would happen to this city? Do you think there would be an orderly evacuation? Women and children first? Cooler heads prevailing? You think that's how the citizenry of Miami would react?"

Baker thought about it.

"What would happen," continued Greer, "is that every idiot in this town who owns a gun, which is basically every idiot in this town, would grab his gun, jump into his car, or somebody else's car, and lay rubber for I-95. Inside of ten minutes the city is gridlocked, and what happens next makes Iwo Jima look like a maypole dance. This whole town turns into the end of a Stephen King novel."

"Good point," said Baker.

"Number three," said Greer, "if word gets around about what's in the suitcase, it eventually gets to the morons who *have* the suitcase. Long as they don't know what they got, which apparently they don't, they ain't gonna think about trying to use it, like as a bargaining chip."

"*Could* they set it off?" asked Baker. "I mean, doesn't it have, like, whaddyacallem, fail-safe things?"

"This thing wasn't built by good guys," Greer said. "It's not like in the movies, where the president has to give the Secret Code and two trusty soldiers have to turn their keys simultaneously. This thing was built by bad guys who wanna be able to set it down in a public place in a crowded city and arm it quickly. We don't know for sure about this suitcase, but the other one? The one they recovered? All you had to do there was open it up and flip three electrical switches, and that starts a forty-five-minute timer."

"Forty-five minutes?" said Baker.

"Forty-five," said Greer. "We think the True Believer was planning to hop a subway, be up in the Bronx, facing north, by the time it blew."

"And now it's here," said Baker, staring out the window.

"Looks like it," said Greer.

"Jesus," said Baker, shaking his head. "I mean, you see this shit in the movies, and you think it's fiction, but I guess it was bound to happen one day."

Seitz snorted.

"What?" asked Baker.

"What makes you think this is the first time?" said Seitz.

"This *isn't* the first time?" said Baker.

Seitz snorted again.

"Never mind which time this is," said Greer. "Here's the thing. What I told you here, it's because, like I said, you're a cop, and you got cops involved. But what I'm also telling you is, when we get these scumbags, we take them, and the suitcase, and we leave, and that's the end of this as far as you are concerned, understand?"

"What do you mean?" asked Baker.

"What I mean," said Greer, "is that as far as the federal government is concerned — and I am talking about way, way, *way* the fuck high up in the federal government — none of this happened. There was no nuclear bomb in Miami. There never have been any nuclear bombs going around loose in suitcases anywhere in this great land of ours. Because if people start thinking there are, we are gonna have panic like you cannot imagine — people leaving for Montana, hoarding food, taking all their money outta the banks, lynching every guy with a beard, you get the picture. The economy goes into the toilet, civilization collapses, end of story. So this did not happen. Understand? Whatever happens, *it did not happen.*"

Baker said, "But I have to report . . ."

"You don't have to report shit," said Greer. "You repeat any of this, Agent Seitz and I, backed by pretty much the entire federal government, will deny it. You push it, and we will push back on you, hard. *Very* hard. Nothing personal, because seems to me like you're a good cop, but we can and will fuck your career up so bad you won't be able to get a job policing Porta Potties."

Baker sat back in his seat, staring out the window again. He said, "What you said before, about if you told me what was going on, you might have to kill me . . ."

Greer turned and looked back at him. "What about it?"

Baker said, "You weren't kidding, were you?"

Greer looked forward again. "Traffic's getting bad," he said.

ELEVEN

Even veteran air travelers find Miami International Airport disorienting. It's often crowded, and it seems to have been designed so that every passenger, no matter where he or she is coming from or going to, has to jostle past every other passenger. The main concourse looks like a combination international bazaar and refugee camp. There are big clots of people everywhere — tour groups, school trips, salsa bands, soccer teams, vast extended families — all waiting for planes that will not leave for hours, maybe days. There aren't enough places to sit, so the clots plop down and sprawl on the mungy carpet, surrounded by Appalachian-foothill-sized mounds of luggage, including gigantic suitcases stuffed to bursting, as well as a vast array of consumer goods purchased in South Florida for transport back to Latin America, including TVs, stereos, toys, major appliances, and complete sets of tires. Many of these items have been wrapped in thick cocoons of greenish stretch plastic to deter baggage theft, which is an important airport industry, another one being the constant "improvements" to the airport, which seem to consist mainly of the installation of permanent-looking signs asking the public to excuse the inconvenience while the airport is being improved.

The airport air smells of musty tropical rot, and it's filled with the sounds of various languages — Spanish, predominantly, but also English, Creole, German, French, Italian, and, perhaps most distinct of all, Cruise Ship Passenger. The cruisers just arriving are usually wearing brand-new cruisewear. They follow in groups close behind cruise-line employees holding signs displaying cruise-line names; they tell each other what other cruises they have been on, and they laugh loudly whenever anybody makes a joke — which somebody does every forty-five seconds — about how much they're going to drink, gamble, or buy. The cruisers heading home are more subdued — tired, sunburned, hungover, and bloated from eating eleven times per day, whether they were hungry or not, because . . . it's all included! Some of the women have had their hair braided and beaded, a style that looks fine on young Caribbean girls, but on most women over sixteen looks comical or outright hideous. Some passengers are clutching badly mass-produced "folk art" — large, unattractive, nonfunctional sticks are popular — and a great many of them are lugging boxes containing the ultimate cruise-ship passenger trophy: discount booze! Never mind that they spent thousands of dollars to take this vacation: They're thrilled to have saved as much as *ten dol-*

lars a bottle on scotch and brandy and liqueurs that they will never actually drink, but which they lug through miles of airports, on and off various planes, so that when they get back home they can haul it out and display it proudly to visitors in the months and years to come ("We got this for twenty-three-fifty in the Virgin Islands! Guess what it costs here!").

On the night that Snake and his party walked in with a nuclear bomb, the airport was even more chaotic than usual. There was bad weather in Chicago, which of course meant that virtually every flight in the western hemisphere, including space shuttle launches, had been delayed. And now some airlines were noticing a problem getting clearance for outgoing flights to push back, although the control tower was not saying why. Most airline ticket counters had sprouted long lines of pissed-off passengers shoving to get to the counter so they could argue fruitlessly with pissed-off airline employees. Police had already been summoned to arrest one returning cruise passenger who had threatened a ticket agent with his souvenir stick.

Eddie came through the airport door first, followed by Puggy, lugging the suitcase, and then Snake, who had one hand under the sweatshirt and the other holding Jenny's arm. Like Eddie and Puggy, Snake had never been inside MIA before, and for a moment, when he saw the roiling mob, he thought about turning and running. But then he squeezed his gun, his wand, and the moment passed. He was *not* going back to scamming dimes.

"Where we goin'?" asked Eddie, staring at the airport scene. He had never felt less like he belonged somewhere, and Eddie was the kind of person who never felt he belonged anywhere.

"That way," said Snake, pointing, pretty much randomly, toward a line of ticket counters. He jabbed the barrel of the sweatshirt-swathed gun into Puggy's back and said, "You stay close, punk. You don't go one step farther away from me'n you are now."

They moved slowly through the crowd — first Eddie, then Puggy lugging the suitcase, followed closely by Snake, who limped next to Jenny, who shuffled her feet and stared ahead, zombielike. The first airline they came to had a name Snake did not understand and a sign listing departures for cities that Snake had never heard of; everyone at the counter was talking in Spanish. Snake jerked his head to indicate to Eddie that he should move ahead. They went past a half dozen more airlines that Snake found incomprehensible, then came to a small counter with a half dozen people waiting in line for a lone agent. Over the counter was an orange sign that said:

AIR IMPACT!

You're Gateway to the Bahamas
Sheduled Departures Daily

232

Snake felt a good-vibe jolt. *The Bahamas!* He motioned Eddie to get in line. They shuffled forward, Snake keeping his grip on Jenny and periodically letting Puggy feel the gun in his back. In ten minutes, they were standing in front of the agent.

The agent was a single mom named Sheila who had been on duty for fourteen hours without a break, because two of her three coworkers had quit that very day. Air Impact! had trouble keeping employees because its paychecks were behind schedule as often as its flights, which was quite often. Air Impact! was owned by two brothers from North Miami Beach who had done well in the pest-control business and had hatched the plan of starting an airline so that they would have a legitimate business excuse to fly to the Bahamas and gamble and have sex with women who were not technically their wives. The airline was in its second year, and the brothers were spending more and more time in the Bahamas and less and less time on business details such as payroll and schedules and hiring competent personnel.

The Federal Aviation Administration had begun to take a special interest in Air Impact! after receiving an unusually high number of passenger complaints about flight delays and cancellations. Eyebrows had also been raised two weeks earlier when an Air Impact! flight from Miami to Nassau, flown by pilots with questionable credentials, had in fact landed in Key West, which

233

even non-aviators noted was several hundred miles in the diametrically opposite direction. Rumor had it that the FAA was about to shut Air Impact! down, and morale was very low among the employees who had not already quit. Nobody's morale was any lower than Sheila's; aside from having been on her feet for what seemed like forever dealing with unhappy customers, she had just received a call from the baby-sitter she could barely afford telling her that her two-year-old daughter was throwing up, this coming on top of the call from the mechanic telling her that her 1987 Taurus, which always needed something, needed major transmission work.

Had Sheila been in a state of higher morale, she probably would have cared enough to be suspicious of the quartet now standing at the counter — a zoned-out young woman with three scuzzy-looking men. But Sheila had long since passed the point of giving a shit.

"Yes?" she said to Snake.

"We need four tickets to the Bahamas, one-way, next flight you got," said Snake.

"Nassau or Freeport?" she asked.

Snake frowned. "The Bahamas," he said.

"Nassau and Freeport are *in* the Bahamas," said Sheila, mentally adding *you moron.*

Snake thought about it.

"Freeport," he said. He liked the sound of it.

"There's a ten-ten flight," said Sheila, checking her watch, which said nine-fifteen. "Four one-way tickets is" — she tapped the computer keyboard — "three hundred sixty dollars."

Snake let go of Jenny for a moment while he dug his free hand into his pocket. He pulled out the fat wad of bills he'd taken from Arthur Herk at the house. He set it on the counter, in front of Sheila, and, one-handed, started counting off twenties out loud . . . "twenty, forty, sixty. . . ." At 120, his brain fogged up — he'd always struggled with arithmetic — and he had to start again. He did this twice, said "fuck," and pushed the wad off the counter, scattering bills across Sheila's keyboard.

"Take it outta there," he said.

Sheila gathered up the wad, feeling the heft of it, this *big* bunch of money being carried around by this guy who didn't even know how to count it. Sheila peeled off $360. Then, after glancing at Snake, who was looking around nervously, she peeled off another $480, which was what she needed to get her transmission fixed, and then another $140, which was roughly what she owed the baby-sitter for the past week. She put the rest of the wad back on the counter. Snake looked at it. He almost said something, but he didn't want any trouble here. Plus he figured he had plenty of money left. Plus a suitcase full of drugs. Maybe emeralds.

"I need the names of the passengers," said Sheila, tapping on her terminal.

Snake hesitated, then said, "John Smith."

Sheila looked up for a second, then went back to tapping.

"And the other passengers?" she said.

"John Smith," said Snake.

Sheila looked up again, at Eddie, Puggy, Snake, and Jenny. "You're all John Smith?" she asked.

"Everybody," said Snake.

"I need to see photo IDs," said Sheila.

Snake grabbed a handful of bills and dropped them on her keyboard.

"Here you go," he said.

Sheila looked at the bills. It looked to be at least two hundred.

"OK, then, Mr. Smith," she said.

Monica, leaning on the horn, swerved the Kia past a car-rental courtesy shuttle on the airport access road.

"OK, listen," she said. "We're looking for the police car. You see it, you yell, OK?"

"OK," said Matt and Eliot. Anna was quiet. Nina was praying.

"Once we see the car," said Monica — who was thinking, *Jesus, I hope we see the car* — "if they're not in it, we go into the terminal and we look for them. There will be police officers at the airport to help us. It's gonna be OK, Mrs. Herk."

In the back, Anna said nothing.

Monica gunned the Kia up the ramp under the Departures sign. They were approaching the terminal building now, Monica, Matt, and Eliot scanning the mass of cars ahead. It was Matt

236

who saw the cruiser in the unfinished garage.

"Over there," he said, pointing.

Monica swerved left into the garage, screeching to a stop behind the cruiser. She was out of the Kia before it stopped rocking. She saw that the cruiser was empty, slammed her hand on the trunk, spun around, and raced, dodging traffic, across the roadway into the terminal. Matt was right behind her, followed by Eliot, holding Anna's hand.

"This ain't gonna work," said Seitz, looking at the string of unmoving brake lights disappearing into the distance northbound on Le Jeune.

"If you can make a right up there," said Baker, "you can swing over to Douglas, go up that way."

"See if that guy'll let me squeeze in front of him," said Seitz, nodding toward a Humvee in the right-hand lane next to their rental. Humvees are a common sight in Miami. They're especially popular with wealthy trend-followers who like to cruise the streets in these large, impractical pseudomilitary vehicles, as though awaiting orders to proceed to Baghdad. The Humvee next to the FBI rental car was occupied by three young males whose buzz-cut heads bobbed simultaneously to the whomping, churning bass notes blasting from a speaker the size of a doghouse filling the entire rear of the vehicle. The driver had received the car two days earlier as a nineteenth-birthday present from his father, a prosperous and respected local cocaine importer.

The Humvee occupants didn't hear Seitz honk his horn, so Greer lowered his window and waved to get the driver's attention. When the Humvee driver looked over, Greer made a cranking signal with his hand. The driver lowered his window; Greer, Seitz, and Baker winced as they were pounded by the music.

I want your sex pootie!
I want your sex pootie!
I want your sex pootie!
I want your sex pootie!

Greer, squinting into the howling gale of sound, made a gesture to the Humvee driver asking him to let the rental car squeeze in front. The Humvee driver made a gesture indicating that Greer should go fuck himself. The driver raised his window; he and his friends were laughing.

"Ah, youth," said Greer.

"You want me to show 'em my badge?" asked Baker.

"Nah," said Greer, opening the door and getting out.

"You ever hear of Special Executive Order 768 dash 4?" Seitz asked Baker.

"No," said Baker. "What's that?"

"Powerful law-enforcement tool," said Seitz.

Greer rapped his knuckles on the Humvee window. The driver glanced sideways, then again flipped Greer the bird. He and his buddies laughed. They stopped when Greer drove the butt of his revolver through the window with his right hand, then reached in with his left, grabbed the driver by the front of his Tommy Hilfiger shirt, and yanked him out the window and onto the street. The driver broke his fall with his hands, scrambled to his feet, and ran ahead into the mass of traffic without looking back. The other two young males exited on the passenger side without being asked. Greer climbed into the driver's seat, turned off the sound system, ejected the CD, and drove the Humvee up over the sidewalk and into a Burger King parking lot, clearing a path for Seitz to move over. Then he climbed out of the Humvee, dropped the CD onto the pavement, stepped on it, and got back in the rental.

"I could've just showed 'em my badge," said Baker.

"Nah," said Greer.

Seitz, aided by the helpful maneuvers of surrounding drivers who had watched Greer in action and did not wish to be viewed as uncooperative, was able to squeeze around to the right and onto a cross street, heading east to Douglas. When they were northbound again, Baker said, "What do you think this guy's gonna do? I mean, why's he going to the airport?"

"My guess," said Greer, "based on crime-fighter deductions, he's gonna try to get on a plane."

"How?" asked Baker. "I mean, there's security at the airport, right?"

That got a large snort from Seitz.

When Snake and his small, unhappy group reached the concourse for their Air Impact! flight, they found a long line of people waiting to go through the security checkpoint.

"Hold it," said Snake, pulling back on Jenny's arm. He wanted to watch a little bit, see what was going on.

It was the standard airport-security operation, which meant it appeared to have been designed to hassle law-abiding passengers just enough to reassure them, while at the same time providing virtually no protection against criminals with an IQ higher than celery. Passengers put their belongings on a conveyor belt that went through the X-ray machine; they put their phones, keys, beepers, and other metal objects on a little pass-through shelf; then they walked through the metal detector. This operation was being overseen by harried, distracted employees who seemed primarily concerned with keeping the line moving.

It took Snake, who had never before seen an airport security checkpoint, about two minutes to figure out how he would get his gun through. He actually had three guns on him, one in his hand and one in each side pocket. He thought he could probably get them all through, but decided not to get greedy. He herded his group over to a trash can and, after glancing around to make sure nobody was looking, dropped Monica's and Walter's official-issue Glocks into the slot. Then he waited for another minute, until he saw a businessman with a laptop-computer bag slung over his shoulder approaching the checkpoint line. As the man walked past, Snake shoved Puggy after him, into the line. As they shuffled forward, Snake whispered to Puggy and Jenny:

"We get up there, you" — he jabbed Puggy — "put that suitcase on that belt and then you walk through. Girlie, you walk through right after. I will be right fucking behind you. Either one a ya says a fuckin' *word,* you are both fuckin' *dead,* unnerstan'?"

"Snake," said Eddie. "This ain't gonna work, man. They got *machines* up there and shit."

"Shut up," said Snake. He was sick of Eddie's attitude.

They were now almost to the checkpoint. Just on the other side of the metal detector was a rotund man whose job, as he interpreted it, was to wave people through as fast as possible.

"Step through, please!" he said, over and over, waving at the passengers.

The businessman in front of Puggy put his laptop bag on the belt, and the rotund man waved him through, then started waving Puggy through. Puggy, prodded by the feel of the gun under Snake's sweatshirt, hefted the suitcase onto the belt and went through the metal detector. As he did this, the woman operating the X-ray machine, seeing the businessman's laptop, said, "Computer check!" They were very vigilant about computers at the security checkpoint.

The rotund man turned toward a stern-looking woman at a table at the end of the conveyor belt and said, "Computer check!" The woman waved the businessman over. She would make him turn on the computer. That was the heart of her job: making people turn on their computers. In the world of the security checkpoint, the fact that a computer could be turned on served as absolute proof that it was not a bomb.

The instant that the rotund man turned his head away, Snake, in one motion, pushed Jenny through the metal detector and placed the sweatshirt, with the gun in it, on the pass-though shelf. He stepped quickly through the detector right behind Jenny and picked up the sweatshirt; this took maybe two seconds. By this time the rotund man had turned his head back and was looking past Snake, to the next person in line.

"Step through, please!" he said.

"Bag check!" said the X-ray woman. She was pointing at the metal suitcase. "Bag check!" said the rotund man, to the stern woman, who was watching the businessman turn on his laptop. When he was done, she pointed at the metal suitcase at the end of the conveyor belt and said to Puggy, "Is this yours?"

"It's mine," Snake said. He was right behind

Puggy, letting him feel the gun in his back.

"Bring it over here and open it, please," the woman said.

"Do it," Snake said to Puggy.

Puggy lifted the suitcase onto the table. He unlatched the four latches and raised the suitcase lid. The stern woman looked inside, saw the steel canister, the black box with the foreign writing, the bank of switches.

"What is this?" she asked.

"Garbage disposal," said Snake.

"A garbage disposal?" asked the stern woman. This had not been covered in security-checkpoint training.

"It's portable," explained Snake.

The stern woman hesitated for a second. She thought about calling for her supervisor. But she also thought about what had happened the last time she'd asked him to look at something she thought was suspicious: It had turned out to be a *latte* machine, and the supervisor had chewed her out for letting the line back up. The supervisor had been hearing from *his* supervisor; there'd been a lot of complaints lately from passengers who had missed, or nearly missed, their flights because of delays at security.

As the stern woman was thinking about this, the X-ray woman called out, "Computer check!" Another potentially deadly laptop was coming down the belt.

"Computer check!" echoed the rotund man. Passengers were still streaming through the metal detector. The checkpoint was backing up.

The stern woman looked at the line, looked at the suitcase, looked at Snake.

"You'll have to turn it on," she said.

Snake studied the interior of the suitcase. On the black box next to the metal cylinder were three switches, which Snake figured were some kind of security system, to protect the drugs or emeralds or whatever was in there. He reached down and flipped the first switch. Nothing happened. He flipped the second. Nothing. He flipped the third. Some digital lights started blinking under a dark plastic panel on the bottom left corner of the box. They said:

00:00

The stern woman frowned at the blinking zeroes, then at Snake.

"It's got a timer," he explained. "Like a whaddyacallit. VCR."

"Computer check!" called the X-ray woman.

"Computer check!" echoed the rotund man. The laptops were stacking up.

"OK," said the stern woman, waving Snake's party away. Snake closed the suitcase, not noticing, as he did, that the digits had stopped blinking and were now registering:

45:00

And then:

44:59

Snake latched the suitcase, then jabbed Puggy. "Move it," he said. Puggy picked up the suitcase, and the little party headed down the concourse toward the planes. Behind them, the stern woman turned her attention to the next passenger, a pension actuary who was already, without having to be asked, turning his computer on, knowing that this was the price that a free society had to pay to combat terrorism.

43:47

Monica trotted through the automatic doorway into the main concourse, darting her eyes back and forth. She was hoping to see another officer, but as bad luck would have it, all the available airport police had been summoned to the extreme other end of the large, semicircular concourse, where trouble had flared at the Delta counter. It had started when a Delta agent had informed a would-be passenger that he would not be permitted to board his flight with his thirteen-foot python, Daphne, wrapped around his body. The passenger, attempting to show what a well-behaved snake Daphne was, had placed her on the counter. As the Delta agent and the nearby passengers backed away in terror, Daphne had spotted, on the floor a few feet away, a small plastic pet transporter containing two Yorkshire terriers named Pinky and Enid. In a flash, she had slithered off the counter and was snaking toward them, as screaming passengers frantically scrambled to get out of her way, clubbing each other with boxes of duty-free liquor.

Within seconds, Daphne had wrapped herself around the pet transporter and was trying to figure out how to get at Pinky and Enid, whose terrified yipping inspired their devoted owner, a seventy-four-year-old widow with an artificial hip, to overcome her lifelong fear of reptiles and flail away at Daphne's muscular body with a rolled-up *Modern Maturity* magazine, until she was tackled from behind by Daphne's owner, who was no less devoted to his pet and had also played linebacker at the junior-college level.

Within a minute, the Delta end of the concourse was in near-riot mode, with virtually the entire airport police force sprinting in that direction, walkie-talkies squawking. Thus, when, a few minutes later, Monica entered the concourse at the other end, looking for reinforcements, she saw none.

"Shit," she said. She turned and saw Matt, Anna, and Eliot right behind her, with Nina just coming through the door.

"OK," said Monica. "We're gonna split up and look for them. I'll take that side" — she gestured left — "you all go that way. If you see them, you keep an eye on them, but *don't approach them,* and, Matt, you come running and find me. Got it?"

Matt and Eliot nodded.

"OK," said Monica, turning left and plunging into the concourse traffic flow. Matt turned right, with Eliot and Anna a step behind, and Nina trotting after. Nina's main concern was not being left behind. The other four, as they scanned the crowd, were all troubled by variations of the same nagging thought: *What if they were in the wrong place?*

42:21

Air Impact! Flight 2038 for Freeport was a two-engine propeller plane with a seating capacity of twenty-two people. It had no flight attendant, and was too small for a jetway; to board it, passengers walked down a stairway from the concourse gate, then across the tarmac about thirty yards to where the plane was parked.

There were supposed to be two Air Impact! employees working the gate that evening, but neither of them had shown up, which meant that the passengers' tickets were being taken by the baggage handler, a man named Arnold Unger who had joined the Air Impact! team after being fired from two other airlines for suspected baggage theft. Unger had worked the same no-break double shift that had seriously undermined Sheila the ticket agent's desire to be Employee of the Month. He'd been keeping his spirits up by swigging from a bottle of Bacardi rum that he'd swiped from a cruise passenger and kept hidden under the stairs. He was eager to get Flight

2038, Air Impact!'s last of the evening, on its way, so that he could go get really hammered.

It figured to be an easy flight. Most of the scheduled passengers had missed their connecting flights into Miami because of the bad weather in Chicago. Unger had loaded just eleven bags onto the plane. When he came up the stairs into the waiting area and punched up the passenger list on the computer, he found only eight names, half of which, he noted with mild interest, were John Smith. There were four passengers in the waiting area; these were two couples, retired postal workers and their wives, all originally from Ohio, now living in Naples, Florida. They had driven across the state that afternoon to take advantage of the bargain Air Impact! fares on flights to the Bahamas, where they planned to play keno. They were anxious to get out of Miami International Airport, which they regarded as the most foreign place they had ever been, including Italy, which they had visited once on a group tour with other retired postal workers.

They looked up expectantly, as Unger, wearing grimy dark blue shorts, a blue short-sleeved work shirt, work boots, and kneepads, propped open the door to the stairwell. He picked up the receiver of a wall-mounted phone, punched in a code, and said, in a booming voice, "Good evening, ladies and gentlemen. Air Impact! Flight 2038 to beautiful downtown Freeport is now ready for passenger boarding through this door right here. We'd like to begin our boarding to-night with . . ." — he pretended to look around the almost-deserted waiting area, then pointed at the retirees — "YOU lovely people!" The re-tirees shuffled over and gave him their tickets. He told them to go downstairs and head out to the plane. They asked him how they would know which plane. He told them it was the plane that said Air Impact! in great big letters on the side. They did not like his tone one bit.

It was now ten minutes before the scheduled departure, and Unger was thinking about clos-ing the door, when Puggy, lugging the suitcase, entered the waiting area, followed closely by Snake and Jenny, followed by Eddie. They moved in a tight, strange-looking little clot over to Unger. Snake handed Unger the tickets.

"Ah," said Unger. "The John Smiths."

Snake gave Unger a don't-fuck-with-me stare. Unger responded with an I-don't-give-a-shit shrug. His feeling was, whoever these people were, they were soon going to be not his prob-lem. He gestured toward the doorway.

"Plane's downstairs," he said.

The clot went down the stairs, with Unger closing the door behind them and following them out to the tarmac. He gestured toward the plane, where the retired couples, complaining loudly about not getting any help, were ascend-ing the narrow fold-down stairway at the rear of the plane, slowly and laboriously, as though it were the last fifty feet of the Everest summit.

Unger followed Snake's clot to the plane. When they reached it, he reached for the suitcase, telling Puggy, "I'll take that."

Snake grabbed Unger's arm. "It goes onna plane," he said.

"I'm gonna *put* it on the plane," said Unger. "You get it back in Freeport."

"I mean it rides with us," said Snake.

"Can't," said Unger. "Too big. FAA regulations."

Snake reached into his pants pocket, pulled out a wad of bills, and handed them to Unger.

"Lemme give you a hand with that suitcase," Unger said. As Snake watched him closely, he grabbed the suitcase — *damn,* this thing was heavy — and manhandled it to the folding stairs. He was a strong man, but he just barely got it to the top. He left it just inside the doorway opening.

Panting, Unger came back down the stairs. He looked past Snake, toward the terminal.

"Where's your friend going?" he asked.

Snake whirled. Puggy, who had been right next to him, was gone. Snake looked back toward the terminal and saw the stocky shape disappearing through the doorway.

"Mother*fucker,*" said Snake, furious, squeezing Jenny's arm so hard that she cried out. "That punk mother*FUCKER.*" He spun back to Unger.

"When's this plane leave?" he said.

"You wanna go back and get your friend?" asked Unger.

"No, I want this fuckin' plane to leave *right now*," said Snake.

"It'll leave soon's you get on and the pilots finish the preflight," Unger said. "Five, ten minutes."

"Get on," Snake said to Eddie. Eddie was looking back to where Puggy had disappeared.

"Snake," said Eddie, "I don't think this is . . ."

"I said *get on the plane*," said Snake, using his sweatshirt-gun to prod Eddie exactly the way he had been prodding Puggy. Eddie turned slowly away from the terminal and trudged up the stairs. Snake shoved Jenny up after him. They had to step over the suitcase to get into the aisle.

Unger walked around to the front and signaled to the pilot to slide open his side windshield panel. When the pilot did so, Unger said, "You're set to go."

"What about the guy who ran back to the terminal?" asked the pilot. "He forget something?"

"Nah," said Unger. "Looks like he just changed his mind." Unger almost said something else then, something along the lines of, *You got a weird passenger back there,* but decided not to. He'd seen weird people get on planes before; South Florida was full of weird people. This guy was definitely carrying drugs or some damn thing. But Unger viewed that as somebody else's problem. It was late, time to get to drinking, and besides, he didn't know this flight crew, a couple of young guys who'd just been hired to replace a couple of other young guys who'd gotten fed up with Air Impact! and quit. Unger, stepping away from the plane, gave the pilot a thumbs-up sign.

TWELVE

35:08

Puggy was trotting away from the Air Impact! gate area, trying to decide what to do. His main thought was to get away from the crazy man with the gun, to just keep going, get out of the crowded, scary, alien airport. But he was also thinking about the girl back there. She was scared to death of the crazy man, Puggy could see that, and he could also see that she was right to be scared to death of him. Puggy thought he should tell somebody about her. But who? Puggy didn't like cops — he'd had bad experiences with cops — but he wished there was one right here that he could tell about the girl.

Ahead, he a saw a counter with two agents, a young man and an older woman, standing behind it, counting pieces of paper, doing the final paperwork on a Miami-to-Philadelphia flight that had been delayed nearly three hours. He hesitated, then went up to the counter. The young man looked up.

"Yes?" he said, not pleasantly.

"Um," said Puggy. "There's . . . I need to . . ."

"I'm sorry," said the young man, who was clearly not sorry, "this flight is closed. No seats, OK?"

"No, there's a guy down there," said Puggy, gesturing back toward the Air Impact! area. "He has this girl."

"Sir," said the woman agent, even less pleasantly than the man. "We have to get this flight out of here *right now*, OK? So whatever it is, we don't have time for it."

"He's makin' her go," said Puggy. "He has a . . ."

"We don't have time for it right now, *sir*," said the man, and he went back to counting pieces of paper, and so did the woman, both of them shaking their heads at how people could be.

34:02

"So what's the plan?" said Baker. "We get in there and sound the alarm?" The rental car was weaving through traffic on the airport Departures ramp.

"Negative," said Greer. "Like I said, the more people know, the more likely we have people getting killed. So we keep it quiet unless we absolutely have to."

"So how're we supposed to find them?" asked Baker.

"We find them because, number one, they're gonna be moving slow, schlepping that suitcase," said Greer. "Number two, what I know about these scuzzballs from our friend back at the Jolly Jackal, they are not gifted in the brains department. Plus they got hostages. They are definitely gonna stand out in the crowd."

"I dunno," said Baker. "This airport, it can be hard to stand out."

33:34

In front of the Delta counter, two police officers were trying to revive Daphne's owner. He had resisted efforts by officers to pry him off the dog-owning widow, and finally one of them had clubbed him with a heavy-duty four-cell flashlight, rendering him, for the moment, unconscious. This was bad, because the police needed him to subdue Daphne, who had abandoned her fruitless efforts to get at Pinky and Enid and let go of the pet transporter. She was now surveying the rapidly growing mob of gawkers, thinking whatever it is that large, hungry snakes think.

The police had a problem. Obviously, they could not allow this creature to remain loose in the airport. Just as obviously, they could not risk trying to shoot it with all these civilians around. That meant that somebody had to capture it, but its owner was currently out cold, and none of the police officers present wanted any part of trying to apprehend Daphne manually. As one of them put it, "What're you gonna do? Slap handcuffs on it?"

And so, for the moment, it was a standoff. On

the one side stood the police, trying to hold back
the crowd; on the other side stood, or, more ac-
curately, coiled, Daphne. An officer had radioed
headquarters to request that an animal-control
unit be dispatched to the airport immediately,
but he had just been informed that the closest
such unit was tied up with a major traffic jam on
Le Jeune, involving goats.

33:17

"Where are the police?" Anna was asking, her
voice right on the edge of hysterical. *"How can
there not be any police?"*

"We'll find some," Eliot said. "There have to
be some around here." But he was wondering,
too. There were *always* police here.

Eliot and Anna were trotting through the
crowd a few steps behind Matt, with Nina bringing up the rear. Their search was becoming more
desperate by the second as they realized how
many people were in the airport, how many concourses, how many gates.

They came to a security checkpoint, where at
least two hundred people were waiting in two
lines to pass through the metal detectors into the
flight concourse. Matt, Anna, and Eliot separated and moved up and down the lines, scanning the faces. No luck. They had just started
moving down the main concourse again when
they heard Nina cry out. They turned and saw
Nina running back toward the checkpoint, call-

ing a name that sounded like "Pogey." Matt was the first to see where she was going.

"It's the little guy!" he shouted. "With the beard! From the house! The guy who carried the suitcase!"

Anna and Eliot saw Puggy then, on the other side of the security checkpoint, trotting toward Nina, a look of wonder on his face.

"Matt," said Eliot, "go find the lady cop. We'll stay here with this guy. *Run.*" But Matt was already sprinting through the crowd.

29:32

"You said Delta, right?" asked the driver.

"Delta," said Henry.

Henry and Leonard were in a U-Drive-It Rental Car shuttle bus approaching the main terminal. They had flagged down the bus — actually, they had stepped in front of it, forcing it to stop — on the airport access road, after abandoning their rental car and hiking through the mass of stopped traffic on Le Jeune. The bus driver had at first been reluctant to open the door, but Henry had persuaded him by pressing a twenty-dollar bill against the windshield.

Henry and Leonard were hot and sweaty and not in a good mood. Every minute or so, Leonard shook his head and announced to the other bus passengers, who were carefully not looking at him, "Fuckin' *goats.*" Henry, though more restrained, was also fed up with this frustrating,

257

nonproductive trip. He'd decided that once they got their boarding passes for the Newark flight, he was going to call his Penultimate contact and tell him that, sorry, but they could find somebody else to kill Arthur Herk, because he, personally, was never coming back to this insane city, where every time you try to execute somebody in a careful, professional manner, another shooter shows up, or the police show up, or a dog attacks you, or some maniac jumps on you out of a tree.

"Delta," the driver said, stopping the courtesy bus and opening the door.

Henry and Leonard got off, with Leonard pausing to tell the bus driver, by way of a farewell, "Fuckin' *goats.*"

As the bus pulled away, Henry and Leonard looked through the automatic glass doors to the terminal. It was packed with people, some of them running. From somewhere inside came the sound of a woman screaming.

"*Now* what?" said Henry.

"Whatever it is," said Leonard, "it can't be any worse than goats."

28:49

"C'mon," said Snake. "*C'mon,* let's fuckin' *go,* here." He was talking mainly to himself, but the postal retirees, sitting four rows ahead, in the front of the Air Impact! plane, could hear him, and they did not approve of his language.

In the cockpit, separated from the cabin by a half-open black curtain, the newly hired Air Impact! pilots were going through their preflight checklist. They looked to Snake to be, based on zit count, maybe seventeen years old, although in fact they were both twenty-three. Their names were Justin Hobert and Frank Teeterman, Jr., and they had been close friends since elementary school, when they'd discovered that they both passionately loved airplanes. They had taken a lot of shit in junior high for continuing to build model airplanes when all their friends had become interested in titty mags.

Justin and Frank had remained single-mindedly obsessed with aviation, and their social lives had suffered. But they felt that it had all been worth it, because, after years of lessons and study, they had become commercial pilots, and tonight they were going to fly together professionally for their very first time. They could not believe their good fortune; most airlines made you fly for *years* with more experienced pilots. Sure, the pay at Air Impact! was not great — $14,200 a year — but the important thing was, they were flying. They were wearing new pilot shirts and new pilot pants, and they were *in command*.

Justin — who had won the coin toss to see who would be the captain on this flight — turned to the seven passengers in the cabin and, deepening his voice and developing a drawl, said: "Folks, welcome to Air Impact! Flight 2036 to . . ."

"Flight 2038," whispered Frank.

"Right, Flight 2038, to, ah, Freeport," said Justin. "I'm Captain Justin Hobert and this is my copilot, Frank Teeterman."

Frank waved a little salute.

"We're almost through our checklist," said Justin, "so in just a few minutes we'll be closing the door and giving you a safety briefing, then we'll be on our way." Justin had practiced this speech in front of his bathroom mirror. He thought it came out pretty good. He turned back to his checklist.

"Hey." It was Snake's voice, from the back. "How 'bout we go now."

"What?" said Justin, turning back around. The retirees also turned around to administer a group glare at Snake, who was sitting next to Jenny, who had her eyes closed and was leaning her head against the window. Eddie was across the aisle, looking glum.

"I said, let's go now," said Snake. He was thinking about the punk getting away. Snake figured the punk, being basically a lowlife like Snake, would not go to the cops. He was probably just saving his own ass, which was what Snake would have done. But Snake still wanted to get out of there.

"Sir," said Justin, "we have to finish our preflight checklist, then we'll go. It's for your safety, sir."

Snake almost showed him the gun right then. He even thought of a good line: *I got my safety*

right here, asshole. But he decided to give it another minute or two.

27:16

"Officer!" shouted Matt, darting through the
airport congestion and waving his arms at
Monica, whom Matt had spotted near the American Airlines domestic counter. "Officer!"

"You found them?" asked Monica, running
toward him.

"We found the little guy," said Matt. "With
the beard. Back this way." They were running
together now.

"Just him?" asked Monica. "Alone?"

"Yeah," said Matt.

"Did he say where the others are?" asked
Monica.

"I didn't talk to him," said Matt. "My dad said
come get you."

"Good work," said Monica.

26:02

"The airport is laid out how?" asked Greer.

"The main concourse is a big semicircle," said
Baker. "Gate concourses radiate off it."

"This about the middle?" asked Greer.

"Pretty close," said Baker.

"OK, then," said Greer. "We'll stop here."

Seitz pulled over and stopped next to a NO
STOPPING ANYTIME sign. They got out of the

car and headed for the terminal entrance.

Greer, talking to Baker, said, "My guess is, these morons already fucked up somehow, attracted the attention of the cops here. Should be easy to find 'em. When we do, we need your help to get the suitcase, get custody of the perps, and get outta here quick and quiet as possible. OK?"

"OK," said Baker.

"But no matter what," said Greer, now talking to both Seitz and Baker, *we get the suitcase.*"

As they entered the terminal, they were almost knocked over by two men with walkie-talkies, running toward their left, the direction of the Delta counter. They could hear shouting coming from that direction, then a scream.

"Bingo," said Greer.

25:41

Puggy could not believe it: his angel! Here! He held her hand and looked into her eyes, which were at exactly the level of his eyes. For a minute, he couldn't even hear what the other lady was saying to him.

"Please," Anna said, for the third time, "where is my daughter? *Please.*"

"Puggy, you must help," said Nina. *Pogey, you mus help.*

Puggy got it now. *The girl.*

"They're down that way," he said, pointing back through the security checkpoint, down the flight concourse toward the Air Impact! gate. "They got on a plane."

"Oh my God!" said Anna. She grabbed Eliot's arm. "We have to get down there!"

"Right," said Eliot, looking around desperately. *Where the hell was Matt? Where was the lady . . . there she was!*

"Over here!" he yelled, waving to Monica and Matt, who were sprinting through the crowd.

"What's he say?" said Monica, reaching the group, panting.

"He says they're on a plane," said Eliot. "Down that way."

"Show me where," said Monica, grabbing Puggy's arm and striding toward the security checkpoint. Puggy, reluctantly letting go of Nina's hand, stumbled behind Monica.

"Police emergency!" shouted Monica, as she reached the head of the checkpoint line. "Out of the way, please!" Dragging Puggy, she went through the metal detector, which beeped because of her badge. Immediately, she found her path blocked by the rotund man.

"Listen," said Monica. "This is a police emergency. I need to go down that concourse with this man, and I need you to notify the airport police right now that . . ."

"I have to scan him," said the rotund man, waving a handheld scanner toward Puggy.

"Did you *hear* me, for God's sake?" shouted Monica. "I said we have an *emergency* down there. We have a hostage sit—"

"AND I SAID I HAVE TO SCAN HIM," replied the rotund man, brandishing the scanner in Monica's face. Rules were rules.

"Scan *this*," said Monica, yanking the scanner from his grasp and flinging it over her shoulder. She shoved past the rotund man, dragging Puggy behind her.

"Hey!" said the rotund man. "Hold it! You can't . . . HEY!"

"Excuse me," said Eliot, coming through the metal detector and pushing past the rotund man, followed closely by Anna, Matt, and Nina. "We're with them."

"STOP!" shouted the rotund man, trying unsuccessfully to block this renegade group. "SECURITY!"

"SECURITY!" chorused the X-ray woman, and the stern woman at the end of the conveyor belt, and the other checkpoint workers. "SECURITY! SECURITY!"

There was an officer assigned to this checkpoint: His name was Ralph Pendick, and he happened to be the older, but not a whole lot smarter, brother of Jack Pendick, the man who earlier that evening had alertly foiled the attempted squirting of Jenny Herk by firing bullets randomly in a parking lot. Ralph Pendick's orders were to remain at the security checkpoint at all times, and he had tried mightily to comply with these orders when he first heard, on his walkie-talkie, about the trouble down at the Delta counter. He had watched, with mounting envy, as other officers ran past, headed for the action; there was *never* any action, here at the checkpoint. Finally, unable to stand it any longer, Ralph had abandoned his post and headed for Delta, which meant there was nobody to heed the cries of the personnel at his assigned checkpoint, who were still yelling "SECURITY!" at the rapidly receding figures of Monica, Puggy, Eliot, Matt, Anna, and Nina.

The rotund man waddled quickly over to a wall-mounted phone, grabbed the receiver, punched a code, and began shouting into it, nearly incoherent with excitement. Security had been breached! A police officer was involved! People had gotten through *without being properly scanned!* They could be carrying . . . *concealed laptops!*

23:24

"You see what it is?" asked Leonard. They were at the edge of the now huge mob in front of the Delta counter.

"Nope," said Henry, craning his neck. "All's I see is people tryin' to see."

"Well, fuck it," said Leonard. "I say we go to the counter."

"Worth a try," said Henry. He led the way, pushing through the crowd, which was shouting in several languages. From what snatches of English they picked up, they gathered that there were police ahead, and somebody hurt, and something crawling. As the crowd got denser, they struggled forward, Henry shoving people aside, each labored step strengthening their resolve to *get . . . out . . . of . . . this . . . crazy . . . fucking . . . place.*

As they approached the Delta counter, the crowd became almost impenetrably dense, squeezed from behind by people trying to see what was going on, and from in front by people pushing back, apparently trying to get away from something. There was a lot of shouting, the loudest coming from an area directly ahead of Henry and Leonard. Suddenly, the volume of the shouting intensified, accompanied by terrified shrieks; the crowd lunged backward violently just as Henry and Leonard pushed forward. They stumbled ahead and were suddenly in the clear, alone, surrounded by a vast ring of shouting and screaming faces. Henry caught his balance, but Leonard kept going, tripping over the pet transporter containing Pinky and Enid, who yipped and yelped in terror. Leonard pitched forward onto the floor. He groaned, then raised his head slightly and saw, on the floor two inches from his eyes . . . a *really long tongue.*

22:58

Snake was going nuts. The minutes were ticking past, and the two zitface pilots were still up there farting around, talking into their headset microphones, and the plane was *not moving*. Snake kept glancing out the window toward the door to the terminal, expecting it to open. Finally, he couldn't stand it. He stood in the aisle of the plane.

"Hey!" he shouted. "Start the fuckin' motors!"

Justin, Frank, and the retirees turned, all of them glaring, until they saw the gun pointed at the cockpit. The retirees gasped and pulled back in their seats, out of the line of fire. Justin and Frank stared at the hole in the end of the barrel, their brains frozen. Frank wet his new pilot pants.

"Start the fuckin' motors NOW," said Snake.

"We . . . we . . ." stammered Justin. "I mean, the door. We have to close the door."

"I'll close the fuckin' door, zitface," said Snake. He wasn't letting anybody else get away. "Now START THE FUCKIN' MOTORS AND FLY TO THE FUCKIN' BAHAMAS OR I BLOW BOTH YOUR FUCKIN' HEADS OFF."

This caused three of the four retirees to wet their pants.

Justin and Frank began working furiously on starting the motors.

The propeller on the right side of the plane started to turn, very slowly.

"Snake," said Eddie. He was looking out the window.

"What?" said Snake. He bent down and

looked where Eddie was looking, then said, "Shit. *SHIT.*"

The terminal door was open. The little punk — that mother*fucker* — was coming out of the building pointing the plane out to . . . *the lady cop.* That fucking *bitch.*

Snake screamed at Justin and Frank, "GET THIS FUCKIN' PLANE MOVIN' RIGHT NOW." He whirled and gimped back to the airplane doorway, aimed his gun toward the lady cop, and fired a shot. Instantly, she ducked back into the building, yanking the punk with her and closing the door.

"WHY THE FUCK AREN'T WE MOVING?" shouted Snake.

"We gotta start the other engine," Justin shouted back. The right-side engine, after a few coughs and sputters, was roaring. The left-hand propeller was starting to turn. Snake looked back toward the terminal door; it was open a crack now, but he couldn't see inside. He turned toward the front of the plane, where he saw Justin speaking into his headset microphone.

"WHO'RE YOU TALKIN' TO?" he screamed.

"NOBODY," said Justin, talking loud over the sound of the engines. "JUST HIM." He pointed at Frank.

"TAKE THOSE THINGS OFF," said Snake.

"WE NEED THEM TO TALK TO THE TOWER," said Justin.

"TAKE 'EM OFF, ZITFACE," said Snake, pointing the gun at the cockpit. Justin and Frank removed their headsets.

"NOW," said Snake, "GET US THE FUCK OUT OF HERE."

"WHAT ABOUT THE DOOR?" asked Justin.

"I'LL WORRY ABOUT THE DOOR," said Snake. He was going to leave it open, for now, in case he had to shoot again.

Justin, shaking his head, released the brake and gently advanced the throttles. Very slowly, the plane started to move.

20:40

She did not appear to be in any hurry, but it took Daphne only a few seconds to coil herself several times around Leonard. Leonard knew exactly what was happening, but found that there was nothing he could do to stop it: No matter how he moved his body, or where he put his arms, Daphne oozed effortlessly, *casually*, around him. Leonard sensed her astonishing strength, but only barely; she never seemed to need it. Leonard was terrified, but even with his terror, and the screaming around him, and the visceral revulsion he felt at being embraced by this *thing*, his brain found room and time to speculate on an unexpected phenomenon: He did not feel any great pressure; did not feel really *squeezed*. Instead, he noticed that, each time he exhaled, it became more difficult, and then impossible, to inhale, as Daphne calmly, relentlessly, took up the slack. Leonard was blacking out; he was dying, he could tell. *Just like that, it's over*, he thought. *I'll never see New Jersey again.*

And then, in his last moment of consciousness, he thought: *Fucking snakes.*

20:31

The stairwell was empty except for Monica and Matt. After Snake had fired the wild shot, Monica had told Eliot and Anna to take Puggy back to the main concourse and do whatever they had to do — "set something on fire if you have to" was how she put it — to get police attention and tell them what was going on. Anna had wanted to stay near the plane, but Monica told her that the best thing she could do for her daughter was to get help.

"What about Matt?" Eliot had asked.

"I need him here, in case I need a messenger," Monica had answered. "He'll be OK."

Eliot and Anna raced back up the stairs, followed by Puggy and Nina, who were holding hands. Monica opened the door a crack and peered out at the Air Impact! plane. It was parked so that the plane's fuselage was parallel to the terminal building. To taxi toward the runway, it would have to turn perpendicular to the terminal, meaning that the plane's occupants would no longer be able to see the doorway. The plane's right engine was roaring, its propeller a blur; the left engine was almost there.

"You stay here," Monica told Matt. "You watch through this crack, but you don't go out there. When your dad gets back here with help, you tell them what happened."

The plane had started to move, making a slow turn toward the right. When its windows were no longer visible, Monica opened the door.

"What're you gonna do?" asked Matt.

"Try and stop the plane," said Monica.

"How?" asked Matt.

"I have no idea," said Monica. And then she was sprinting across the tarmac. She did not look back.

20:17

Agent Greer led the way through the crowd, shunting people to either side, like a V-bladed snowplow. Those who didn't get out of his way quickly enough got picked up and tossed like hay bales. Still, it took Greer, Seitz, and Baker a good five minutes from the time they reached the edge of the mob until they could actually see the Delta counter. They heard shouts and screams; they saw uniformed officers, some trying to hold back the crowd, some yelling instructions to each other and pointing toward . . . *something* going on down on the floor, out of sight.

"OK," said Greer, over his shoulder, as he drove his body forward, through the last few feet

271

of crowd. "Remember, *we get the suitcase.*"

19:58

The Air Impact! plane was starting to pick up speed, but it was still moving slowly enough that Monica — who, until sixth grade, when she developed breasts, had been the fastest runner of any gender in her school — was able to close on it. She angled to the left, where she could see the door at the rear of the plane, still open, with a little folding stairway hanging down. She tried not to think about the gun. She would worry about the gun when she caught the plane.

19:50

Henry had never killed a snake, large or small, in his life. But he was a professional, and he gave careful thought — quick, but careful — to how he would handle this situation. He had to shoot the snake's head, that much was obvious; the problem was that the bullet would keep going. Henry didn't want it to hit Leonard, of course, but he also didn't want it to go into the crowd. He didn't want to shoot down, because the bullet would ricochet off the floor, which would be concrete, under the carpeting. Henry decided his best bet was to shoot up, toward the ceiling.

Henry knelt and pulled his revolver from his ankle holster. Then he stood and circled Leonard, whose eyes were bulging sightlessly and whose face was turning maroon. Two brave cops had their hands on Daphne's neck and were pulling with all their strength, with no noticeable effect on Daphne. As Henry approached them, another cop ran toward him, yelling something that Henry couldn't make out in the general din; seeing the gun in Henry's hand, he backed off. Henry showed the gun to the two brave cops; they looked at each other, then let go of Daphne and stood. As they did, Henry dropped to his stomach, rolled onto his back directly next to Leonard. As Daphne, who was never in a hurry, gracefully turned her head to see what was happening, he stuck the barrel of the gun into the underside of her jaw, pulled the trigger, and blew out her brains, not that she had many.

One second later, Greer burst through the crowd, drawing his own gun as he heard the shot and the ensuing screams. He ran forward, and then stopped, gun in hand, staring down at the scene on the floor — first at the unconscious Leonard, then at the now headless Daphne, and finally at Henry, who was on his back, gun still pointing straight up.

The two men studied each other for a moment. Then Henry spoke.

"Agent Greer," he said. "What brings you to Miami?"

19:22

The plane was moving faster now. Monica, tiring fast, was not sure she'd catch it. She was not entirely sure she *wanted* to catch it. But she found some reserve energy somewhere and got to within a few feet of the hanging stairs. She reached her left hand out, and for a second, caught hold of the plastic-covered steel cable that served as the stair's railing, but the effort of reaching forward slowed her slightly, and the railing was yanked away. Straining, her lungs burning, she lunged forward again, and this time she had the railing, but she was starting to stumble and *shit she was going down and the plane was going to get away and* . . .

. . . and Matt, sprinting next to her now, pulled her upright and gave her a push forward, and she grabbed the other railing and swung on to the ladder. She moved up to the second step and turned and held out her hand to Matt, and he grabbed it and she pulled, and in a second Matt was on the lower step, and in the next second the plane suddenly accelerated, and the fastest runner on earth would not have caught it.

18:37

Eliot, drenched in sweat, with the others trailing behind him, ran back toward the security checkpoint.

"POLICE!" he shouted. "POLICE!"

In front of him, a herd of returning cruise-ship passengers watched his approach, open-mouthed.

"CALL 911," Eliot shouted at them as he went past. "PLEASE. THERE'S A MAN SHOOTING BACK THERE."

The passengers stared as Eliot disappeared down the concourse, with Anna, Puggy, and Nina behind him. One passenger went to a pay phone, dialed 911, and told the operator what Eliot had said. The 911 operator said the police were aware of the shooting at the airport and had the situation under control. The passenger reported this news, and the herd relaxed.

18:08

Monica hauled herself to the top of the folding stairs and wriggled past the heavy suitcase partially blocking the doorway, keeping low. She peered around the last row of seats on the left and saw Snake standing in the middle of the plane, his back — *thank God* — to her. He was watching the pilots.

The pilot on the left yelled something to Snake, which Monica thought was about the door. Snake yelled something that Monica couldn't make out, and he pointed his gun at the pilot. The pilot shrugged and turned back to the controls.

Monica crawled across the aisle and into the last row of seats on the right sight of the plane. Matt crawled in and went to the left side. He gave her a look that said, *Now what?* Monica held up her hand in a gesture that said, *Wait.* She had no idea what for. The plane had reached the end of the taxiway and was turning onto the runway. The engines were very loud now. They were taking off.

17:41

As they turned into Garbanzo Street, the couple in the Lexus was arguing. They had been arguing for two hours now, since the start of their dinner at the Italian restaurant in Coral Gables. The issue was whether to stay in Miami, where the husband had been transferred by his bank a year and a half ago, or move back to Cedar Rapids, where they were both from. He thought that, for career reasons, they should stay; she wanted to go.

They were arguing so heatedly that the husband almost ran into the large man standing in the street, waving his arms. The man seemed to be wearing a uniform, but it was filthy and drenched in sweat, and there was blood running down his arm, which was . . . *handcuffed* to some big, mangled piece of metal, which was . . . *my God*, it was handcuffed to *another* man, a strange-looking man, off to the side there. With a big dog.

"I think we should get out of here," the husband said.

"They look like they need help," the wife said.

"OK," said the husband, "but we stay in the car."

Keeping the car in gear, the husband pressed the power-door-lock button and lowered his window two inches.

"Listen," said the large man. "I'm a Miami police officer, and I need you to . . ."

"GET OUT WHILE YOU CAN!" said the strange-looking man.

"SHUT UP!" said the large man. Turning back to the couple, he said, "I need you to . . ."

"SHE WANTS YOUR SOUL!" said the strange-looking man. He was pointing at the dog, who sniffed his finger, then barked.

"I SAID SHUT THE FUCK UP GOD-DAMMIT!" said the large man, shoving the big metal thing hard, knocking the strange man over. "THAT IS NOT ELIZABETH FUCK-ING DOLE!"

The husband pressed the accelerator. The car shot forward, tires squealing.

"NO!" screamed the large man. "COME BACK!"

The husband drove three blocks before speaking.

"OK," he said. "You call the movers."

17:01

"You *know* this guy?" Baker asked Greer. They were standing with Henry, who was watching three police officers and two paramedics un-wrap Daphne from Leonard, who had regained consciousness. So had Daphne's owner, who

277

was being formally taken into police custody and had already been handed business cards by four personal-injury attorneys who happened to be on the scene.

"Oh yeah," said Greer, "I know Henry from the old days, in Jersey. I used to interrogate him alla time, back when I worked organized crime."

"Wasn't *that* organized," said Henry. "Which is why I got out of it."

"You're saying you're retired now?" asked Greer. "Workin' on the stamp collection? Drinkin' Ensure?"

"More or less," said Henry.

"Sure," said Greer. "Listen, much as I would enjoy hearin' you explain to these officers why you come to their airport wearin' a piece on your ankle, I got important federal business, OK?"

"Real good chattin' with you," said Henry, turning back to Leonard.

"OK," said Greer, to Baker and Seitz. "These are assholes, but not the *right* assholes. I need to talk to somebody in charge."

"That guy there, I'm pretty sure he's the head airport cop," said Baker, pointing to a white-haired man in a shirt and tie, talking on a cell phone and holding a walkie-talkie, which was emitting a drumbeat of messages and static. Greer walked over.

"No, nobody got hit," the white-haired man was saying. "Just the snake." He listened for a moment, then said, "I don't *know* what kind. A *big* snake."

Greer was holding his badge wallet in the man's face.

"FBI," he said.

The man waved the wallet away.

"We don't need any help," he said. "We got this."

"No," said Greer, "I need somethin' from *you.*"

"Well, it's gonna have to wait," said the white-haired man, turning away.

Greer stepped a few paces away. He pulled the odd-looking phone from his pocket and pressed a button on it. He waited for two seconds, then spoke for about twenty. He pressed another button and put the phone back in his pocket, then walked back and stood next to the white-haired man, waiting. The white-haired man, ignoring him, continued talking on his cell phone for about thirty seconds, then stopped and listened.

"What?" he said. He looked up at Greer. Greer showed him his badge again.

"Yes," said the white-haired man, into the phone. "He's right here." He listened some more, frowning.

"But . . ." he said, then listened some more.

"OK," he said. "I got it." He shut off his phone, looked at Greer.

"My name's Arch Ridley," he said. "Tell me what you need."

"I need you to find out if anything else unusual has happened in this airport in the last thirty minutes," said Greer. "Besides this mess here."

"Lemme call the security office," said the

man. He dialed a number, waited, and said, "Doris. Arch. Listen, is there . . . *What?* Oh, Jesus. When?"

"What?" asked Greer. Ridley raised his hand, indicating *wait a sec*.

"No, that's not your fault," he was saying, "all this radio traffic. So what else did they . . . OK . . . OK . . . *shit*. OK. Keep the phone line open. I'll call right back." He shut off the phone.

"*What?*" said Greer.

"Five minutes ago," Ridley said, "the tower here got a message from a pilot on the ground, saying he had a guy on his plane, with a gun, telling him to take off."

"Oh Jesus," said Greer.

"The tower tried to get more, but they're not responding," said Ridley. "The plane taxied out and just took off, just now."

"*Shit,*" said Greer. "For where?"

"It's an Air Impact! flight," said Ridley. "Prop plane. It's supposed to go to the Bahamas."

"OK," said Greer, "listen. Call the tower, tell 'em to watch the plane, keep trying to raise 'em. Which way is the Air Impact! counter?"

"That way," said Ridley, pointing, "little over halfway around the concourse. I can . . ."

But Greer, Seitz, and Baker were already running.

15:21

Flight 2038 took off into the prevailing winds,

to the west. As the plane gained altitude over the Everglades, Justin banked left, making a long, slow turn until he was heading almost due east, toward downtown Miami, with Biscayne Bay beyond, then the southern end of Miami Beach, then the Atlantic. Justin was praying that air traffic control was telling the other air traffic where he was, since without his radio he had no way to get flight instructions.

Justin glanced over at Frank, and what he saw was not good: Frank was a zombie. It was up to Justin, the captain, alone, to handle this maniac with the gun. He figured the main thing was don't piss him off, do what he said, fly him to Freeport. They'd be tracked on radar; the authorities would be alerted; rescuers would be sent.

Justin clung to that thought. Help was coming.

15:06

As he ran, Greer was talking into his special phone. Baker was behind him and missed most of what he said. The only word he heard clearly was "fighters."

THIRTEEN

14:16

The security personnel had heard Eliot running down the concourse toward them, shouting for the police. They were looking his way, and as he approached the checkpoint, they recognized him as one of the perpetrators who had violated their scanning procedures a few minutes earlier.

"STOP HIM!" shouted the rotund man, pointing at Eliot.

"STOP HIM!" echoed the X-ray woman, the stern conveyor-belt woman, and the other checkpoint personnel. "STOP HIM!"

As Eliot veered to his right toward the checkpoint exit, three young men, on their way home to Pittsburgh after a week in South Beach, jumped in front of him. All three of them lifted weights regularly, focusing especially on biceps development. All three were wearing tank tops. They always wore tank tops, unless the ambient temperature dropped below forty degrees.

"Out of the way!" shouted Eliot, trying to push past the biceps men. "I need to find a police officer."

"GET HIM!" shouted the rotund security man.

One of the biceps men grabbed Eliot by the arm.

"Hold it, buddy," he said.

"Listen," said Eliot, fighting to sound calm. "I need to find a cop *now*. There's a man shooting back there." He yanked his arm free.

"HOLD HIM THERE!" shouted the rotund man.

The biceps men were inclined to follow orders from the rotund man, because he was wearing an official blazer. All three of them grabbed Eliot.

"NO!" Eliot shouted, struggling. "I HAVE TO GET *ooof*."

Eliot's breath was knocked out of him as he went down hard onto the carpet, with the three biceps men on top of him. They had been knocked over by Anna, who had hit the struggling huddle running and was now pounding one of the biceps men on the back of the head.

"Let him GO, you idiots!" she shouted. "He's trying to get help!"

"GRAB HER!" shouted the rotund man. "SHE'S ONE OF THEM!"

One of the biceps men threw a hard elbow that caught Anna in the gut and sent her rolling off the pile, moaning. The other two each had one of Eliot's arms and were pressing him hard, face-first, to the floor. Eliot could no longer open his mouth to yell, and his right arm felt as though it were coming out of its socket. Knowing it was hopeless, he gave one last, desperate heave, and . . .

. . . and one of the biceps men was gone. And then another one. Eliot rolled to his right and saw the third biceps man flying through the air, hitting the concourse wall, and landing next to the other two.

The thrower was Puggy, who had never lifted a weight in his life, but had always had a knack for picking up heavy objects. He reached down — he did not have to reach far — and raised Eliot easily to his feet. Nina was helping Anna, who was still gasping for air.

"SOMEBODY GRAB THEM!" shouted the rotund man, not making any moves in their direction personally.

"We gotta get outta here," Eliot said to Anna, who nodded *I'm OK* and waved him forward. The four of them, Eliot in the lead, ran out of the checkpoint area and turned right. A couple of security people trailed behind, still shouting for somebody to stop them. As he ran, Eliot frantically scanned the gawking crowd; *where the hell were the cops?*

13:36

When Greer, Seitz, and Baker reached the Air Impact! counter, it was abandoned; there were no more flights that night, and Sheila had gone home to her sick child.

"Now what?" asked Baker.

Greer was looking at the Air Impact! schedule on the wall behind the counter.

"I'm thinkin' we go to the gate," he said. "Find whoever loaded the plane, find out who was on it."

"This way," said Seitz.

13:00

Flight 2038 was crossing Miami Beach now, the vast glowing blob of Dade County behind it, the blackness of the Atlantic ahead, dotted with the lights of a few seemingly motionless north-bound freighters out in the Gulf Stream shipping lanes. Justin was feeling very lonely. Next to him, Frank was catatonic with fear. Immediately behind him, the postal-retiree couples were huddled in their seats, both women sobbing, both men staring at the floor. Behind them, the maniac was still standing in the aisle, holding the gun, watching. He had spoken to Justin only once, shouting over the noise of the plane.

"Two things, zitface," he'd said. "You touch that radio, you're dead. This plane don't come down in the fuckin' Bahamas, you're dead."

Justin knew the guy would be crazy to shoot him, because then who would fly the plane? But he also knew that the guy *was* crazy, because why else would he be doing this?

Adding to Justin's discomfort was a nagging alarm, beeping in his ear, telling him that the rear door was open. The door, and the hanging stairs, were making the plane handle weird. Justin was worried about the landing in Freeport. If they made it to Freeport.

Please, he thought — although he was not sure to whom he was beaming the thought — *please send some help.*

12:26

The two F-16s had used rockets to accelerate their takeoff from Homestead Air Reserve Base in South Dade County. The instant they were airborne, they turned sharply toward the northeast, and in under a minute, they were approaching the speed of sound, closing on the civilian plane over Miami Beach as though it were moving no faster than the freighters out in the Gulf Stream. The fighter pilots' orders were to stay behind and above the civilian plane, out of sight but nearby. They were not to arm their missiles. Yet.

11:49

As Greer, Seitz, and Baker trotted through the crowd, they saw a man in shorts and T-shirt running in their direction, looking upset.

"POLICE!" the man shouted.

Greer and Seitz ignored him; whatever this guy's problem was, they weren't interested. But Baker stared at the man's face. He'd seen this guy, but he couldn't remember where. Then he saw the woman running behind the upset man, and it clicked.

"Mrs. Herk!" he shouted. The man and woman both stopped, looked at him.

"I'm Detective Baker," he said, "Miami PD."

"Oh, thank God!" Anna said, grabbing Baker's arm. "You have to . . ."

"Hold it," said Baker. He shouted ahead to Greer and Seitz, who were disappearing in the crowd ahead, "Agent Greer! Back here!"

Greer turned and trotted back, impatient. *"What?"* he said.

"This is Mrs. Herk," said Baker. "It was her house. Where the suitcase was."

In an instant, Greer had his hand on Anna's arm.

"Mrs. Greer," he said, "I'm with the FBI. I need you to . . ."

"My daughter," said Anna. "She's in the plane with that man, and he shot at us, and you have to . . ."

"*Listen*, Mrs. Herk," said Greer, now gripping her arms with both his hands. "We're concerned about your daughter, but we have to know, *Where is that metal suitcase now?"*

Anna shook her head. "I don't know," she said. "They had it, they took it when they left the house . . ."

"Is it on the plane?" asked Greer. "Did they take the metal suitcase on the plane?"

"I don't *know*," said Anna, starting to cry. "I don't *know* about the suitcase."

"Mrs. Herk," said Greer, shaking her, "you have to . . ."

Eliot pulled Anna away and stepped right in front of Greer. Their noses were a half inch apart.

"She says she doesn't *know* where the goddamn suitcase is, OK?" Eliot said. "She wants her *daughter*. She doesn't care about your fucking suitcase."

"Who're you?" asked Greer.

"I'm her friend," said Eliot.

"Well, *friend*," said Greer, "if you want to help her daughter, you better care about the fucking suitcase."

"She wasn't with the suitcase," said Eliot. "She was with me. *This* guy was with the suitcase." Eliot pointed to Puggy, who had just trotted up.

Greer turned to Puggy.

"Who're you?" he asked.

"Puggy," said Puggy.

"You were with the suitcase?" asked Greer. "A metal suitcase? You saw it?"

"I carried it," said Puggy. "It's heavy."

"You *carried* it?" asked Greer. "*Where?*"

"To the plane," said Puggy.

"It's on the plane?"

"Yeah," said Puggy.

Greer thought for a second, then said, "Did anybody open the suitcase?"

"Over there," said Puggy, pointing toward the security checkpoint.

288

"They opened it there?" asked Greer.

"Yeah," said Puggy. "They made him turn it on."

Greer's face went pale.

"How did he turn it on?" he asked.

"There was these, like, switches, that he . . ." Puggy made a hand motion, flipping up imaginary switches.

"Then what happened?" asked Greer. "Did anything happen when he did that?"

"Lights," said Puggy. "Little numbers."

Greer glanced at Seitz and Baker, who were both listening. Seitz's face was blank. Baker looked sick.

Greer looked back at Puggy. "When did this happen?" he asked. "How long ago did he turn it on?"

Puggy thought about it.

"It's been a while now," he said.

07:43

Monica's legs ached from crouching in the tiny space allotted for legroom in front of the seat. She was trying to think, but it was hard with the horrendous roar of wind and engines coming through the open door.

Twice, very carefully, she'd moved her head just enough to look around the seat in front of her toward the front of the plane. Both times, Snake was facing forward. Once she'd heard him say something to the pilot, but she couldn't make out what it was.

From time to time, she made eye contact with Matt, crouching across the aisle. She tried to look confident, but she definitely didn't feel confident. She had no plan. The only thing she'd thought of was to jump Snake from behind, but he'd almost certainly fire his gun, and there were passengers — Monica didn't know how many — in front of him. And of course the pilots. If he shot them, everybody would die. On the other hand, if she didn't try to grab him, he might kill everybody anyway. He was definitely crazy.

Monica looked over at Matt, gave him another confident expression. He stared back. He was clearly scared.

Monica thought, *he's right.*

06:22

Greer was standing at the edge of the main concourse traffic, next to an abandoned airline counter, talking into his special phone. Seitz and Baker were next to him. A few feet away were Eliot, who had his arm around Anna, and Puggy, who was holding hands with Nina.

"Still nothing from the pilot?" Greer said to the phone. "OK, and his location is . . . OK. How about Homestead? They're . . . right, OK, good." Greer looked at his watch. "Right, that's affirmative."

"I don't understand," Anna said to Baker. "Why aren't you going out to the plane? Why aren't there police out there?"

"Mrs. Herk," said Baker, "the plane took off."

"Oh my God," she said, putting her hand to her face. Eliot hugged her tight, imagining how awful he'd feel if Matt were in that plane.

"But they're tracking it," said Baker. "They have it on radar. That's what he's talking to them about now."

"So what happens?" asked Eliot. "When the plane lands, they arrest him?"

Baker looked at Seitz.

Seitz said, "They'll do whatever it takes."

05:55

The noise was driving Snake crazy. He decided to try to close the door. Facing the cockpit, he walked backward slowly toward the rear of the plane.

05:45

Baker pulled Seitz aside, close to where Greer was talking on the special phone.

"What do you mean, 'Whatever it takes'?" asked Baker.

"Just what I said."

Baker stared at Seitz. A few feet away, Greer was saying, "Has that been cleared? Can I talk to . . . Sorry, I didn't realize. Yes, sir. I understand, sir. Yes, sir, they've acquired it."

"Who's acquired what?" Baker asked Seitz.

"Keep it down," said Seitz, nodding toward Anna.

"It's fighter jets, isn't it?" said Baker, his voice low. "From Homestead. You're gonna shoot this plane down, aren't you?"

Seitz said, "Whatever it takes."

05:12

Snake was backing slowly toward the rear of the plane, keeping his eye on the pilot. He was now even with the third row from the last. And now he was even with the second from the last. One more step, and he'd be right next to Monica and Matt; he'd see them for sure. Monica saw she was going to have no choice.

04:52

"We got no choice," said Greer. Baker was right in his face. They were talking quietly, so Anna and Eliot couldn't hear.

"There are innocent people on that plane," said Baker. "This woman's *daughter* is on there."

"With a nuclear weapon that's gonna go off," said Greer. "If it goes off in Freeport, *many* innocent people die, you understand? *Many.* We have to get it *now.*"

A man wearing an official Greg Norman golf shirt, official Greg Norman hat, and official Greg Norman slacks tapped Baker on the shoulder. He tapped several times before Baker turned to him.

"What?" Baker said.

"Which way is Northwest Airlines?" the man asked.

"I don't know," Baker said. He turned back to Greer. "Can't you signal to them somehow?" he asked. "Tell them to . . ."

The man tapped Baker's shoulder again, and said, "Is there some kind of . . ."

"NOT NOW," Baker said.

"Well, you don't have to *shout*," the man said. He went back over to his wife, who was wearing a muumuu the size of a wedding tent, to tell her how rude this jerk was.

"Can't you tell 'em the situation?" Baker said to Greer. "Tell 'em throw the suitcase out of the plane?"

"We tried," said Greer. "We're still trying. Pilot doesn't respond."

"But how can you just . . ." Baker held up his hands, let them drop.

"We *have* to," Greer said. "We fucking *have* to, that's how. Listen, nobody likes this. Nobody wants this. But this has been discussed, believe me, as high as it can be, every scenario, and this is the only way outta this."

Baker looked over at Anna. She was watching him and Greer, the representatives of Law and Order, waiting for them to tell her that her daughter was OK. Baker looked back at Greer.

"When does this happen?" he asked.

"When the plane's over the middle of the Gulf Stream," said Greer. "Over deep water."

"How long is that?" Baker asked.

Greer looked at his watch.

"Three minutes," he said.

03:17

Snake had stopped one row in front of where Monica crouched. She could see the back of his legs; he still hadn't turned. He was yelling something Monica couldn't quite hear to the pilot, something about the radio.

Monica looked across the aisle at Matt, nodded her head toward Snake, and made a grabbing gesture with both hands, to indicate, *We're gonna jump him.* Matt nodded. Monica held her right hand out with the forefinger and middle finger pointed down, like legs, then tapped upward between the legs with the forefinger of her left hand, to indicate *Kick him in the balls.* Matt puzzled over that one for a moment, then got it and nodded again. The thought flashed through Monica's mind, just for an instant, that Matt was a lot quicker on the uptake than her partner, Walter.

02:37

The F-16s carried both the AIM-9M heat-seeking missile, known as the "Sidewinder," and the AIM-120 AMRAAM, or advanced medium-range air-to-air missile, which is radar-guided. Because they were at close range, and because Flight 2038 had turboprop engines that generated enough heat, the pilots had elected to go with the Sidewinders. They radioed this decision in and were told to go ahead and arm.

01:58

Snake took another step back. He was right next to Monica and turning to his left, toward the door, which meant his gun was turning toward Matt. Monica came up out of her crouch and grabbed for his right arm, the one with the gun in it. She gripped it for an instant, but then a cramp sent a vicious jolt of pain through her right hamstring, buckling her leg. As she fell sideways, Snake shook off her arm and whirled, pulling the trigger. Monica's body jerked violently backward into the window, then crumpled to the floor. There was a softball-sized hole in the window, its edges spattered with blood.

As she went down, Matt came up, wrapping his arms around Snake, trying to pin him; but Snake was stronger, and he twisted quickly back to his left inside Matt's arms, whipping the gun around hard into the side of Matt's head. Matt lurched to his right and went down onto the plane seat.

In the front of the plane, the postal retirees had gone to the floor at the sound of the gunshot, as had Frank the copilot. Justin had turned around and seen that the maniac was fighting somebody — Justin had no idea who it was — back there. Turning forward again, Justin quickly reached for his radio headset.

01:14

"Yes," said Greer, into his special phone. He was looking at his watch. "That's affirmative. I repeat, affirmative. When you're ready."

01:12

Snake was furious. *The cop bitch and the punk! How the fuck did they get here?* He looked down at the bitch; her eyes were open, but he couldn't tell if she was seeing anything. He turned back toward the punk, who was groaning, moving a little. Definitely alive. *Not for long, punk.*

00:59

Greer had his ear pressed tight to the special phone. *"What?"* he said, his voice rising. *"What'd he say?"*

"What?" asked Baker, pressing close to Greer. *"What?"*

"They heard from the pilot," said Greer. "He's . . . hold it." He listened on the phone. "OK," he said, looking at his watch. "Ask him is the suitcase on the airplane. Got that? Ask him can he get the suitcase off the airplane right now." He looked at his watch. *Shit.*

Snake raised the gun, aimed it at Matt's head.

"Snake!" a voice shouted. Snake jerked his head right. It was Eddie, standing in the aisle.

Snake, still aiming the gun at Matt, shouted, "The fuck you want?"

"Snake, Jesus," shouted Eddie, pointing down at Monica. "You shot a cop."

"That's right," shouted Snake. "Now I'm gonna shoot this punk."

"Snake," shouted Eddie, "You're fuckin' *crazy*. I don't *wa*. . ."

Snake grabbed Eddie by the shirt, yanked him hard, pivoting and hurling him past Matt against the wall in the rear of the plane. Eddie's back hit the wall and slumped to the floor next to the suitcase.

"DON'T CALL ME CRAZY," shouted Snake.

"Snake," shouted Eddie, "When we land, I ain't goin' with you."

Snake fired the gun. Eddie screamed and rolled sideways, grabbing his thigh.

"That's right," shouted Snake. "You ain't goin' with me." He turned back toward Matt, raising the gun.

Jenny landed on Snake chest high, wrapping her legs around his waist, grabbing his hair with one hand and furiously clawing at his eyes with the other. He raised his left hand to shove her off and she bit into it, her teeth sinking in to the bone.

00:26

The F-16s were directly behind the target, in textbook firing position. The target was slow and taking no evasive measures. There was essentially zero chance the Sidewinders would miss.

00:24

Snake screamed and yanked his bleeding hand away from Jenny's mouth. He brought his other hand up hard, hitting Jenny with the gun barrel under her jaw. Her head snapped back and she dropped off of him, into the aisle.

"You fuckin' BITCH," he screamed, kicking at her. "I'm gonna KILL YOU, YOU FUCKIN' BITCH." Jenny, on her back, tried to scrabble away up the aisle.

"YOU AIN'T GETTIN' AWAY, BITCH," screamed Snake, raising the gun.

Then he heard it, over the plane noise, a thump behind him. He spun and looked. Eddie, blood spreading quickly over his thigh, had managed to shove the suitcase against the lower lip of the open doorway. His eyes closed, his teeth gritted, he was pushing it over the lip. It was leaning out now, into the shrieking wind.

"NO!" screamed Snake. He dove to the back of the plane. As he got there, Eddie gave the suitcase a last desperate shove, toppling it slowly over the lip. Kicking Eddie aside, Snake leaned out of the doorway and grabbed for the suitcase handle with his left hand. He caught the handle, and he almost got the suitcase pulled back. But he'd leaned forward a little too far, and the weight of the suitcase was a little too much. Snake felt it pulling him out of the plane. He grabbed for the side of the door with his right, but he still had the gun in that hand, and he couldn't get a good grip. If he'd have let go of the suitcase, he could have grabbed the stairs, could have stayed on the plane and saved himself. But he wanted that suitcase; that was his kingpin suitcase. Snake held on to it as it bounced down to the bottom of the hanging stairs, then off the last stair, dragging Snake along, into the rushing black nothingness, over the vast black ocean.

00:14

Justin heard the bumps and felt the sudden weight change at the back of the plane. He looked back where the maniac had been, where the suitcase had been. He began shouting into his headset microphone.

00:11

Greer was shouting into the special phone, now, causing airline passengers to stop on the concourse and stare at him.

"ABORT ABORT ABORT," he shouted. "DO YOU HEAR ME? ABORT ABORT ABORT."

Snake was falling, falling. He was very afraid, but he was still thinking clearly. He had not let go of the suitcase. He would not let go of the suitcase. This was his kingpin suitcase. He would hold on to it for the rest of his life.

FOURTEEN

The next day's newspaper was full of news.

The big story was the rogue wave, estimated to be somewhere between eight and twelve feet high, that hit both South Florida and the Bahamas. The wave was felt by even the big freighters; it capsized a number of smaller boats, although fortunately nobody was hurt. It was also fortunate that the wave hit at night, when there were few people on the beaches. There were some scary moments and a fair amount of damage, but nobody drowned.

The cause of the wave was, for the moment, a mystery. The best guess from the experts was that it was caused by some freak seismic event on the seafloor under the Gulf Stream. Rogue waves had hit Florida before; Daytona Beach had had one in July of 1992. As one oceanographer quoted in the newspaper put it: "Every now and then, Mother Nature throws you a curve."

There was also a dramatic story of a hijacking attempt aboard an Air Impact! turboprop flight from Miami to Freeport. A man — described by one of a group of retirees who'd been on the plane as "a complete lunatic" — managed to smuggle a gun on board and ordered the pilot to take off without clearance. A Miami police officer, Monica Ramirez, had somehow — details were not yet available — gotten on the plane and tried to apprehend the hijacker, who had shot her. Other passengers had also fought the hijacker, and during the struggle, he had apparently fallen from the plane to his certain death in the ocean. Officer Ramirez, who was described by the police chief as a hero, was still alive when the plane returned to Miami; she was in critical condition, but doctors said her chances for survival were good. A passenger identified as Edward Porter also sustained a gunshot wound to the leg; he was listed in satisfactory condition.

By bizarre coincidence, there was another, totally unrelated story involving the airport at around the same time. Somehow, a thirteen-foot python had gotten loose in the main concourse and attacked a passenger, identified as Leonard Pflund, a forty-two-year-old consultant from East Orange, New Jersey. He was rescued by his business associate, identified as forty-seven-year-old Henry Algott, also of East Orange, who killed the snake with a handgun. Police had taken possession of the handgun and detained Algott pending further investigation of the incident. Police said they would file charges against the snake's owner, Neil Hart, when he was released from the hospital, where he was being treated for injuries sustained while resisting arrest.

Police reported two unusual incidents in Coconut Grove. In one, a man identified as Jack Pendick, twenty-eight, of the Harbour Oakes Manour Trailer Court in Cutler Ridge, had been apprehended after firing a handgun several times near the CocoWalk shopping complex. Nobody had been hurt, but the incident and subsequent apprehension of Pendick had attracted a crowd of tourists, who had temporarily blocked Grand Avenue. A few hours later, in a residential section of the Grove, a Miami police officer identified as Walter Kramitz had been discovered in the middle of Garbanzo Street handcuffed to a large metal object, along with a local business executive identified as Arthur Herk. This apparently was the result of a home-invasion-style robbery at Herk's home, but the details of the incident, and especially how Kramitz and Herk ended up in the street, were still sketchy.

Finally, traffic on busy Le Jeune Road had been shut down completely for several hours when a group of goats had somehow gotten loose on the roadway. The newspaper ran this story as a "bright" on the bottom right-hand corner of the front page, with a picture of a sweating animal-control officer, surrounded by cars, chasing a frisky, cheerful-looking goat. This picture produced identical reactions in thousands of readers: They shook their heads, smiled, and said, "Only in Miami."

EPILOGUE

In the weeks that followed, oceanographers up the Atlantic coast detected elevated radioactivity levels in the waters of the Gulf Stream; in addition, some mariners noted an unusually large quantity of dead deepwater fish floating on the ocean surface. Various explanations were offered for these phenomena, including the possibility that they, and the rogue wave, were caused by a catastrophic malfunction aboard a nuclear submarine. This allegation was aggressively advanced on the Internet by a number of people, most notably Pierre Salinger; the fact that the U.S. government said there had been no submarines of any kind in that area only reinforced their belief that they were right. But no concrete evidence ever surfaced, and eventually the matter became just another random piece of conspiracy-nut lore.

The Federal Aviation Administration immediately suspended all flights on Air Impact!, which soon filed for bankruptcy. In response to outrage expressed by the public and political leaders over the apparently lax security at Miami International Airport, a high-level task force was formed to root out problems and recommend solutions. After months of hearings, a number of measures were implemented, the most significant being the hiring of an expert consulting firm to oversee passenger checkpoint operations. This lucrative contract was awarded to See-Cure Tech, Inc., a wholly owned subsidary of Penultimate, Inc.

Eddie Porter was visited at the hospital by investigators from various law-enforcement agencies, some of them quite curious about how he came to be on Flight 2038. But the FBI took over the investigation and ultimately found no reason to detain Eddie, who returned to Coconut Grove, where he joined the local Hare Krishna temple and became known as Ram Baba Ram.

Nobody ever asked what happened to Snake.

Henry Algott was arrested and tried on several weapons-related charges stemming from the incident in front of the Delta counter. At the trial, the prosecution introduced evidence showing that Algott was a convicted felon and suggesting that he was linked to organized crime. Henry's lawyer — who coincidentally was one of the lawyers Henry had lectured on cigar etiquette, specifically Lawyer C — received permission from the judge, over heated prosecution objections, to bring a mature python into the courtroom, so the jury could appreciate the threat Henry had courageously confronted in the airport. The snake somehow — the prosecution claimed it was intentional — got loose and had to be subdued in a struggle that left the courtroom in a shambles and one bailiff with a dislocated shoulder. The jury took less than ten minutes to return a "not guilty" verdict. Henry returned to East Orange, where he and Leonard continued to operate a successful freelance business killing people, although they refused to take any more jobs in South Florida.

Daphne's owner sued Dade County for pain and suffering related to getting knocked out, plus the loss of a beloved pet. A jury awarded him $3.2 million.

After Arthur Herk got out of the mental hospital, he went to the U.S. attorney's office and told a wild story about corruption and payoffs and hit men and a place in Coconut Grove that sold bombs and missiles. But when investigators went to the address, all they found was a deserted, boarded-up bar, with nothing inside but old beer signs and a busted TV. Arthur died a few months later in what was ruled a fishing accident, which seemed odd because nobody could ever remember his having gone fishing before.

Ivan Chukov and Leonid Yudanski were taken to a secure federal facility and questioned for several weeks. Then they were deported to Moscow, where they opened a very successful Star-bucks.

Walter Kramitz finally grew tired of hearing snide comments from his fellow police officers and quit the force to become a dancer at a night-club for women called "Thrust." His stage name is Buck Lance.

Jack Pendick pleaded no contest to a number of charges related to the Coconut Grove shoot-ings. He served a year in prison, and after an early release because of good behavior, he even-tually found a job as a security guard.

Monica Ramirez recovered slowly but steadily. Once she got out of intensive care, she was vis-ited regularly by Harvey Baker, and when she got out of the hospital, they started dating. One night, after they finished a bottle of wine — the first time her doctor had allowed her to have al-cohol — he proposed to her, and she accepted, and then they made love, and then, after she promised, cross her heart, that she would not tell anybody ever, he told her what had been inside the suitcase. And she said, you're telling me they let a scuzzball get through airport security with a gun *and* a nuclear weapon? And he said, yup. And she said, what a world. And they hardly ever talked about it again.

Eliot Arnold fell even deeper into debt, and

came very close to being evicted from his office for nonpayment of rent. On the day that his landlord had intended to kick him out, he got a visit in his office from two young partners of the hottest advertising agency in New York. They asked him if he was the guy who'd done the Hammerhead Beer ads, and he started to say it wasn't really his idea, but before he could get the words out, they told him they LOVED those ads, they were so RUDE, and they wanted to hire Eliot to do a national campaign, print and TV, with a huge budget, for a new type of nonalcoholic youth beverage called SpewTum, which was going to feature a high-profile involvement by the Seminal Fluids.

Anna filed for, and quickly got, a divorce from Arthur. He didn't have much in the way of assets, but she did get to keep the house. She and Eliot had agreed that they would not jump into anything, that they would take it slow and be really sure. They were married four days later.

Jenny and Matt dated for a while and went to the prom together, but they decided it was just too weird, their mom and dad being married and all, and they decided to be good friends, which they remained for the rest of their lives.

The enemy toad, perhaps traumatized by its encounter with Arthur, hopped away and never returned. Roger could never say so in so many words, but the truth was he kind of missed it.

Puggy moved in with Nina in the maid's room, although every now and then, for old time's sake, they slept in the tree. Puggy did odd jobs around the house for Eliot and Anna; sometimes he earned extra money by voting in Miami municipal elections, which were ordered by the courts at frequent intervals. He wanted Nina to teach him Spanish, but all he ever learned to say was *Te quiero*. Which turned out to be all he ever really needed.